FATED HEARTS

An Echoes of Darkness Prequel – Book 0.5

Published by Skye Publishing

Copyright © 2024 Lucia Skye

No part of this publication may be reproduced, distributed, or transmitted in any form or by any means, including photocopying, recording, or other electronic or mechanical methods, without the prior written permission of the publisher, except in the case of brief quotations embodied in critical reviews and other non-commercial uses permitted by copyright law.

This book is a work of fiction. All names, characters, places and incidents either are products of the author's imagination or are used fictitiously. Any resemblance to events, locales, or persons, living or dead, is coincidental.

The author acknowledges all songs titles, song lyrics, film titles, film characters, trademarked statuses, brands, mentioned in this book are the property of, and belong to their respective owners. The publication/use of these trademarks is not authorized/associated with, or sponsored by the trademark owners.

Lucia Skye is in no way affiliated with any of the brands, songs, musicians or artists mentioned in this book.

Paperback ISBN: 978-1-0687616-1-4

E-book ISBN: 978-1-0687616-0-7

All rights reserved ©

FATED HEARTS

LUCIA SKYE

Content Warning

This book contains graphic violence and sexual content. It is not intended for anyone under the age of legal adulthood. All characters depicted herein are over 18 years of age. This book is not to be used as a resource for sexual education, or as an informational guide to sex or BDSM.

Some contents within this book may be triggering or disturbing to some readers

Reader discretion is strongly advised.

TRIGGER WARNINGS include but are not limited to:
- **Alcohol consumption and use of drugs**
- **Blood**
- **Death**
- Gore
- Grief
- **Hospitalization**
- **Kidnapping**
- **Physical abuse**
- Sexual assault
- **Sexually explicit scenes**
- **Strong language/ profanity**
- **Torture**
- **Breathe play/choking**
- **Swallowing bodily fluids**
- **Restraint**
- **Spanking**
- **Raw sex/sex without a condom.**

Playlist

1. Billie Eilish - What Was I Made For?
2. Sia - Courage To Change
3. Linkin Park - Numb
4. Labrinth - Still Don't Know My Name
5. Sleep Token - Aqua Regia
6. K.Flay - High Enough
7. Evanescence - Bring Me To Life
8. Sia – Alive
9. Teddy Swims - Bad Dreams
10. Teddy Swims - Lose Control
11. Gracie Abrams - That's So True
12. Sleep Token – Mine
13. Sleep Token – Chokehold
14. The Weeknd - Shut up and Listen x Often (Mashup Remix)
15. David Kushner - Skin and Bones
16. P!nk - Just Like A Pill
17. Måneskin - THE LONELIEST
18. Christina Aguilera - Fighter
19. Sia - Bird Set Free
20. Billie Eilish - BIRDS OF A FEATHER

To you,

May you find the courage to follow your heart.

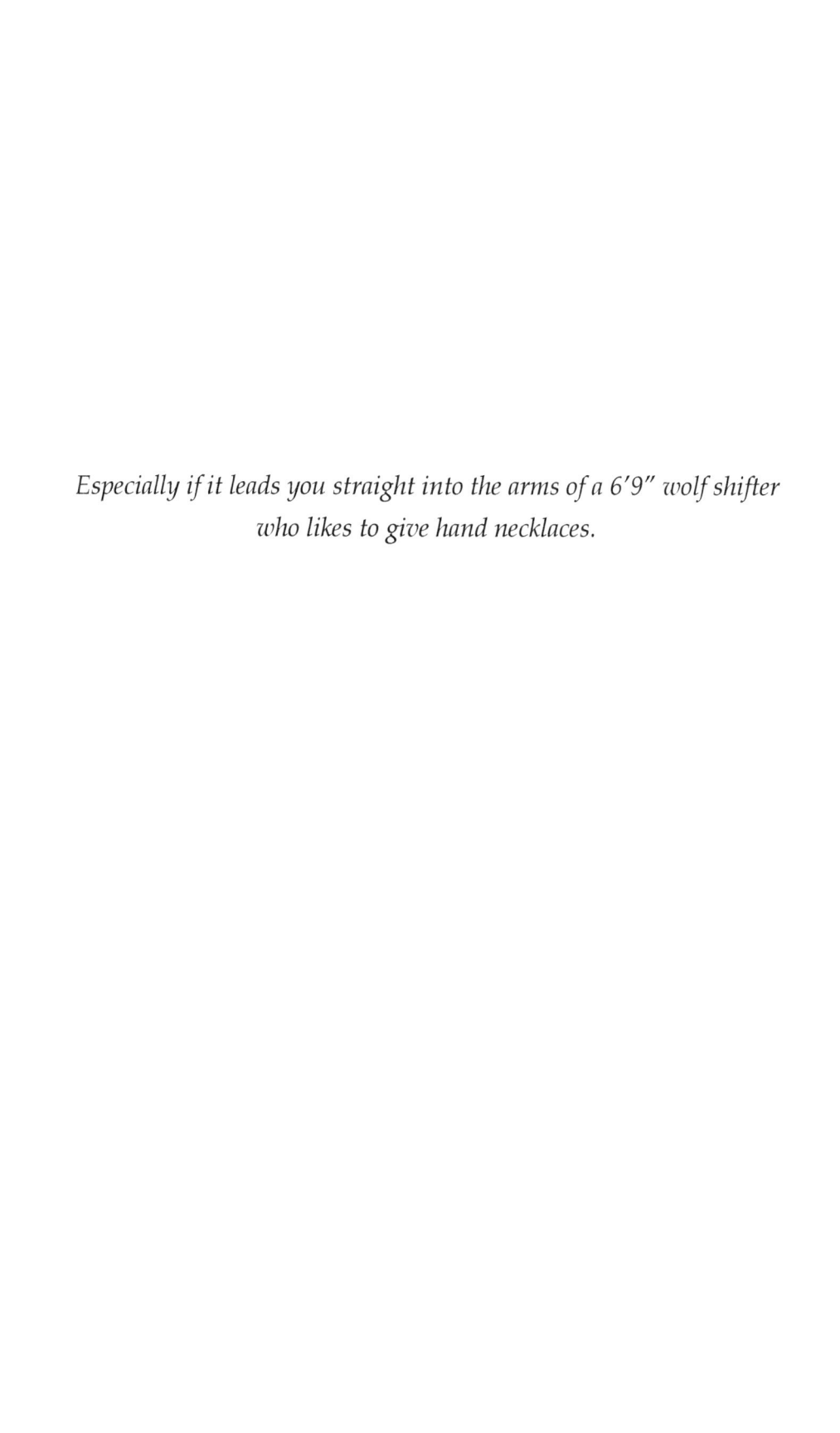

Especially if it leads you straight into the arms of a 6'9" wolf shifter who likes to give hand necklaces.

1

Ava

It's a strange feeling knowing you're going to die. The doctor's voice drowns in the sound of the blood rushing into my ears.

Whoosh. Whoosh. Whoosh.

I can only hear my weak heart pounding. The cold metal of the bed's armrest chills me to the bone as I grip it so hard I'm afraid I might break a finger. Sweat dots my forehead, and my already shallow breath leaves my lungs in a huff.

A clammy, trembling hand placed over mine brings me into the present. I shake my head and look to my right, where my mother stands beside my bed. Three days ago, I was rushed into the hospital.

Who suffers a heart attack at twenty-one?

"So, what are you saying? How much time does my daughter have?" my mother asks in disbelief, her lips drawn in a thin line. Her whiskey-colored eyes are swimming with tears.

"We can't be sure. A few months, maybe six if she's lucky," Doctor

Anderson replies, his lined face stoic. He is a handsome man past the age of fifty, with salt and pepper hair and kind denim blue eyes that are now focused on my mother.

She clings to my hand with a bruising grip. "No, you can't let my daughter die!" she pleads. "There has to be something you can do."

"Unfortunately, the underlying cardiomyopathy that went undiscovered for years weakened her heart muscles too much. And now, with the heart attack she just suffered, I'm afraid there's not much else we can do. We're going to put Ava on the transplant list and hope for the best."

I scoff. "Hope for what? For another person to die just so I can live?" My voice is laced with bitterness.

My mother sucks in a sharp breath. "Ava Juanita Perez!"

The doctor smiles kindly at me, unfazed by my question. "Ava, not many people are faced with the possibility of dying at your age. I understand you must be upset. In shock, even. We have counselors here that can help you. I can arrange for one to see you—"

"I just want to go home," I grit out through clenched teeth and snap my eyes shut, resting my head on the pillow that now feels like a block of cement.

"Thank you," my mother says.

The doctor's disappearing footsteps reverberate in the weighted silence that blankets the room.

Rain pelts the window furiously, and the wind howls outside before a menacing clap of thunder booms, making me flinch. At least the sky is crying, raging. I can't. I feel cold. Emotionless. The clock perched on the wall in front of me is a ticking bomb, its taunt cruel…unforgiving. With each second that passes, my lungs constrict.

Tik. Tok.
Tik. Tok.
Tik. Tok.

I want to laugh in the face of the cruel destiny I've been dealt. I'm twenty-one years old, and I haven't lived. I am but a mere shadow of a person, always too afraid to step out of the boundaries my mother imposed on me. A puppet on her strings, every decision I have ever made pondered greatly as to not cause her distress.

Ava, the good girl. Always too quiet. Always the pushover. The straight-A student who never parties. The girl who never says no to her mother. I didn't even get drunk on my twenty-first birthday because I was too afraid I was going to upset her. There were so many things I wanted to do and experience, but I always backed down because I knew my mother would disapprove. But now, I want to set fire to those strings. I want to take a sharp knife and cut into my back and force wings to spring free from the cuts, so I can experience flying for the first time in my life. To at least get a taste of freedom before the stuttering organ inside my chest gives out and takes my last breath with it.

"We're going to see another specialist, *mija. Ya hablé con tu tía Paula.* She said she heard about a doctor, and we're going to make an appointment." My mother's voice pulls me out of my thoughts as she plops down on the chair next to my bed, making it scrape loudly against the vinyl floor.

"Doctor Anderson is the best cardiothoracic surgeon in the country, *Mamá*," I say before I open my eyes and look at her.

Her jet-black hair is disheveled, and her face is gaunt. Dark circles paint her under eyes, and she looks like she aged ten years in the span of a few days. She is wearing the same clothes as yesterday, her shirt rumpled with a stain of coffee on the sleeve. I hate that I did this to her. My stomach constricts painfully at the thought of what my mother will have to face once I'm gone.

She purses her lips. "I'm not giving up, Ava. We will find a solution. Tomorrow, I'll pack up your things, and you will move back in with me so I can take good care of you. I have already spoken to my boss. He agreed to give me some time off given the situation and—"

"I'm not moving back with you, *Mamá*," I snap, and she flinches at my tone.

I never talk back to my mother. It was a miracle she let me move out of the house I grew up in. She threw a fit when I told her I wanted to be more independent, but I finally managed to convince her because the apartment I moved into was just a few blocks away from our house. She didn't even let me attend an out-of-state college. And like a good girl, I did everything she wanted. Even now, I don't want to hurt her, but she is smothering me. No more. I am tired of living my life for others.

"Ava, I know what is best for you. I spoke to your landlord. *Tu tía* is coming tomorrow, and she'll help me move the boxes. I already cleaned up your old room—"

I suck on my teeth then cut her off. "You didn't hear me, *Mamá*. I'm not moving. I only have a few months to live, and I want to live the rest of my short life on my terms, not yours."

2

Logan

We run, nothing more than a blur in the thick canopy of trees, the winding forest trails as familiar as a second home while we hunt for our next meal. The pine-scented air fills my snout and ruffles my fur as fallen leaves and branches crunch under my paws. I look at her. At my mate. Her wolf form is a sight to behold. Sparkling blue eyes and a beautiful coat of golden fur that shines in the silver light cast by the full moon. She stops all of a sudden, making me halt and turn around. Her snout lifts, and she starts sniffing the air.

"Over there," she says through our mental link as her head points to the trees a few feet away. Following her lead, I start running again. It doesn't take long to pick up the scent of the stag we've been following since the full moon took sentry in the night sky.

"Rise and shine, little bro!" My sister's voice breaks through my dream as something wet and cold assaults my head.

Groaning loudly, I turn around, open my eyes, and blink a few times in order to adjust to the bright light. "Was this really necessary, Em?"

I mumble grouchily as I push myself up from the forest floor where I have fallen asleep after running with the pack last night. A few leaves stick to my naked body, so I brush them off. Then, I shake the water from my wet hair and throw my sister a dirty look.

"Dude, can you at least cover your junk before you turn around and flash me with it?" she screeches and uses her forearm to shield her eyes as she throws clothes at me.

"Really, Em? You've seen everyone from the pack naked like a thousand times before. How is this any different?" I roll my eyes at her as I start dressing in the jeans and T-shirt she brought from my closet.

She turns around so her back is facing me. "Um, eww. Are you for real right now? You're my brother; that's how this is different. I really, really don't want to see your junk."

Well, now that I think about it, I don't want to see my sister naked either. It's a miracle we haven't seen each other without clothes until now. Being a wolf shifter means you have to be in the nude a lot more than one would think.

The happy trill of bird songs fills the air as the morning sun warms my back. "Did something happen?" I fall into step with her, and we start walking toward my truck as pine needles and fallen branches crunch under the soles of my boots.

She heaves out a deep sigh and turns to look at me. Emily is not only my sister; she is my twin. She has the same deep amber hue to her skin—though a little darker—honey-colored eyes, and ash-brown curls that are longer than mine touching her shoulders. Her features are softer and feminine, her lips a little fuller, and she is much shorter than me. "Yeah…it's Josh's son. He's not waking up. I think it's the weakness. You can't ignore your responsibilities. You can't keep running away."

My nostrils flare. "I'm not running away."

She arches a perfectly trimmed eyebrow at me. "C'mon, Logan, be real. This is the fourth time this month I've come to get you from the forest. You always wander off after the pack run. The pack needs y—"

"I know, okay?" A muscle thrums in my jaw as I cut her off. "I just…I feel like I'm not doing enough. Like I'm disappointing everyone. I need to find her, but I'm running out of time. This is the only way I know how. I dream about her, when I fall asleep by myself in my wolf form after our runs."

She bites her lip pensively. "You need to search for her in the real world. Not in your dreams."

I huff and push at a semi-wet curl that falls over my eye. "And how do you suggest I do that? I haven't seen her in her human form yet. All I know is the color of her eyes and hair. That's all. Besides, the mating bond should have made her come to me; that's how it works."

"Yeah, but the bond must be faulty or something, since she hasn't shown her face. If you only stay in our community, you'll never find her. Mom wants to throw some kind of old-fashioned ball and invite the packs from all over the country. She said that's how she and dad met."

"I know. She's only mentioned it like a hundred times," I grumble.

"She wants you to take a chosen mate, a Luna, for our pack."

Instead of replying, I round the hood of my new Hennessey Mammoth truck and stop at the driver's door. "Aren't you going to toss me the keys?"

"Nu-uh, I've been looking for you for two hours. The least you could do is let me drive us back," she says as she pushes me away, unlocks the door, and opens it.

"Fine. But take it slow on the potholes, okay? This is not your beat-up Kia." I circle the car again and settle into the passenger seat.

"Hey, don't you dare insult Rusty!"

I snicker. "I don't even have to. That name is enough of an insult." Before I can even close the door on my side properly, she peels off at warp speed and then pushes on the brake so hard I almost take a bite out of the dashboard. "What the hell?" I yell. Throwing daggers at her with my eyes, I fumble with the seat belt and snap it in place as fast as I can. My sister is a freakin' maniac.

She belts out a deep belly laugh. "Told you not to insult Rusty," she singsongs.

"How bad is it?" I ask after a few beats of silence. My question is overshadowed, though, by terror for my life. I grip the edge of my seat. "Slow down. You're going to crash into a fucking pine tree at this rate, and I just bought this car."

"Oh, stop being a sissy," she chuckles out. But her smile dies quickly on her lips as she looks at me briefly, her forehead crinkled in worry. "It's pretty bad. It started with a high temperature and a headache a few days ago. Layla thought it was just a cold."

"What the fuck?! Wolf shifters don't get sick like humans do. Layla should have known better and said something." My jaw locks with anger.

"I know. I think she just hoped it would pass…but when she tried to wake Ryan up for school this morning, she couldn't. He's running a high fever, and he is unresponsive. She's tried everything."

I pinch the bridge of my nose. "Fuck! Did you happen to bring my phone? I need to call Malik." Malik is a warlock coming from a very powerful line of dark witches, and he is also one of my closest friends. He has extraordinary healing powers, which is unheard of for a dark magic wielder, and is the only one who's managed to heal the other kids when they were touched by the weakness.

"Already called him. He came over before I left looking for you."

I place my hand on her arm and squeeze it lightly. "Thanks, sis. I don't know what I would do without you."

A soft smile tugs at her lips. "That's why I'm the best Beta ever. But no more running away, Lo. The pack needs its Alpha now more than ever."

I nod. Emily is right. I can't run away anymore. This is the third case of a child touched by the weakness in the last few months, and it's because I didn't want to marry a chosen mate. But how could I when I know my fated mate is out there, and I keep seeing her in my dreams? The bond between fated mates is sacred and highly revered by our kind, but it's extremely rare, and most wolf shifters never meet their fated mates. They settle for a chosen mate instead. My pack is growing restless because I refuse to settle.

When I became the unchallenged Alpha of the pack the moment our father died seven years ago, I knew I had to get married to my mate—chosen or fated—before the age of twenty-five; otherwise, my pack would be weakened. My twenty-fifth birthday is only a few months away.

My mother keeps pressuring me to forget about my fated mate. I've managed to convince her to give me more time by promising that if I don't find her before my twenty-fifth birthday, I will choose another woman to be my Luna. Until then, our pack is suffering, and it's all my fault. With every day that passes, I feel like I'm being crushed under the weight of my guilt and responsibilities.

Emily parks the car in front of Josh and Layla's house, snapping me out of my thoughts. We get out of the truck at the same time. It's a fucking miracle I didn't throw up with how recklessly my sister drove us here. At least we arrived in record time.

Josh doesn't let a second pass after I rap my knuckles against the front door. He swings it open like he's escaping a magnitude nine earthquake. I guess he must be feeling like his world is crumbling around him. It's made pretty clear by his auburn hair pointing every which way as if he spent hours pulling at it and the stiffness in his shoulders. Red, blotchy hazel eyes meet mine, filling with stark relief.

"Alpha," he says before stepping out of the way for us to enter.

"How's Layla holding up?" my sister asks.

"She's pretty shaken up. She kept sobbing uncontrollably. I had to give her some pills so she could calm down. She's sleeping right now."

"Is Malik still here?" I inquire as we shake hands.

"Yeah, he's in Ryan's room."

We follow Josh through the narrow corridor, then climb the stairs to his son's room on the second floor. Josh opens the door, and we step inside. Ryan is lying on the floor in the center of a pentagram drawn with white chalk, and Malik is crouched beside his small body, both of his palms on the boy's chest, his protruding veins swirling with the inky, black magic while he chants softly in a language I don't understand. The magic flows in the room like a thick fog.

His slanted cat-like eyes snap open, finding mine. He pushes to his feet, grim tension evident in the tight lines around his mouth, as the thick fog caused by the black magic starts to dissipate. He is dressed in his usual black leather duster, lively silver hair pulled in a bun at the nape of his neck. "His fever is gone. But I'm sorry, Logan, his forced slumber won't end until the pack gets stronger. They let too much time pass between the first symptoms and now," Malik says and bends over, gingerly picking up the kid in his arms and settling him on top of the bed.

"Fuck!" Josh bellows as he punches the door. A tornado of splinters follows his fist plowing through the wood with a loud thud.

A heavy weight settles on top of my chest, and my stomach plummets at Malik's words. To add insult to injury, birth rates are down. Moreover, the last cub was born a year ago. If any other children get touched by the weakness…Motherfucking fuck! I also want to throw fists left and right and break something, but I am the Alpha; I have to stay level-headed. So, instead of showing how fucking scared I am, I grip Josh's shoulders with both of my hands and look into his eyes, imbuing my gaze with as much reassurance as I can.

"It's going to be okay. Have faith. We'll get through this. I'll find a solution." I turn on my heel and make my way to the front door with Malik and my sister at my back.

"You need to take a chosen mate, Logan. Giving the pack a Luna is the only way to strengthen it and heal the kids," Malik says grimly as we step out of the house.

I inhale deeply and ball my hands into tight, eager fists at my sides. "I know."

3

Ava

A drop of sweat falls directly into my eye as the guy I picked up at the bar earlier grunts like a rutting pig on top of me. *Eww.* He calls out for his mother as he comes, and then his sweaty body gives out, crushing me under the weight.

Great. Another weirdo with mommy issues.

I didn't think it was possible, but he lasted even less than the last guy. I wonder why people like sex so much. Since losing my virginity at sixteen and two other unfortunate sexual experiences after that, I hadn't had sex again until this past month. Why bother when men only care about themselves and their pleasure? Most of them wouldn't know what a clit is if it hit them in the face. But since I was given only a few months to live, I decided to give sex another try. In the last month, I've had sex with seven guys. Spoiler alert: none of them made me come.

"Can you move? You're crushing me," I mutter as I push at his heavy body. I have enough trouble breathing on my own, thank you very much. I don't need to be reminded of how bad of a job my weak heart is doing at pumping blood to my lungs.

He finally takes his weight off me as he slides out of me and slumps to the side. "You came too, right?" he asks smugly as he fluffs his pillow and rests his back on it. He weaves his hands behind his head and throws me a megawatt smile with perfectly straight, pearly white teeth. He is really good-looking. I have to give him that. A bit too preppy if you ask me, but he has that old money charm with his perfectly coiffed blond hair and blue eyes. Well, I learned my lesson. Being good-looking doesn't necessarily mean a guy is good in bed. I swear I'm ready to write off sex for good this time.

"No, I didn't come, Brad." I mean, the fact that I wasn't making any sounds, lying like a stiff board beneath him, should have been an indicator that I didn't enjoy what he was doing all that much.

His eyebrows shoot up. "But I touched your clit like you asked me to. And my name's not Brad. It's William the Third."

Huh, I could have sworn his name is Brad.

A laugh bubbles out of me before I can stifle it. "Sorry, William. You kind of look like a Brad. Anyway, you should maybe study the female anatomy more because that surely wasn't my clit." He kept stabbing at my labia with his finger like he wanted to make a shish kebab out of it. I did try to move it and redirect him, but he told me he knew where the clit is because he was a man. Honestly, I should have pushed him off me in that moment, but I kept hoping it would get better.

The vein on the side of his forehead looks like it's going to pop any minute now. "I'm sure that's where the clit is. My mother showed me," he snaps.

WHOA! This is definitely not something I was expecting to hear from a guy I just had sex with. I clear my throat, trying to recuperate from my shock. Why do I pick up all the weirdos? I'm blaming tequila for this one. "A piece of advice, Willy boy, maybe keep that to yourself the next time you decide to have sex. That is something you should unpack in therapy," I mumble the last part to myself.

Hell, I think I'll need therapy after this.

I shudder and push up from the bed. *Mierda.* The dizziness hits me badly this time, and little white dots swim in my vision. It's getting worse and worse with each day that passes. I blink a few times and grip the bed frame, waiting for the universe to stop twirling.

"I'm going to take a shower, and I don't expect to find you here when I'm done. Please don't leave the condom on the floor; toss it in the trash can on your way out," I say as I put on my robe and amble toward the bathroom.

"What? Wait! We can go again."

I snort a very unladylike laugh as I stop in my tracks and turn around to face him. "Yeah, no, thank you. I think I had enough for tonight."

His nostrils flare as he gets up from the bed, kicking my bedside table. Luckily, he didn't do any damage, but he does look at me like he wishes it was me he kicked instead. So he has anger issues on top of mommy issues.

I really know how to pick them…

"You're a fat bitch," he grumbles, then throws the condom to the hardwood floor and starts getting dressed. "I only fuck models. You should consider yourself lucky that I chose to pity fuck you."

I arch an unimpressed eyebrow. "Oh, Willy boy, it's funny how you think anyone would want to fuck you with that micro penis . Don't let the door hit you on your way out," I fire back as I spin on my heel and stalk into the bathroom, locking the door, hoping he will leave without any more incidents because he's starting to scare me.

Ugh, I can't wait to wash his disgusting sweat off my body.

"To finally finding a guy that knows how to fuck," Chloe, my best friend, toasts as she clinks her shot glass with mine.

"Hopefully, I can find him before I croak," I reply and throw my head back, downing the shot of tequila. It burns my insides as it travels to the bottom of my stomach. I bite into the lime wedge and shudder. The first shot is always the hardest to stomach, and this tequila is so strong I think I just grew a few hairs on my chest.

She throws me a dirty look that's distorted because her face is all scrunched up from the awful taste. But her eyes are glassy, more from my words than from the burning spirit. "Fuck, Ava. Stop saying shit like that. You're going to make me cry." She takes the beer bottle from the floor and passes it to me.

I take a big swig, wipe at my mouth with the back of my hand, and give it back to her. "Well, I'm going to die, Chlo. There's not much I can do about it." Shrugging, I take the tiny hand-held mirror from my lap and resume doing my makeup.

We are both sitting cross-legged on the hardwood floor of my small bedroom, resting our backs on the bed frame. Simba, my orange tabby cat, is a tiny purring ball between us as we get ready for tonight. Chloe won VIP tickets to a rock concert of a famous band, Deadly Sins. We even have backstage access to meet the members.

"I don't need a reminder every single time we see each other that you're going to die," she mutters and starts painting her nails a deep purple to match the top she is going to wear.

"I know you don't like to talk about it, but it's my reality, and eventually, you will have to come to terms with it." I line my waterline with a black waterproof pencil and start applying eyeshadow. I'm doing a deep black smokey eye to bring out my pale seafoam- green irises. Hopefully, I won't end up with panda eyes.

"I also wanted to talk to you about Simba. Will you take him after I die? Mom's allergic, and I don't want to give him back to the shelter." The chances of older cats getting adopted are low, and he was already eight years old when I brought him home from the shelter two years ago. I can't stand the fact that he might end up never being adopted again and spend his last years in a crate.

"Oh my God. You might get that heart transplant; you never know," she exasperates, a muscle feathering in her taut jaw.

"Please, Chlo—"

"Fine. I'll take him. You know I love this little monster." She uses her baby voice as she pets Simba's head carefully to not ruin her freshly painted nails. "Who's the best boy in the whole world? You wanna come live with Auntie Chloe, you sweet orange angel?"

He lets out a cute little meow and turns belly up so he can receive more pets. It's a trap; the little shit is going to bite her the minute she touches his belly.

I throw my arms around her neck, her peach scent enveloping me. Simba lets out a disgruntled *meow* when he ends up squished between us. "Thanks. It means the world to me." I pull back when my phone starts vibrating on the floor.

Taking a deep breath, I mentally prepare myself before I tap my finger on the screen to accept my mother's call.

"Are you insane, Ava?!" her bellowing scream almost makes me deaf in my right ear. Chloe cringes and throws me a knowing look when I put my mother on speaker so I can still have an intact eardrum at the end of this conversation.

"How could you go skydiving with your heart condition? You have become so reckless. *Ya no te reconozco.* You were such a good girl before."

She starts crying, her favorite form of manipulation.

She probably traced my phone again. She is dating a cop, and every time she catches the stalker itch, he traces my phone so she can find out where I am or what I have been up to at all times. I tried talking to him on several occasions, but he is too infatuated with my mother and always dismisses me because he thinks she only wants to know if I'm safe. Well, I think it's a deep violation of my privacy. I even threatened to file an official complaint if he tracks my phone again. I guess he doesn't care.

"It was on my list. It's something that I wanted to do before I die," I say when she finally stops sobbing.

"*Tu tía* Paula called me and told me you froze your school year. Are you trying to get me killed? I might die of a heart attack before you if you don't stop ruining your life."

Wow, that's a low blow, even for her. I cut her off before she starts the hour-long rant I know is coming. "I never wanted to go to law school. That was your dream, not mine," I clip out.

"This nonsense stops now. I already called the school and made the arrangements for you to go back."

I push to my feet so fast I almost get whiplash, managing to scare Simba in the process. He hides under the bed as I exit the bedroom and start pacing the small apartment. The red-hot anger makes my blood thicken in my veins so much that my weak heart starts sputtering in my chest. My breath turns ragged, and I can barely speak at this point.

"I'm not going back to school, *Mamá*. You keep pushing me to do things I never wanted. I am tired of living the perfect life you chose for me. I have only a few months left to live. You need to accept that reality once and for all." I stab at the screen furiously to end the call and plop down on the cream-colored loveseat, pressing my hand over my heaving chest. Fuck. No one gets on my nerves like my mother.

"You okay?" Chloe asks as she passes me a glass of water, a deep frown marring her forehead. I didn't even notice she followed me out of the bedroom. A glint of worry shines in her dark eyes as she looks at the hand clutching my chest.

I nod and take a sip. *C'mon, Ava, take a few deep breaths; you don't need another trip to the hospital.* Blinking and exhaling loudly, I look at my best friend. "Yeah, thanks. I just…Fuck. I know she is like this because of my deadbeat of a father running away when I was just a baby, but I can't excuse her behavior anymore. The way she wants to control my life is beyond crazy. I should have seen it before. I don't know how I could let it go on for so many years."

She sits beside me and holds my hand, waiting for me to calm down completely. Chloe is very well acquainted with my mother's special brand of craziness.

"C'mon," I say, standing up when I finally get my heart and breathing under control. "Let's finish getting ready. I'm not going to let my mother ruin our night." I pull on her hand and stride back into the bedroom with determination.

I am tired of my mother suffocating me. She dragged me to see so many doctors this past month, and every single one gave the same verdict. I understand why she can't accept what awaits me, but I've come to terms with the fact my time is limited. I was furious at first, sure. Who wouldn't be? But I am doing my best to move past it and live my life to the fullest until I can't anymore.

4

Ava

The venue the band is playing at tonight is packed to the brim with sweaty, gyrating bodies that crowd us near the raised, wooden stage. I am one with them; sweat trickles between my shoulder blades and makes my hair stick to my back as I jump up and down with Chloe, losing myself to the music. My heart is fluttering, and I feel like something heavy is pressing on my chest, but what else is new? Nausea hits me all of a sudden. I push the uncomfortable feeling aside and concentrate on dancing. It's probably just the alcohol. I refuse to think of what else it might be.

"You sexy bitch!" Chloe screams in my ear, slurring her words as she grinds against me and cops a feel of my ass.

I am wearing a leather mini dress I paired with combat boots for the full rock chick vibe. It has thin spaghetti straps, a plunging V-neck, and an open back. Smiling drunkenly at my best friend, I look at her from head to toe. "You're the one to talk. Every guy in this place is drooling over you."

Chloe is a bombshell with legs a mile long. Her thick, inky black hair reaches the middle of her back, and she is the spitting image of her Filipina mother. She looks like a runway model. Whereas me…I couldn't be any different. I'm a mix of my white Argentinian father with jade-green eyes and my Mexican mother with a much darker complexion. My skin is golden, thanks to the time I spent sunbathing at the pool with Chloe, and my hair is brunette with natural caramel highlights. I am also shorter than her and a lot curvier.

I have a belly that hangs a little over my waistband, probably because I love baking and eating anything sweet, and thick thighs that chafe like a bitch in the summer. But, I would rather die than eat food I don't like just because society tells me I'm not exactly the perfect body size. Fuck them. I starved myself enough over the venomous words thrown at me by insecure girls who hate themselves more than anything and want others to feel as miserable as they feel inside. Finding out I was going to die had one advantage, I didn't give a shit about their opinion anymore.

"Um, hello, I'm not the one Jude's been eye fucking the whole night. I bet he wants to fuck you for real," she giggles.

She is right. The lead singer of the band keeps roving his gaze over me. He is looking more at my boobs than at my face, though. I do have a decent rack, so I can't blame him. We are so close to the stage that my chest vibrates with the deep bass, and I can see every single drop of sweat that courses in rivulets on Jude's half-naked body.

To the delight of every woman in attendance, he took off his shirt at the middle of their set, tucking it in the back pocket of his leather pants. He keeps throwing smoldering looks toward the crowd as he grips the microphone, flexing his chiseled abs. He has that bad boy look with slicked back raven hair, hazel eyes, and tattoos that cover his muscular yet slender body. Like a swimmer rather than a bodybuilder. It also doesn't hurt that he sings so damn well. There's something about a man who can sing that turns a woman into a crazed, hormonal teenager.

"And Knox hasn't stopped looking at you," I shoot back, referring to the drummer who has eyes only for Chloe. He is good-looking, too, with warm brown eyes and dirty blond hair that touches his shoulders and moves every time his sticks hit the drums.

We keep dancing and screaming until the band finishes their last song. I need to pee really bad, and I can't wait for people to clear a path so we can go to the bathroom and then go backstage to meet the band.

Before I can turn around, a behemoth of a man with a buzz cut and a mean mug appears next to me. "Miss," he says.

I look around, confusion pulling at my eyebrows.

"He's talking to you, Ave," Chloe chuckles out.

Heat blooms in my cheeks. "Yeah?" I reply and cringe because I screamed the word, my ears not fully recovered from being so close to the blasting speakers.

The corners of his lips turn up in amusement. "The band wanted you to have these." He extends two backstage passes toward me.

"Oh, we already have those." I rummage through my small, black leather fanny pack to get them out. We took the badges off at some point because they kept smacking into our faces with those sharp edges when we jumped to the music. I swear I almost lost an eyeball.

"These are special ones." He winks, and Chloe takes the passes, giving one to me. We both put them around our necks. "If you can follow me, please."

"Oh my God, we're getting the VIP of the VIP treatment. I think I'm going to faint." Chloe jumps on the balls of her feet as she lets out an excited scream. I honestly don't know how she can do that and still keep her balance on those high heels with how much we drank until now. "Told you that mini leather dress was the way to go for tonight," she whispers as she elbows me in the ribs.

I grunt and give her a dirty look because I swear she doesn't realize how freakishly sharp her elbow is. "Wait, can we swing by the bathroom first? I need to pee." At this point, my bladder is about to burst, and I'm beyond getting embarrassed talking about bodily functions in front of this mountain of a man.

"There's a bathroom you can use on the bus," he replies.

Chloe and I look at each other at the same time. Her eyes almost bulge out of her head. "Holy shit, we're going to their tour bus!" She grips my arm so hard I am sure I'm going to have an imprint of her fingers the next day.

Twenty minutes later, we climb the steps and enter the bus as the bodyguard shuts the door behind us. It took us forever to get here since we had to wait in line as everyone made their way to exit the venue. The band is still outside, giving autographs to the mass of people waiting for them near the bus.

I let my eyes take in my surroundings as Chloe brims with excitement next to me. The front lounge is dimly lit and decked with two dark brown leather couches. A big flat TV screen is embedded into one of the shiny, dark wood-paneled walls. Everything looks luxurious and screams money.

Chloe takes a seat on one of the couches. "Damn, this leather is buttery smooth," she says as she runs her fingers over the material of the couch.

I chuckle at her enthusiasm and hastily cut through the corridor in pursuit of the bathroom. I'm glad no one can see my weird attempt at walking with my inner thighs pressed together.

Passing the kitchen with state-of-the-art appliances and a round booth with a table in the middle, I stop at a closed door before the bunk beds. I turn the knob and thank God it's the bathroom. I was about to pee in the middle of the bus, and I don't think the band would have been too happy about that. The bathroom is nicer than the one in my small apartment. It has a full walk-in shower, two sinks, and a big LED-lit mirror that hangs above the black marble countertop.

After I've taken care of my business and am washing my hands, I suddenly become lightheaded, my breath coming out in shallow spurts. My reflection in the mirror whirls in a way that tells me I'm about to faint. *Fuck.* White-knuckling the edges of the sink, I try to stabilize myself.

My jaw starts hurting as a dull headache blooms in the back of my head. Bile burns the back of my throat until it spills into my mouth. I quickly open the lid of the toilet and start heaving my last meal along with all the alcohol I have ingested. The moment I finish throwing up, I stand up on shaky legs and throw some ice-cold water onto my face. Whatever reprieve that gave me, though, is shot to pieces when a sharp pain pierces my chest. It shackles my lungs with heavy steel chains and forces me down onto the toilet with my head between my knees, struggling to breathe. My fingers tremble as I push a wet strand of hair out of my face.

After a few minutes, the pain has subsided enough that I feel I can finally stand without fear of tearing down a towel rack. There is a bottle of mouthwash near the sink. I use it to rinse my mouth, hoping no one will mind or notice. Taking a tissue from the holder in front of me, I pat my face dry and fix my makeup as best as I can.

A loud knock reverberates in the small space, making me flinch. "Ava, are you okay? You've been in there for a long time," Chloe's voice travels through the door, thick with worry.

"Yeah, I got sick because of the tequila," I say weakly.

"Do you want me to hold your hair?"

"No, I'm fine. I'll be out in a minute."

"'Kay."

I step out of the bathroom not into the sleek designer bus I left, but into a fully raging nightclub complete with blasting music and dizzying

LED lights flashing blues and reds and purples. The band has arrived.

Knox is sponging every word that comes out of Chloe's mouth as she animatedly gestures something. They sit close to one another on a couch in the front lounge, lost in their own bubble. She twirls her hair on one of her fingers and bats her eyelashes at him before taking a drag of her beer, a clear sign that she is into him. As I pass the kitchen, I quickly avert my eyes at the image before me. Slouched in the kitchen booth, a blissful look on his face, and gripping a fistful of blond hair, the bassist pushes down the head of the woman sucking his cock. I cringe at the slurpy, suction noises she is making.

So…that's how a rock star lives.

The other two guitarists are in the lounge area on the couch opposite Chloe and Knox. They each have two girls sitting in their laps. As I advance on the corridor, I stop when I feel a hand at the small of my back.

"Hello, gorgeous," someone whispers roughly in my ear, making a shiver pass down my spine.

I turn around, and I am hit full force with how good-looking Jude is this close. And he smells delicious. He definitely showered because he has fresh clothes on, now wearing black distressed jeans and a tee with their band name written over the chest in bold, bloody letters.

"Hey," I say.

"God, you're so fucking beautiful." He leans closer and brushes a strand of hair out of my face, eliciting tingles all over my body. "What's your name, gorgeous?" he purrs.

Damn, he's good. I already feel weak in the knees. I bet he has a lot of experience seducing women. "Ava," I shoot back.

His eyes rake over my body, stopping at my cleavage. "What do you say we party somewhere private, Ava?"

"Um…sure." But as soon as I say it, my stomach constricts painfully, almost making me bend over. *Mierda.* I'm getting sick again. With a few deep breaths through my nose, I engage in a battle of wills with my rioting organ. *You will not ruin this moment for me, you little shit*, I mentally chastise, as if I'm in control over that sort of thing. Luckily, it finally settles. *Thank God*. Before I can change my mind, Jude takes my hand in his and drags me to the back of the bus.

The bassist and the blond are no longer in the kitchen. They surely moved to one of the bunk beds since the curtain is drawn, and it's doing nothing to muffle the loud moans. Huh, either she is faking it, or he is really good because I've only heard those kinds of sounds in porn movies.

We enter the bedroom at the end of the bus. A round double bed with crimson satin sheets sits in the middle, and there's another bathroom through the open door at my right. Jude closes the door behind him and prowls toward me. He doesn't waste any time as he closes the space between us and presses his body to mine, a hand gripping my ass and the other at the nape of my neck. He dips and crashes his lips to mine, his tongue licking at my mouth with languid strokes. As he brushes his finger over my nipple, making it pebble, my heart speeds dangerously in my chest. Honestly, I don't know if it is because of him or because of my defective heart at this point.

Jude pulls back and licks his lips. "Damn, you taste good, gorgeous. Let's have some fun." He winks and smoothly takes out a small transparent bag of white powder from the back pocket of his jeans. He swings it in the air like a pendulum as if trying to hypnotize me before he saunters to the small wooden desk near the bed and pours the bag's contents onto a small mirror-like tray.

It brings me back to those moments in law school, sprawled on the couch while taking a break from the mountain of textbooks on my desk. Instead of dancing on tables alongside Chloe, I would watch movies to pass my time. As if following the script in my head, Jude starts cutting the cocaine into tiny lines, using a card he fished out of his wallet. Predictably, he takes out a hundred-dollar bill and rolls it until it resembles a straw.

I swallow hard. How many times did I wish I played the main character? Only to feel something…anything other than suffocating apathy.

A loud, nasally sound snaps me out of it, and I realize Jude just snorted all three lines. He rubs at his powdered nostrils before sniffing sharply. "Want a bump?" he asks as he blatantly eyes my boobs, his pupils increasing in size as we speak.

"Um…I don't know," I reply. My mother's horrified expression flashes through my mind, followed by a deep disappointment that sets her mouth in a tight line. I brush her haunting apparition off my shoulders and think about it without the heavy cloud of her judgment hanging over me. As far as drugs go, since finding out I'm going to die, I've only smoked weed a couple of times—which my weak lungs didn't like all that much—and done half a Molly once. I was afraid, with it being an upper, that it would affect my heart. I was right; I nearly passed out.

Snorting cocaine feels like playing a game of Russian roulette, though.

"C'mon," he pauses as if searching for my name in his head. He must have already forgotten it because he says "gorgeous" after a few awkward beats of silence. "You're only going to be this young once, right?" He smiles sheepishly and extends the hundred-dollar straw toward me.

He's dangling in my face the starring role I've been craving for years. All I have to do to escape the numbness is go on a wild ride with him. What else could go wrong? I'm dying already. I stride toward the desk and take the makeshift straw. Bending over, I start snorting the first line. The powder tickles the inside of my nose before it slightly stings. I weirdly feel it between my eyes.

"I can't wait to fuck you," Jude says gravelly as one of his hands smacks my left ass cheek, and the other sneaks under my dress and palms my pussy over my panties. "C'mon, snort another. One is not enough."

As soon as I finish snorting the second line, a rush of euphoria hits me. My insides pitch as my heart starts thudding at the speed of light. Straightening, I blink a few times, trying to clear the dancing white spots in my vision, but the room moves with me like I'm in one of those spinning roller coasters and my knees buckle while my arm begins to throb. I go down hard as a heavy weight presses on top of my lungs, like a building has collapsed on top of my chest.

"Fuck, you okay?" Jude asks, alarmed.

I try to answer, but my tongue is filled with lead, and my vision blackens at the edges. I hear Jude screaming.

Then nothing.

5

Logan

I pinch the bridge of my nose in an attempt to calm my throbbing temples as my eyes skitter over the endless pages in front of me. I've been at this for hours. I wish someone would have told me before becoming an Alpha that I would spend most of my time chained to this fucking office chair by my responsibilities.

"You don't look too good, little bro," Emily's voice travels through the room, pulling my attention toward the door.

"You were born thirty seconds before me," I shoot back, throwing the documents I'm holding onto the desk in frustration and running a hand over my face. For a whole month, I've been trying to find a cure for the weakness affecting the children of the pack. Two more kids have fallen into the deep sleep and won't wake up. Endless hours of research have amounted to nothing. Needless to say, I am beyond desperate.

"That still makes me the bigger sister," she teases. A wry grin pulls at her lips as she enters my office, her high heels clicking against the hardwood floor. She is wearing a long, light blue dress that floats at her back with every step. The sigil of Baphomet etched on her right bicep, marking her as an Obsidian Conclave member, stands out against the deep amber hue of her skin, enhanced by the color of the dress. Everyone in the pack wears the same sigil tattooed on their wrists, but only my family wears it on their biceps.

All dark creatures are under the jurisdiction of the Obsidian Conclave. We all have to abide by the rules of not killing humans and, in the case of wolf shifters, not transforming anyone by biting them. It's pretty easy if you ask me, but some rogue wolf shifters don't believe in following the rules.

"Aren't you going to start getting ready? Mom's gonna be pissed if you're late to your own ball." She takes a seat on one of the chairs in front of my desk.

I run my hand over the back of my neck and snap my eyes shut. I'm sure wrinkles form at the corners with the pressure. *God, I just want a minute to fucking breathe.* "I'll go take a shower," I say as I stand and push the swivel chair backward.

"Wait, have you seen this?" Emily looks above my head, where a flat-screen TV is perched on the black-painted wall behind me. I turned the volume down earlier because it made me lose my focus. "Where's the remote?" she asks as she starts searching under the mountain of paper covering the top of my desk.

I open the top drawer, take out the remote control, and pass it to her. She turns the volume up while I spin to face the TV. The voice of the news anchor announces a brutal animal attack two towns over.

My phone starts vibrating in my jeans pocket. I take it out and tap on the screen. It's Kaiden Black, the head of the Obsidian Conclave and one of my closest friends. I accept the call.

"Have you seen the news?" he asks.

"I'm watching it right now. Another animal attack. Do you think it's a rogue?"

"Yeah, I sent Dominic to investigate. I got wind of it yesterday before it hit the news. He said it's a wolf shifter for sure; there were no signs of fang marks on the victim."

"Shit. You think it's the same one from a few months ago?"

"It looks that way. Same claw marks, and the heart was ripped out brutally from the chest cavity," he says grimly.

I swear under my breath and look at my sister. Her face is etched with worry as she listens to our conversation.

"I wanted to let you know so you can have everyone in the pack on alert. It's pretty close to Ashville. The rogue wolf shifter might travel toward our city next."

"So far, we haven't picked up a strange scent, but I'll keep you posted if anything changes. Thanks for letting me know, man."

"We are having a Conclave meeting tomorrow night. Are you coming?"

"I'll be there," I respond and end the call. I've been ignoring my Conclave responsibilities lately since the weakness was—*is* my top priority. But aside from being the Alpha of my pack, I also represent wolf shifters around the world within the Obsidian Conclave. There has been a lot of blood spilled in wars between our species, but when Kaiden became head of the Conclave, he made sure all of the dark creatures' voices were heard, and the wars stopped. I am the representative for wolf shifters, Dominic for vampires, and Malik for the dark witches. It also helps that we are all close friends.

My gaze locks with Emily's. "You heard all that?"

"Yeah, should I prepare a statement? You need to announce this as quickly as possible. With the pack being weakened…"

"I know. Fuck, this is the last thing we needed right now," I mutter, pinching the bridge of my nose. "I'll announce it at the ball tonight. I'll go get ready," I say and make my way to the door.

"Maybe wait until the ball is over. Mom will kill you if you ruin the celebration. If you start with that kind of speech, no one will want to have fun anymore. The pack needs a breather just for one night. We've all been so wound up with the kids being touched by the weakness."

"Yeah, you're right. Tomorrow morning, then." With slumped shoulders, I stride out of the room to get ready for the ball my mother is throwing in the hopes I will finally choose a mate and get married.

"Would it hurt you to smile a little?" my mother scolds as she arches a dark eyebrow at me. She is wearing a golden, sparkly dress that enhances the deep hue of her umber skin. Her usually curly, dark-chestnut hair is straightened and styled in an intricate updo.

"She's not here, Mom," I grumble before downing a hearty sip from the whiskey tumbler. With a deep sigh through my nose, I glance over the ballroom. The spirit burns the back of my throat as it carves a path to my stomach and kindles a low burning fire that warms my insides. I don't usually drink hard liquor, but tonight, I seem to need it more than anything.

My mother put a lot of work into organizing this event, and it truly shows. Crystal chandeliers hang from the embellished, vaulted ceilings. Their soft, glittering light bathes the marble floor, along with every guest in attendance. Men in their best suits and women dripped in diamonds and shapely gowns that flow and swish with every move are engaged in animated conversations or gracious waltzes as the lively tune played by the band bounces off the ornate plaster-smothered walls.

Strangely, I feel exactly like one of the stupid walls while my mother parades me around like a prized stud at auction.

"Two more packs need to arrive. I asked them to bring all the single women with blond hair and blue eyes. In the meantime, you should at least mingle. These people came all this way for us." She takes a sip of champagne. "And Logan, you promised if you can't find your fated mate tonight, you will get engaged and married as soon as possible."

"I know, Mom. Trust me, I'm trying. It's just…I can't seem to do anything right, and I know everyone is blaming me for the children falling into the deep sleep. I hate that I haven't found a cure." I crook a finger in my shirt collar and pull at it. The suit I'm wearing is custom-made to fit my big frame, but I feel like it's constricting me, and I can't breathe. I want to rip it to pieces.

She lets out a deep sigh. "I don't tell you this enough, but your father would have been proud of you, Logan. I know I am. You are the best Alpha this pack could ask for. You simply need to let go of the idea that you will find your fated mate. Taking a chosen mate and getting married is the only way the children will wake up. The pack needs a Luna desperately." She places the empty flute of champagne on the cocktail table near us and curls her fingers around my bicep. "Now come, I want you to meet someone. I think she will be the perfect chosen mate for you."

We descend the stairs from the private balcony on the second floor and make our way to greet every guest in attendance—at least those of significant importance. My mother knows how to work the room, making everyone eat out of the palm of her hand while exchanging graceful pleasantries left and right. You can see how much she enjoys this type of life. On the other hand, I would rather take a silver bullet dipped in aconite than sit ten more minutes through the surface-level stilted conversations.

Fuck, how I wish I were at my small cabin high up in the mountains right now, away from everything and everyone.

"That man doesn't know when to shut up," my mother mumbles with a grimace when we finally manage to escape a conversation with the Alpha of a northern pack who is under the impression we still live in the dark ages and have to fight vampires and dark witches to death. He doesn't realize how lucky we are that Kaiden put a stop to all the bloodshed. My father lost his life because of an injury he sustained in one of the wars against vampires. The fact that we now live in peace shouldn't be taken for granted.

She swipes a flute of champagne from a server's tray that passes near us and takes a delicate sip. As she turns around, a big smile spreads over her face. "There she is. The girl I've been telling you about. Isn't she beautiful?" my mother gushes in my ear as we approach Conrad, the Alpha of the Ironclaw pack.

"Hello, Conrad, thank you for coming! It's wonderful to see you again," my mother says from beside me.

"Thank you for inviting us, Deborah. It's always a pleasure to see you and your Silverfang pack." He bends at the waist slightly and kisses the back of my mother's hand.

We exchange a firm handshake. "Conrad."

He is almost as tall as me, with hair that is more salt than pepper and wise ocean-blue eyes. "This is Grace, my oldest daughter. I hope you'll find her to your liking."

His daughter takes a step forward and curtsies like we are in a period movie. She is angelic, with pale blond hair and eyes the same color as her father's, her body lithe like a ballerina's, enhanced by her soft pink dress. But I don't feel even an ounce of attraction to her; I prefer my women a lot curvier and with more fire in their eyes. However, it wouldn't matter if she was my fated mate. My fated mate will always be the most beautiful woman for me, perfect in every way.

I know what my mother is trying to do. She thinks that if she picks a girl for me with features similar to my fated mate, I will surely consider her my future bride, my Luna. At the end of the day, it doesn't even matter what my fated mate looks like. It's the bond that matters. The feeling of rightness that courses through me when I simply dream about her. I can't even imagine how it would feel to have her in my arms. I'm getting hard just at the thought of her, and surely this isn't the moment for that.

Clearing my throat, I get my mind out of the gutter and bring my thoughts into the present. "She is beautiful," I reply politely, and Grace smiles demurely at my remark.

"I think it's safe to say my son won't find a woman more striking than Grace tonight. Maybe you should invite Grace to dance with you, Logan." She pushes me slightly toward her like I'm a child.

My sister suddenly appears at my side. "I'm so sorry for interrupting your conversation." She nods toward Conrad and Grace.

My mother's lips thin. "This is Emily, my daughter. She's Logan's Beta."

"I'm afraid something that requires your immediate attention has come up," Emily says, her tone dripping with urgency, earning a look from my mother that could cut through skin and bone.

"I'm so sorry," I echo and dip my chin toward Conrad. "Please enjoy the rest of your evening." I turn on my heel with Emily at my side, my strides long and purposeful as I let out a deep breath of relief. "Did something really happen?"

She arches an eyebrow while throwing me a conspiratorial glance. "Dude, you looked like someone shoved something up your ass. More so than usual," she chuckles out. "I decided to play the good Samaritan and save you. You owe me one."

"You get on my nerves every single day, sis, but damn if I don't want to kiss you right now."

"Eww, I don't want your dumb face anywhere near mine, thank you very much. What you need to do is give me a fat raise for how smoothly I saved your ass. I surely don't make enough if I have to bartend and be your Beta."

"You bartend because you want to, Em, not because you need to. I'll give you a bonus and a raise if you keep Mom away from me for the rest of the night, though."

She puckers her lips, seemingly pondering my offer. "Deal."

6

Ava

A garbled sound leaves from deep within my chest as I try to open my eyes. *Try* being the operative word there; my eyelids feel so damn heavy the millimeters I do gain feel like a Herculean effort. When I finally manage to open them, bright light burns through my retinas, and I have to blink for what seems like an eternity before my vision adjusts to the space I'm in. I am lying on a hospital bed with tubes and wires coming out of seemingly every limb. Why am I in the hospital again? The last thing I remember is the concert and then…then…Jude pulling me into the back room of the band's bus and the cocaine.

Mierda…the cocaine.

My heart quickens dangerously at the memories assaulting my brain, but somehow, it feels different. Stronger. It has a more constant, steady rhythm. That isn't the only oddity, however. Because as the sound of the blood rushing in my ears dims, the beeping of machines scrapes against my eardrums alongside heavy steps and roaring conversations that seem to be happening all at once around me. I can even hear the traffic from outside, the blaring of honks, and angry drivers shouting at each other. Is that…someone changing the radio station in their car?

What the fuck?

Not only that, but the strong, bitter smell of antiseptic mixed with the artificial fragrance of harsh cleaning products burns my nostrils and the back of my throat but does nothing to distract from the pungent stench of bodily fluids and ammonia. Then the smell of fresh and already decaying flowers hits me like a ton of bricks, and bile surges into my throat at the confusing odors mingling all at once.

The distinct slapping sound of shoes making contact with the floor reaches my ears long before a nurse walks into the room, shock passing over her features. Her strong perfume gives me a headache, even though she's nowhere near my bed. God, did she have to bathe in it? She hurries to the side of my bed and uses a remote to lift the upper half of my body into an upright position.

Her eyebrows pull together in concern. "You shouldn't be awake so soon; you barely just got out of surgery. Can you take a deep breath in and then out for me?"

I do as she says, and the moment I start exhaling, she expertly pulls the breathing tube out of my throat. Which, surprisingly, I didn't even notice beyond the absolute chaos assaulting my ears and nose.

"Oh my God! You're awake already." Chloe's panicked voice pulls my attention toward her as she enters the room and ambles to the side of my bed. "The doctor said it would probably take up to twenty-four hours."

"Hey," I manage to whisper in a hoarse, deep voice.

"Do you want water?" the petite nurse asks. Her hair is cut in a razor-sharp bob, and she is wearing thick-framed glasses. She reminds me of that designer lady from *The Incredibles*.

I nod, so she takes a glass already filled with water from the tray next to the bed and places the straw right at my lips. I take a few sips, the cold liquid like a balm to my abused throat. "Thank you."

"I'll notify the doctor you're awake," she says and scurries out of the room.

Chloe squeezes my hand gently. "How are you feeling?"

"Surprisingly well. I feel different somehow…What happened, Chlo?"

She grimaces and wrinkles her nose. "How much do you remember?"

"The last thing I remember was being with Jude on the bus and then snorting some cocaine and then nothing…" I mumble weakly.

She shakes her head, eyes brimming with tears. "Fuck, Ava. You scared me to death." Taking a deep breath in, she continues, "Jude came from the back of the bus in a panic and told us you collapsed. We called an ambulance, and if Knox didn't know how to do CPR, you would be dead right now. You were brought into the hospital, and the doctor said you would be dead in a few hours…that there was nothing they could do."

She shudders with a haunted look in her eyes. A tear crests over her eyelid and falls, running down her cheek. "Then the doctor came and told us they received a call. They had found a donor, a perfect match… Ava, you got your heart transplant. You have a new heart." As if she can't contain her emotions, she throws her arms around my neck. I tear up, and I'm not completely sure if it's the new heart or just her newly overpowering peach smell invading my senses.

But the scent of her perfume is the last thing on my mind. I feel like I've been tossed overboard in treacherous waters without a life jacket, and giant tidal waves are smashing into me. For the past month and a half, I've only concentrated on how little time I had left, and it made everything a lot simpler if I'm honest. But now, theoretically, I have all my life in front of me and I should be happy, yet I am terrified. The endless possibilities of what the future holds make me feel like I'm in a boat adrift at sea.

The shock dissolves after a few moments, and then the dam breaks. Tears stream down my face like pouring rain while deep sobs rake my body. Chloe doesn't pull back until I manage to calm myself.

I clear my throat and wipe at my tear-streaked face, finally able to take in my room. It resembles a fancy five-star hotel room with a hospital bed. All the machines look futuristic, and everything is brand-spanking new. The marble floor is so shiny you can see your reflection in it. "Um, Chlo, where am I? I don't think my insurance can cover this room."

"They transported you to a private hospital specifically for the transplant surgery. They couldn't bring the heart to you and refused to let Doctor Anderson do the surgery. They wouldn't even let him assist. He was beyond pissed, but your Mom signed all the consent forms, and you now have a new doctor. It was weird, but everything happened in a blur, and your heart was deteriorating by the minute. She had to act fast. Anyway… they said all costs were taken care of by an anonymous donation."

"For real?" *Was I just this lucky?* "Well, I'm not going to look a gift horse in the mouth. Where's mom?"

"She went home to take a shower and change. The doctor said it would be hours until you woke up."

"How is she?"

"Honestly…she was barely hanging by a thread. But as soon as you got rushed into surgery, she was already making plans to move you back in with her and to speak with the school again so everything could go back to normal."

I shake my head. "Too bad that's not what I want."

I now know how it feels to have your days numbered. I learned the importance of living my life to the fullest, for myself, not for other people. Did I make mistakes? Sure. I spiraled out of control with the men, desperate to feel and experience as much as I could in the limited time I had left. Did I regret anything? Honestly, not really. Well, okay, maybe having sex with William the Turd. And I shouldn't have snorted cocaine with my heart condition. But I let myself make mistakes. I let myself live. And that is what matters most.

Two Months Later

7

Ava

The blaring sound of my alarm breaks through my dream, and I groan, not ready to wake up yet. Fumbling for my phone, searching for it in the tangled sheets, I finally manage to find it and press the snooze button.

Just five more minutes.

I was dreaming about him again, the majestic, giant wolf with honey-colored eyes and a beautiful, thick coat of ash-brown fur. We were howling at the full moon together, and the sense of rightness, of complete belonging, enveloped me like a warm blanket.

Is it weird that I'm sexually attracted to a wolf? Yup, I'm definitely going crazy.

Sighing, I push up into a sitting position as the alarm screams at me again. I stab at the screen, mumbling profanities at it, and rub at my eyes to clear the sleep cobwebs from my mind. Standing up, I accidentally knock into one of the boxes I still haven't had the chance to unpack. It flies across the room. Jesus, I'm so much stronger since the surgery, and I haven't gotten used to it yet. I can't even keep track of how many things I've managed to clumsily break, only by holding them or by pressing my finger on a button. On the bright side, I was able to carry all my boxes to my new apartment without any help in record time.

My body is also toned. Don't get me wrong, I don't have abs or anything like that. I am still my curvy self, but you can start to see some muscle definition here and there, and the weird part is that I didn't do anything for it. I still eat chocolate cake like my life depends on it; you can't pry it from my cold, dead hands even if you want to.

Even though it's small, the studio apartment I moved into is cute, and the space is used efficiently. A glass paneled screen separates the bed from the rest of the space, and the dark brown L-shaped couch is on the other side, with a small walnut coffee table between the couch and the TV console resting against the wall. The kitchen is adjacent to the living room space with white cabinets that are a bitch to clean and a breakfast bar that sits two instead of a dining table.

Making my way to the bathroom, I enter the small room and take care of my business. Then I turn on the shower, take off the sleep shorts and the tank top I'm wearing, and step into the spray of hot water.

To my mother's horror, I moved across the country to the city of Ashville a week ago. One day, I was rotting in bed, still drowning in the endless possibilities of what my life could look like, when this wildlife documentary about Ashville's national park started on TV. With my eyes plastered to the screen and a weird jolt from my heart, I felt this strong compulsion to move here. I took it as a sign to make a new beginning and escape my mother's immediate reach. She drove me nuts after the heart transplant surgery.

As soon as I got the confirmation from my new doctor that everything was all right and I made a full recovery after the surgery, I packed all my things and haven't looked back. He said I was a miracle patient, that no one had ever made such a fast recovery after a heart transplant in all of his career. I was just happy that I could put distance between me and my mother so soon.

Turning off the water, I dry myself and wrap the towel around my body. I have a pep in my step as I shuffle to the small mirror hanging above the square-shaped sink. My heart condition made everything strenuous. So now, I greedily sponge every mundane task I go through without feeling like I'm running up a hill with no lungs. I brush my teeth and then dab a bit of foundation and blush on my face. I tame my unruly eyebrows with a spoolie and curl my eyelashes before coating them in a thin layer of mascara.

When I deem my face presentable enough, I stride to one of the boxes on the floor next to my bed and rummage for something to wear. I finally settle for a pair of straight jeans and a sweatshirt that looks like it doesn't have too many wrinkles and get dressed.

My loudly grumbling stomach guides me to my fridge. Since the surgery, it seems like I can never eat enough. The idea of stuffing my face as soon as I woke up was never appealing to me. Now, I feel like I will wither and die if I don't wolf down a whole continental spread in the morning. Strangely, though, I haven't gained any weight. I'm practically living the dream if you ask me.

I've cracked six eggs and am whisking them in a bowl with a fork when my phone starts ringing on the coffee table. I make a beeline for it, take the phone, and accept the video call from Chloe, bringing it back with me to the kitchen.

"Hey, Chlo."

She smiles brightly, and my chest constricts with how much I miss her. Her hair is piled on top of her head in a messy bun, and her beautiful face is free of makeup. "I see you still haven't unpacked everything."

"Yeah, well, it's not that easy doing it all by yourself," I say as I rest the phone on the kitchen counter next to the induction stove, angling it so she can still see me, and take out a skillet. I drop in a big glob of butter and wait for it to melt under the heat.

She blows on top of the mug she's holding, the window at her back giving a glimpse of the night sky. "You know I would've come to help you if you would've let me."

I arch an eyebrow at her and pour the eggs into the hot skillet. "And miss going on tour with your sexy rockstar boyfriend? Like I would have ever let that happen. How is he, by the way? Where are you guys?" After the night my heart stopped on the tour bus, Knox pursued Chloe relentlessly. She was nervous and had a lot of reservations about dating a rock star, understandably so, but he turned out to be a sweet guy, and I convinced her to give him a shot since life was so short and all that.

She practically has hearts in her eyes at the mention of said hot rock star boyfriend. "I honestly don't know, somewhere in Europe. We just arrived like an hour ago, and Knox left five minutes after that. They're having a late session at the studio recording a new song that Jude wrote." She takes a sip from the mug, and her expression turns serious. "By the way, he won't stop asking about you. He keeps demanding I give him your phone number. Since I joined the band on tour, I haven't seen him with one chick, and he hasn't touched drugs or alcohol. Maybe you should give him a chance."

I huff as I turn off the stove and dump the scrambled eggs on a plate. "How's my baby?" I deflect, referring to Simba, my cat. I don't feel like talking about Jude at the moment.

After the incident in the tour bus, he sent a dozen bouquets to my hospital room with an 'I'm sorry' note and then put a stop to the tour so he could get admitted into one of those exclusivist celebrity rehab centers. He said he had a spiritual awakening the moment my heart stopped and that he realized he was going down a slippery slope with the drugs and the alcohol, and what happened to me made him rethink all of his life choices.

When he got out, he tried to reach me everywhere on my social media, but I ignored his messages. He kept saying we belonged together, but c'mon, we just met, and we kissed once. I am happy he got clean and that they restarted the tour, but honestly…Jude and I, we just used each other. He probably got hung up on the idea that he never got to fuck me after all and that I chose to ignore his messages. I can't see myself with him, and it's silly, but he can't compare to the longing I feel every time I dream about the wolf with amber eyes.

"My mom is spoiling him rotten. I swear to God, he won't even want to come back to my apartment once the tour is over. She refuses to feed him kibble. Last night, she made him the cat-safe version of dinuguan, a traditional Filipino stew. Wait, I'll send you the photos; I forgot to forward them when she sent them last night."

Taking a seat at the breakfast bar, I dig into the scrambled eggs before they get cold. "Oh my God, he's so fat," I chuckle out after swallowing. Tears prickle the back of my eyes when I scroll through the photos Chloe has finished sending me. Simba really is living his best life at her mother's house.

After I got released from the hospital, he kept hissing at me and hiding. He was so terrified of me he refused to eat. It broke my heart into a million pieces, but he was losing weight, and he wasn't happy living with me anymore, so Chloe offered to adopt him, and he is staying with her mother while she's on tour with Knox.

"Yeah, I keep telling her to feed him less, but she won't listen." Chloe rolls her eyes. "What are you up to today?"

"Nothing much. I have to look for a job. The money my *Abuelita* left me is not infinite, and I don't want to blow it all out on rent and food, so I have to find something."

Chloe yawns loudly as she stands up from the couch and plops on the bed. "I think I'm going to turn in for the night. This tour life is fucking exhausting."

"'Kay. Love you."

"Love you too," she replies, ending the call.

HALF AN HOUR later, I'm exiting the apartment building, the slightly chilly air prickling my cheeks and filling my lungs. The morning sun shines brightly on the cloudless sky, but the rays barely convey warmth. It's almost the middle of September, and an array of colorful leaves cover the sidewalk like an autumnal blanket, from bright copper to a fading yellow, the smell of decay filling my nose. The weather here is vastly different from the West Coast, and it definitely needs some getting used to. However, my body temperature is running higher after the surgery so while the people I pass on the street are already wearing jackets, I don't need one.

The city is bustling with people on their commute to work, and the morning traffic is brutal, angry drivers honking and muttering insults at each other. Luckily, I don't have to drive my car today. The building I moved into is a ten-minute walk from the Raven district, where I am on my way to meet the private investigator I hired a month ago to look into my donor. He's in the area with another job and asked me to meet him face-to-face to report his findings.

The Raven district is smack dab in the center of Ashville, and it's filled with people wandering in and out of the small restaurants and cafés. I pass by a help-wanted sign in the window of a bar named the Shabby Shotglass—information I store for later.

A chill skates down my spine with the sensation of being watched, and I frown, turning my head, expecting to find someone following me, but I can't spot anything out of the ordinary. It's not the first time I've felt this way since I was released from the hospital. Every time I step outside, I feel like someone is watching me, and honestly, it's starting to bug me how paranoid I'm becoming for no good reason.

I shake off the unpleasant feeling, berating myself, and open the small café's door to the pleasant smell of cinnamon and freshly roasted coffee. The murmur of conversations, laughter, and the thick whir of the frothing machine fills the air. The café has a cozy urban vibe with two exposed brick walls, other two painted a nice mint green, and a few industrial light fixtures that hang from the ceiling alongside numerous plants. A long line of people at the back of the café are waiting at the wood-paneled counter for their to-go orders.

I take my phone out to call John, the private investigator, because we have never met in person, and I have no idea what he looks like. A man lifts his hand as if to signal me, and I walk to the rounded table in the far-left side corner of the café where he's seated. He stands, scraping the plush velvet chair abrasively against the floor.

"Ava, right?" John asks as we shake hands. He is a stout and scruffy middle-aged man with a thick mustache and intelligent hawk-like green eyes. His dark hair is sprinkled with some gray here and there.

"It's nice to finally meet you, John," I reply, and he gestures with his hand, urging me to sit. I sling my purse on the back of the chair. "So, did you find anything?" I ask, drumming my fingers on the table.

He turns slightly and takes out a file folder from the brown leather satchel that dangles from his chair, opening it and pushing it toward me. "Her name was Hope Moore. I also emailed you everything in case you misplace the folder or lose it."

I nod and look down at the page. I'm immediately riveted by Hope's otherworldly beauty, her hair golden and eyes a vivid azure, her features delicate and regal. My heart starts beating erratically against my ribcage as if it recognizes her, and goosebumps form all over my body as I trace her face with the pad of my finger. "She was so young," I murmur, swallowing hard.

John picks up his coffee from the table and takes a sip. "Actually, that's the last photo I could find of her. She disappeared when she was fifteen years old, and she only appeared the night she was declared dead. She was twenty-three when she died."

A horrible feeling churns in my gut. My eyes snap to his. "That's weird, right? How did she die?"

"She got hit by a car. At least, that's what the hospital records say. Getting that information was hard; I had to hire someone to hack into their system. When the family went to pick her up, she'd been cremated already. They made a big scandal out of it because they wanted to bury her in the woods of the community she grew up in."

"Hello. Can I get you something?" the chirpy voice of the server interrupts our conversation.

"Hi, yes, can I have a cappuccino, please? Oh, and a chocolate croissant?" I reply.

She inserts my order into her tablet and smiles at John. "Can I get you anything else, sir?"

"I'm good, thanks," John says, waiting for the server to leave until he speaks again. "She was from a small town in the mountains called Devil's Creek. Her family lived deep in the woods in a closed community. When I started to ask around town about them, everyone acted strangely, and no one wanted to speak to me. I even got thrown out of a few places. When I almost gave up, I passed this house, and an old woman sitting on the porch called out to me. She told me some weird shit about the people living in that closed community."

Leaning forward in my seat, I wait with bated breath for his next words. Maybe I will finally get an explanation for the weird things happening to me. And the vivid dreams. "Like what?"

"She said the people living there belong to some sort of a weird cult that performs satanic rituals while wearing the skin of wolves. She even said her late father saw one of them transform into a wolf when he was just a child playing in the woods."

Ice fills my veins. It must be some sort of a weird coincidence, right? That woman was probably crazy…right? It's just a fluke that I've dreamed about transforming into a wolf and running through the woods with my amber-eyed companion almost every night since I woke up in the hospital after the surgery. I take a few deep breaths in an attempt to stop the panic crawling in the back of my throat.

John smiles halfway. "I wouldn't believe the ramblings of an old woman, though. You know how these small-town folk are. They get so bored living their lives, they start spinning lies and weird tales."

I try to reciprocate his smile, but it probably looks more like a grimace. What John's saying is logical, and his words should erase this feeling of uncertainty bubbling inside me. But the more I think about the old woman's story, the more I feel my heart racing in my chest, like it's trying to say *Yes, exactly*. My palms turn clammy, and my fingers tremble in my lap. "Anything else?" I ask.

"No, that's everything I could find," he responds, standing and slapping a five-dollar bill on the table for the coffee. "I hope you don't mind, but I have to meet another client in about twenty minutes." He puts his jacket on and takes the leather satchel from the chair.

"Thanks, John. I'll wire you the rest of the money," I say, still sitting. I don't want to be rude, but honestly, I don't think I can stand. My legs feel weak and disjointed.

He leaves hastily with a goodbye thrown over his shoulder, and I remain seated in an almost catatonic state as I stare at Hope's picture with equal amounts of sadness and gratefulness for her saving my life. My eyes silently beg her to tell me what's going on.

I wish you didn't have to die for me to still be here, Hope. I promise I won't waste your precious gift.

8

Ava

The sun makes its lazy descent into the horizon, painting the sky and the four-story Victorian-style buildings in vibrant orange hues as I get out of the art studio in the northern part of Ashville. I've just finished attending an hour-long pottery class, and let's just say it was a bit of a disaster. I have clay stuck in places no one should. I'm looking forward, though, to the other classes, especially the watercolor painting one, since I always loved to paint as a kid, but my mother said it's nonsense, and I shouldn't even bother with it because becoming an artist is not a real job that will earn me money, so she threw out all my art supplies.

After I woke up from the heart transplant surgery, I wanted to start exploring things I've never done before because I was never given the opportunity. Even if pottery is going to be a failure, I'm not easily deterred. I will find something I'm good at, and if I can't make money from it, I will at least enjoy it as a hobby.

Crossing the street, I make my way to where I parked my car and get inside. The traffic is a bitch, moving at a snail's pace, and by the time I park the car on the side street next to my apartment building, dusk is settling around me on the short walk to the front door of the building. I punch in the code and take the elevator to the seventh floor.

As soon as I close the front door of my apartment, I make a beeline for the bathroom and turn on the water in the shower. I peel off the sweaty, clay-splattered clothes and step into the hot spray, letting it pound on my sore muscles. Who knew throwing pottery is a freakin' workout?

I made some pasta for dinner, and now I'm seated cross-legged on the couch with the hot plate in my lap, surfing through the TV channels for something to watch as I eat. I stop on the news and turn the volume up. The news anchor's voice echoes off my apartment walls as she announces a woman has been killed in a horrible animal attack in the national park.

She looks like she has been mauled to death by a lion. What kind of animal does that? A horrible feeling of dread churns in my gut. I wanted to take a walk in the national park today, but I changed my mind at the last minute. That could have easily been me.

After I finish eating, I do my makeup, carefully accentuating my eyes with a sexy brown smokey eye. I then get dressed in a leather skirt with black tights underneath, a cute satiny red top with a deep V-neck, and my leather jacket. I pair the look with my over-the-knee boots that have short high heels, and even take the time to style my hair in voluminous curls.

I've been trying to find a job these past few days, but after scouring the internet for hours, I always come out empty. Today though, I remembered the sign I saw in the window of the dive bar in the Raven district. I'm going to stop by and ask if I can speak with someone about the job. I don't think I will get it since I have no experience working in a bar, but I can at least try. It's better than nothing.

I exit my apartment building and start walking in the direction of the Raven district. The city's sounds and smells travel through the air, assaulting my senses. I haven't been here at night before, especially not on a Saturday night, and it looks like an entirely different neighborhood. People are crowding the streets in groups while stumbling in and out of bars, their speech slurred and loud. As I walk by a dark, dingy alley, the pungent smell of alcohol and vomit makes my stomach roil, and I crinkle my nose, trying to breathe through my mouth for a few seconds.

My mood sours when I see I have to pass a group of drunken men standing and smoking in front of the Shabby Shotglass. All of them look like douchey frat boys. They make disgusting remarks at every woman who passes their group, and their boisterous laughs are like nails on a chalkboard as I approach them.

Inevitably, one of them spots me. His leering gaze travels the length of my body, and I shudder in disgust. "Nice tits," he says, and they all snicker, turning around to look at me.

My jaw ticks, and I curl my fingers into fists at my sides, leaving behind crescent indentations. Exhaling loudly through my nose, I ignore them and reach for the bar's door. But as soon as I turn my back to them, a hand grabs my ass beneath my skirt and squeezes hard.

My blood boils over with rage. Before I can think my actions through, I turn around and swing my arm, punching the blond *pendejo* that grabbed my ass. Don't get me wrong, I know how to throw a good punch: torque your hips to use your body weight, not just your arm strength. At least my mother's boyfriend did one thing right; he taught me how to defend myself against sleazy *cabrones como este*. But even so, I don't expect to send him flying backward. He would have skidded on the asphalt a few feet back if it wasn't for one of his friends stopping his momentum.

WHOA!

I look at my fist, my brows furrowing in confusion. My knuckles don't even hurt. The old Ava would have just clamped her mouth shut and kept going. I think I like this new Ava that doesn't take shit from anyone. Pretending like I'm a badass bitch, I smirk. "Nice face," I retort. "Maybe next time you'll use your brain, if you even have any, before putting your hands on a woman."

"You bitch," one of the other pricks spews and staggers toward me.

"If I were you, I would be mindful of the next words that leave your mouth before I decide to rearrange your face," a deep, gravelly voice booms from behind me. The asswipe stops in his tracks, face ashen. Then they collectively scurry away like their asses are on fire, stepping all over each other as they cross the street.

"You okay?" he asks.

"Yeah, thanks," I say while turning around. I almost have to do a double take at how freakin' attractive this guy is. His muscular body is decked in a very expensive-looking suit, the top buttons of his shirt left undone to allow a tattoo to peek out from underneath. He has a piercing in his left ear, a short beard that stretches across his cheeks, and a razor-sharp jaw that could cut a diamond in two. There's a dangerous air to him. Like he could snap your neck with the flick of his finger. And it's not only because of his artfully styled raven locks.

"No need to thank me. I think you had it covered with how you sent that dipshit almost to his grave. You've got a mean right hook," he chuckles out, his pearly white teeth glinting in the light cast by the street lamppost.

"I'm honestly surprised by my own strength," I reply, laughing.

He bends slightly and opens the door. "After you," he says, gesturing for me to enter.

As soon as I step over the threshold, the smell of tap beer mixed with cloying cologne and fried food overpowers my senses. The low music playing in the speakers is drowned out by the murmur of people talking all at once, laughing, and by the sound of ice clinking and beers being gulped.

"What's your name, *bella*?" the stranger asks with a perfect Italian accent after he closes the door at our back.

I turn to look at him, his piercing blue-green eyes captivating mine. "Ava."

"Well, I guess I'll see you around, Ava." He winks and saunters toward the back of the dive bar, leaving me staring at his fine ass. As soon as he's gone, I realize I was so mesmerized by his eyes that I forgot to ask him his name.

Blinking a few times, I take in my surroundings. The dimly lit interior is far more spacious than the outside let on, with a long bar at my right made out of dark wood and numerous high-top tables, almost all occupied. Two pool tables are on my left in a separate space, crowded by people playing and standing near them, drinking beer. There are some private booths as well toward the back, where the hottie disappeared.

Making a beeline for the bar, I sit on one of the empty brown leather stools, hanging my purse on the wooden backrest. The wall at the back of the bar is entirely made out of shelves stacked with alcohol bottles. A rack with upside-down stem glasses hangs above the bartender's head.

She has to be one of the most beautiful women I have ever seen, her delicate features framed by angular cheekbones and a defined jawline — the kind of bone structure you would kill for. She is mixing a cocktail vigorously, the outline of a tattoo on her muscular right bicep peeking from under the short sleeve of her T-shirt. Damn, she is ripped.

I am munching on a pretzel when the bartender finally makes her way to my side of the bar. "Hey, sorry about the long wait. Do you already know what you want to drink?" she asks, smiling warmly and placing a coaster in front of me.

I smile back. "No worries, it looks like it's a pretty busy night." My eyes skim over the drinks menu I am holding. There aren't many alcohol-free options. "How's the Zombie mocktail? I can't drink alcohol," I say, lifting my head and looking into her honey eyes.

Those eyes, they're so mesmerizing. Why do I have a feeling I have seen them before?

"It's a blend of citrus and tropical flavors. It's okay, but not my favorite. I can make you the Emily Special mocktail if you want. It's not on the menu, but it's delicious. It's my favorite."

I shrug. "Yeah, sure. I trust you."

"Do you want to start a tab?" she asks.

"No, I'll just pay by round."

"'Kay." She dumps some ice in the cocktail shaker. "So, are you visiting Ashville?" She starts pouring from different bottles over the ice, her gaze flitting to me.

"No, actually, I just moved here a week and a half ago, and I'm looking for a job. I saw the sign in the window and thought it's a good idea to come by and ask about it."

"Em, can you please pour twelve tequila shots for table seven?" A willowy guy with dark umber skin places a tray on top of the bar next to me and sighs. "The crowd's rowdy tonight," he mumbles, pats his sweaty forehead with a napkin, then runs a hand over his short buzz cut.

"Tony, is Marnie still here? We have someone asking for the server job."

"Yeah, she went into her office ten minutes ago," he shoots back and turns to look at me. "Oh hey, buttercup. I saw you through the window punching that douche outside. I could hug you right now. Those frat boys were a nightmare to serve, and they didn't even leave a tip. Don't let her pay for her drink, Em. It's on me." He winks at me and picks up the tray of tequila shots, keeping it high above his head while weaving his way through the packed bar.

"Marnie's our boss. You can find her office at the end of the bathroom hallway. Just take a right at the back exit sign, and then her office will be the first door on your left," the bartender says before placing a rounded cocktail glass filled with an amber concoction in front of me.

I take a sip; the flavor explodes on my tongue. A moan escapes my lips at how good it is. "Oh my God, this is incredible. I can't believe it doesn't have any alcohol. What did you put in it?"

"It's an amaretto sour mocktail with a secret blend. I knew you'd love it." Her full lips curve in a knowing smile, and then she moves to the other patrons waiting to be served.

I down what is left of the delicious mocktail. Despite what that server, Tony, said, I place the money for it along with a tip under the empty glass and get off the bar stool. I sling my purse back over my shoulder before making my way toward the toilet sign hanging above the corridor near the pool tables.

As I weave through the packed bar, a burly man that is clearly shit-faced tries to hoist himself up on the stool at one of the high-top tables, but his foot misses, and he ends up spilling his beer on the guy next to him while falling backward and barreling into my side, sending me sprawling forward.

I slam and squeeze my eyes shut to mentally prepare myself to collide with the floor, but instead, I land into a hard, hot body that smells incredible, earthy, and woodsy with a hint of pine. It reminds me of the forest.

A strong arm bands across my middle, and a warm hand presses at the small of my back, fusing me completely to the front of the stranger that caught me. My eyes immediately snap open at his touch, which feels like a live wire of electricity, making my pulse skyrocket and my nipples pebble into diamond-hard tips.

As I look up, intending to thank him, my words die on my lips. My brain absolutely short-circuits. He must be the hottest man alive. He's so freakin' tall, about six foot nine, and he is all hard-cut marble, broad shoulders, and thick, powerful thighs. His muscles are so sculpted you can see the outline through his navy Henley. The color of his skin reminds me of the desert dunes bathing in the sunset light right before the sun disappears completely from the sky, and his hair is an ash-brown mess of curls, longer in the middle and shorter on the sides. Stubble covers his cheeks, giving him a sexy, scruffy appearance.

Time seems to stop as everything disappears around us. The muffled music, the slurred drunken conversations, and the laughter coming from a nearby table all fade away the moment our gazes collide. His eyes are two pools of desire, the amber transforming to burnished gold as he gulps, his breath coming hard through his parted lips.

His eyes…where have I seen his eyes before?

Oh my God. The wolf I've been dreaming about since I woke up from the heart transplant surgery. He has the same eyes. No…that's impossible. I'm just reading too much into things.

We are both breathing as if we've just finished running a marathon. He bends slightly, brushing his knuckles on the side of my face, and then frames my jaw with his calloused fingers while his thumb presses on my bottom lip. My tongue sneaks out to taste his skin, and his eyes darken with desire. Molten lava courses through my veins, and my clit starts to throb as my panties soak completely with the need to feel him between my legs.

Mierda. ¿Qué me está pasando?

He closes the space between us, and I think he is going to kiss me, but instead he buries his face in my hair. "Mmm, you smell so good I could eat you piece by piece," he rumbles in my ear, his deep, gravelly voice like crushed velvet over silk as his breath tingles the side of my neck, sending shivers down the ladder of my spine.

Jesus, I have never been more turned on in my entire life. If he decides to bend me over and fuck me right here in the crowded bar, I won't even lift a finger to stop him.

He turns his head slightly, bringing our faces so close we are practically sharing the same breath. Fiery golden eyes snap to my lips. A hard swallow follows. And as if he can't stop himself, he inches forward when a woman knocks into us and breaks the spell. His dark-winged eyebrows furrow while he shakes his head as though he can't believe what just happened between us. As if I'm poisonous, he lets me go abruptly. Everything comes rushing back all at once. My knees buckle, and I feel like this time I will surely face-plant when his hand shoots out, grabbing my elbow and stabilizing me.

"You okay?" he asks gravelly, clearing his throat, his eyes fixated somewhere above my head as though he's asking for the universe's secrets to unravel at his feet.

"Yeah," I respond, my voice so breathy, I barely recognize it. "Thank you."

He nods sharply, letting go of my elbow as if I burnt him. Shoulders stiff and spine rod-straight, he turns around and hightails toward the private booths at the back like the hounds of hell and Satan himself are nipping at his heels.

What the hell was that?

I have to take a few moments to breathe in and out with my hand pressed to the center of my chest in a feeble attempt to calm my erratic heart. I almost go after him and demand he finish what he started.

When I finally feel I have full control over my body again, I make a beeline for the hallway near the pool tables. After I pass the long line of women waiting to get into the bathroom, I amble toward the exit sign the bartender talked about and make a right on the dark corridor. I rap my knuckles against the first door on the left wall.

"Come in," a raspy voice travels through the door.

Turning the knob, I step over the threshold and can barely see the woman sitting at the desk through the thick wall of cigarette smoke. "Hello, my name is Ava Perez. I'm here for the server position. I saw the help-wanted sign in the window."

She stubs out the cigarette into an ashtray on top of the glass desk and waves her hand in front of her face in a failed attempt to clear the air. "Hi Ava, please come in and sit down." She stands up and opens the window. "Sorry about the smoke. I forgot to open the window. I told my husband I quit a week ago, but running this bar stresses me the fuck out, so I hide in here to wind down," she rambles as she takes a seat back at the desk. "He's been on my case lately about selling the bar and retiring to a tropical island, but this bar has been in my family for generations. I can't just sell it."

Now that the thick billowing smoke starts to dissipate, I can see her clearly. She is a woman past the age of fifty with unruly, curly silver hair. She's wearing a long flowery skirt and a bohemian shirt with flounce sleeves. "I'm Marnie," she says, extending her hand toward me. "So, Ava, do you have any experience serving in bars?" she asks after we shake hands, her kind brown eyes sizing me up.

I sit down. "Um, I don't want to lie to you. I haven't worked much because I was focused on law school. I do have some experience working at a café on campus. I know it's different from working in a bar, but I'm a fast learner."

Marnie purses her lips and drums her fingers on top of the desk. "Why'd you quit law school? Don't tell me your dream is to work in a dive bar," she says, amusement dripping from her tone.

I fumble with my fingers in my lap. "Well, two months ago, I was given a new chance at life. I had a heart transplant, and I realized going to law school was only my mother's dream and that I wasn't happy. So, after I recovered, I decided to move to Ashville and start living on my own terms. The truth is, I don't know what my dream is. I guess I never let myself dream when I only wanted to please my mother and be her perfect little puppet."

She leans back in her seat with a contemplative frown, accentuating the already deep lines on her forehead. "I like your honesty. Can you start tonight?"

My eyebrows shoot up all the way to my hairline. "Wait, what? You want to give me the job?" I can't believe it could be that easy.

"You're not underage, are you?"

"No, but as I said, I don't have any experience—"

"Well, I desperately need a server, and you need a job. Beggers can't be choosers. Schedule's Wednesday to Saturday from nine p.m. to three a.m. You have to come one hour before opening, and then you can leave after cleaning. If you do well tonight, we can manage all the paperwork on Monday." Marnie pushes her chair back, making its legs scrape loudly against the hardwood floor, and stands up. "C'mon, let's go find Tony. He's one of the servers. You'll shadow him tonight, and he'll teach you everything you need to know."

After she shows me the staff room and gives me a locker where I put my jacket and purse, I follow Marnie back into the crowded bar. My feet are already killing me, even if the boot heels are short. I'm not one to wear heels very often, and I want to kick myself for this stupid decision, but I honestly wasn't expecting to start working right away.

Marnie hands me a notepad for orders and explains the last details of what the job entails as we wait for Tony to finish serving a table.

"That's Emily," Marnie says, pointing at the beautiful bartender pouring tequila into some shot glasses.

Wait a minute. The color of her skin, the shape of her face, her hair, and even her eyes. All of her features are so similar to those of the hot guy I landed into twenty minutes ago. "Does she have a brother?" I blurt out.

Marnie throws me a sidelong glance. "Yeah, she does. How did you know?"

I gulp, remembering the way my body responded to the stranger's touch. "Um, I thought I saw a guy that looked exactly like her," I reply, heat blazing in my cheeks. "She's extremely talented. I ordered a mocktail, and I swear I couldn't even tell it didn't have any alcohol," I say, trying to change the subject because I'm feeling flustered all of a sudden.

"Trust me, I know. I'm lucky she loves to bartend so much. Otherwise, I wouldn't be able to afford someone with her skills. Will you be okay waiting for Tony by yourself? I need to head back into the office to deal with some paperwork."

"Yeah, sure, no worries."

She stands. "Okay then, I'll see you Monday morning so we can sort out the contract and everything else. Does ten a.m. work for you?"

"Ten is perfect," I reply, and she gives me a toothless smile and a nod before disappearing through the crowd.

9

Logan

The thick envelope filled with cash makes a hearty *thwack* when I plop it into the coroner's outstretched hand. I use it as my cue to turn on my heel and make my way out of his office. The moment I step outside, I inhale deeply, grateful for the fresh, icy air filling my lungs. But the stench of death still lingers on my skin. Regretfully, I don't have the time to shower. The Conclave awaits.

I came here half an hour ago to inspect the cadaver of the woman found in the national park. It's the first thing I did after my month on the road to search for my fated mate. So far, I have visited all the packs that couldn't come to the ball my mother organized and haven't found her. But I won't give up, not until the last moment.

I can't believe the rogue managed to get on my turf undetected, even with the patrols my pack has been doing every single day and night for two months now. The victim was also found right at the border of our community like he was playing some kind of twisted game with me.

Even worse is that a hiker found her instead of a pack member.

My phone pings with a text message, and I get it out of my pocket as I make my way to where I parked my truck on the side of the street. I open the door and get in the seat, tapping on the screen. The sudden burst of light blinds me momentarily.

> **Malik: Change of location. Meet us at the bar where Em works.**

The drive from the coroner's office to the Raven district, where the bar is located, is short, but I have to find a parking garage to leave my truck. Parking it on the side of the street in the district is not a possibility, especially with the drunks that get shit-faced and crowd the streets like cockroaches. Once, I found the side of my car all scratched up and the hood splattered with vomit. Let's just say I have learned my lesson since then.

The half-moon is perched high on the night sky, the tiny glimmering lights of the stars being dwarfed by the artificial city lights as I make the pungent fifteen-minute walk to the bar. I don't like how you can't see the sky properly here in the city. That's why I prefer to stay mostly in our community, located deep in the national park, surrounded by nature, and even more in my private cabin in the woods where no one can find me. Only my sister knows its location, and I like that no one can reach me there.

However, I haven't been able to go back to the cabin in more than two months. All of my responsibilities and the children of the pack getting touched by the weakness have prevented me from taking any time off. And now the motherfucking rogue decided to come to Ashville and maul a woman on the border of my community where I'm supposed to keep everyone safe. I just can't catch a fucking break.

As soon as I open the door and step through the bar's threshold, I see *her*. Everything disappears around me, my vision tunneling until all I can see is *her*. My wolf takes notice and growls loudly inside my head, "*Mine!*" My eyes are laser-focused on her as she weaves through the crowd of people drinking and laughing near the high-top tables.

She has a curvy body that would fit just perfectly against mine. I immediately get a mental image of my fingers skimming along her naked, naturally bronzed skin, making me instantly hard. Goddammit… those perfect thighs. I would sell my soul to the devil only for a couple of minutes with them wrapped around my ears or to suffocate under them as she rides my face. I'm not picky.

She tucks a wavy strand of shiny brunette hair under her ear, and I forget how to fucking breathe when I get a glimpse of a perfect heart-shaped face with luscious lips and big, expressive eyes.

Before I can process my actions, my legs move under me with long, purposeful strides and a hint of desperation, as though she is the center of my gravity. Just as I'm about to reach her, fingers trembling, a drunken asshole misses his chair by a few inches and falls on his back, sending her sprawling forward, directly into my arms. My wolf growls loudly at him in my head for bringing any sort of pain to her but is immediately settled when her body melds perfectly against mine, sending pulses of desire straight to my dick, hardening it further if that is even possible.

My arm moves on its own accord as it circles along her middle, and my hand splays on her lower back, pressing her even closer to me because even the smallest distance between us is unbearable. She lets out a tiny whimper at the touch, and that sends my wolf screaming inside of my head to claim her right this moment.

Fuck, only her scent can bring me to my knees. She smells deliciously and entirely intoxicating, like caramel and vanilla, with a hint of something flowery. It reminds me of the field of violets near my cabin in the woods.

My heart starts beating like a jackhammer inside my chest when she opens her eyes. I have never seen eyes like hers, so pale green, darker on the outside of her irises and then gradually leaching color toward the dilated pupils that hint she is as affected by me as I am by her. So up close and personal, I can see lighter streaks of color in her hair and the freckles smattered across the bridge of her upturned nose.

The impulse to touch her overtakes me completely as I lift my right hand and let my knuckles caress the side of her perfect face. *Fuck me.* These full sinful lips. Before I can stop myself, I am already pressing my thumb on her lower lip as my hand cradles her jaw. My wolf urges me to close the space between us and take what's mine. Her tongue sneaks out and licks my thumb, and I can smell the musky tang of her desire mixing with her heady aroma.

Suddenly, my body bends to be closer to her, and my nose buries in her hair as I inhale her scent deeply like an addict searching for my next fix. Her perfume, mixed with the scent of her arousal, makes my head spin like a drug and shoots up my veins to fry my nerve endings. "Mmm, you smell so good I could eat you piece by piece," I say gravelly, voicing my wolf's thoughts.

What did I just blurt out? I sound like a creepy idiot.

I turn my head slightly, about to claim those plump lips and finally taste them, when someone knocks into us.

The reality of what I was about to do kicks in like a sucker punch. I can't betray my mate. Not like this. Not when there is still a small chance to find her, even if my days are numbered. I can still fucking find her, dammit. I may not have dreamed about her in over two months, no matter how hard I've tried, but she still has to be out there. I feel it in the very fabric of my being.

I let this woman go immediately, earning a deep, menacing snarl from my wolf. I need to put as much distance between us as possible. Her scent and the feel of her skin on mine muddles my brain.

In an attempt to clear my mind, I shake my head hard. But then she sways in front of me, not being able to withstand her weight. My hand shoots out and grabs her elbow, the heat of her skin burning through mine. Her nipples are taut, pointing at me through the thin material of the shirt she is wearing, and all I want to do is bend and suck on the tiny buds until she melts in my arms and begs for my cock like a good girl.

I clear my throat loudly, trying to stay in the present. "You okay?"

"Yeah," she breathes in a sexy, low, raspy voice that makes my dick twitch in my pants as if I'm still a hormonal teenager.

Down boy! When the fuck did I become so pathetic?

"Thank you," she says, looking at me with those doe-like eyes, and I almost get lost in them again.

Giving a jerky nod in response, I let go of her elbow abruptly because if I keep touching her, I will lose my fucking mind. My wolf is not happy, and my muscles are straining as he's trying to take control of my body, warring with the rational part of my mind. I somehow manage to turn on my heel and reach the back of the bar, where I know the others are waiting for me. Every single step I have to take away from her is physically painful. Sweat drips down my spine with the sheer effort.

10

Ava

A few minutes pass before Tony slides onto the bar stool Marnie vacated. He heaves out a deep sigh and places his tray on top of the bar. "Thank God you got the job. I don't know how much more Rita and I could take," he says, referring to the other server, a woman in her late forties whose blond ponytail swishes against her back as she walks out of a door.

"Okay, so the kitchen is through that door Rita came from. Marnie's husband, Dave, is the cook. The food menu is limited. We only serve bar grub, French fries, wings, and stuff like that. You'll learn it in no time." He lifts his hand in the air, catching Emily's eye. She comes over after a few seconds. "Em, can you pour two glasses of that fancy whiskey you keep only for your brother's friends?"

"Logan's here too?" she asks as she takes a bottle from the shelf behind her. Dumping some ice into two whiskey tumblers, she pours the spirit over it.

So now I have a name to go with the mysterious stranger…Logan. Even his name is hot, and it definitely suits him.

"Yeah, and all of his delicious-looking friends," Tony replies, fanning himself with a dreamy look in his eyes. "What I would let those men do to me. Too bad none of them are gay," he sighs while he stands, takes two beers from the fridge, and places them on top of another tray.

"Look alive, buttercup. Prepare yourself because we're going to serve the hottest men alive. You'll take the beers, and I'll take the whiskey," Tony tells me as he lifts the tumblers, positions them on top of his tray, and saunters toward the private booths in the back, expertly slicing through the crowd. I follow closely while holding the tray with the beer bottles.

As we approach their table, my stomach constricts, and my hands suddenly become clammy and start trembling. I almost drop the tray. *Pull it together, Ava!* Tony is taller than me, and I can't see much besides the back of his head. But, when he moves a little to the side, I swallow hard, not prepared to be hit full force with the raw, sexual energy every single one of them exudes.

Is there something in the water here? How can all of them be this level of hot?

My heart flip-flops inside my chest the moment my eyes land on Logan. All of them are tall and built like some sort of Greek gods, but Logan is the tallest and the Zeus of the group. His big frame dwarfs the others, which is saying a lot because none of them are small men. My eyebrows shoot up in surprise when I realize the guy with blue-green eyes, the one dressed in the expensive-looking suit who threatened the frat boys earlier, is sitting beside Logan at his right, near the wall.

Across suit guy is another ridiculously attractive man with dark eyes and inky black hair that is pulled in a short ponytail, a few strands framing his face. He is decked in black jeans and a black tee, intricate tattoos covering every inch of available skin on his arms. Even his throat and knuckles are tattooed. He wears his arrogance like a dark cloak. But there is also something else about him…something dark and dangerous, sending a shiver down my spine in awareness.

Next to him, in front of Logan, is a guy with such exotic features I can't quite place from where he is. He has high cheekbones and upturned eyes that look almost cat-like. A septum piercing dangles from his nose, and his long hair, the color of lively silver, reminds me of moonlight slanting through a window.

They are all talking low with grim expressions on their faces. Only the tattooed guy, who seems the most dangerous, keeps stealing furtive glances toward the bar as his white-knuckled fingers tighten on the empty whiskey tumbler, anger flashing in his eyes like lightning. His grip is so strong I'm afraid he will shatter the glass any second . They all stop talking the moment we reach their table. Not like I could even decipher what they were saying, which is weird since I can hear much better now after the surgery.

"Here you go, gentlemen," Tony says with a flourish, replacing suit guy and tattooed guy's two empty glasses of whiskey with the full ones. He steps to the side so I can come closer to the table.

Immediately, I feel Logan's gaze on me like a hot brand to the face, but I can't look his way. I'm afraid I'm going to drop the tray if I do.

"Ava, you work here?" Suit guy asks as I bend to place the beer in front of the silver-haired guy. A glint of animalistic hunger shines in his eyes as they slowly rake over my face and land on my neck. They stop on the fluttering vein on the side of my throat for a few seconds before his gaze snaps back to mine. "If I knew, I would have come here more often," he says charmingly with a wink.

I clear my throat loudly, feeling flustered at the attention he is showing me. "I just started tonight. I'm sorry I didn't quite catch your name earlier," I reply with a smile.

"It's Dominic," Silver hair answers for his friend with a shit-eating grin as he looks at Logan. "I'm Malik; that right there is Kaiden," he says, pointing with his thumb at the tattooed guy who isn't paying any attention. His gaze is still fixated on one of the tables near the bar with flared nostrils. Silver hair juts his chin in front of him. "And this angry furball here is Logan."

"Nice to meet you guys. I'm Ava," I murmur.

Tony is standing next to me, a big smile on his face, his eyes volleying between us. He looks like all he misses now is a big bowl of popcorn. Turning toward Logan, I finally let my hungry gaze rake over him. There's a stiffness in his shoulders. Even weirder, anger radiates from him in waves as a muscle ticks along his jaw.

I lift the beer bottle from the tray with trembling fingers, but as I bend to place it in front of Logan on the table, my high heel gets trapped in between the floorboards. In the next second, I fly forward into the side of the table and hit my pelvic bone, spilling the beer all over Logan's lap.

"Oh my God!" I exclaim and immediately straighten. Dislodging the high heel, I hastily pluck all the napkins from the holder. The pain pulsing throughout my pelvis makes my teeth grind. Motherfucking fuck, it hurts, but not as bad as the embarrassment I feel at this moment. I wish the floor would open and swallow me alive.

"I'll bring more napkins," Tony says with urgency as he scurries away.

"I'm so sorry," I mumble, bend over Logan, and press the napkins on top of his crotch. His intoxicating smell wraps around me in a dizzying spell. I gasp when I feel his massive erection digging into the palm of my hand. Scorching fire takes over my entire body, making my core pulse with need.

What the hell is happening to me?

All of a sudden, he grabs my wrist, stopping my movement.

"Enough," he snaps in a voice so thick and raw I freeze and stare back into his eyes that feel like two pieces of hot coals. My pulse quickens as I feel everything around us fade again, until Logan swears loudly under his breath and lets go of my wrist as if I'm radioactive.

I shake my head and blink a few times, attempting to clear my mind, not understanding the deep connection I feel to this guy I just met and why I got so aroused at a mere touch. "I'll bring you a fresh bottle." I offer a small smile. My face is probably ten shades of red at this moment since I feel my cheeks burning fiercely.

"There's no need. You've done enough. Just leave," Logan says coldly, his voice chilling me to the bone.

I recoil as if he slapped me, back rod straight. "I'm so sorry," I whisper. "I'll ask Tony to bring you another, then." I turn on my heel, desperate to get as far away from him as possible, the room hazy through the curtain of unshed tears.

"Sorry! He doesn't get out much," Malik yells at my back as I make a beeline for the bathroom hallway. I shove my way through the sweaty bodies crowding the bar, needing a few moments to compose myself before going back to shadowing Tony for the rest of the night.

Fisting my fingers at my sides, I take a few deep breaths in. A failed attempt to calm my racing heart, really. All I want to do is go home and curl into a ball. I don't understand the visceral reaction I have toward that asshole, but I can't let him ruin my first day at work. I need this job. I just have to stay away from that section for the rest of the night and let Tony handle it alone. Hopefully, he will understand.

11

Logan

I finally reach the private booth where only Kaiden and Malik are seated.

"Are you possessed or something? You looked like you were about to fuck that girl in the middle of the bar," Malik chuckles out before taking a hearty sip from the beer bottle he is holding. "She's hot, but still, I didn't picture you as much of an exhibitionist. That's more my thing."

Kaiden is seated next to him in the black leather booth. A curt nod is the only acknowledgment I receive from him. He is turned slightly with his back to the wall. His gaze is fixated in the direction of the bar, and his silver rings make sharp clinking noises against his whiskey tumbler while he drums his fingers on its side.

"Shut the fuck up, Malik. I'm not in the mood right now," I snap at him, my jaw locking with anger. "Where's Dominic?" I ask, pointedly looking at the empty glass of whiskey on the table opposite Kaiden's vise-like grip, knowing it must be his.

"He got bored and hungry waiting for you, so he stepped out for a quick snack," Malik replies and places the beer bottle back on the table.

"What crawled up your ass, fuckface?" Dominic's voice rings from behind me.

I turn around and step to the side so he can sit at the table. He is dressed in one of his Italian designer suits, as per usual, and his features are relaxed. The hunger that always seems present in his eyes dulled down, and the pale hue that usually settles over his bronzed olive skin absent.

"Nothing," I respond in a clipped tone and sit down next to him, signaling to the server to come take my order. "Since when do we have Conclave meetings someplace other than Kaiden's penthouse?"

Malik tilts his head toward Kaiden. "Since lover boy here had to drag us with him on one of his stalking sessions. Look toward the bar at one of the high-top tables," he tells me as he relaxes back with a shit-eating grin.

"I'm not stalking her," Kaiden says through clenched teeth. The look he throws Malik could level a city to mere ashes.

Dominic snickers. "Oh yeah? Then what are we doing here?"

Tony, the willowy server, blocks my view as he places a beer in front of me and refreshes Dominic's glass of whiskey so I can't see what they're talking about, but I get a feeling I know who this is all about. Even so, I'm allowed a glimpse of the object of Kaiden's obsession as soon as I thank Tony and he steps aside — a young woman with ebony hair, ivory skin, and pale cerulean eyes surrounded by rings of violet.

She is seated at a high-top table near the bar next to a skinny blond guy who rambles like he is in a race with himself. She looks kind of bored, to be honest. He leans forward, places his hand on Iris's naked thigh, and slides it a little upward under her dress. If Kaiden was pissed before, he is going to burn this fucking place to the ground any minute now.

I chance a look at him, and crimson streaks take over the bottomless pits of onyx in his eyes, mixing with the flecks of gold, his power thickening the air in the bar as the dim lights flicker above our heads. Still, it's a good sign if his irises are not completely golden. He comes dangerously close to losing his shit when that happens. The vein on the side of his head looks like it's about to burst, though.

"Kaiden," Dominic rumbles in warning before anyone in this bar can notice what is happening.

Kaiden takes a deep breath in, and his power retreats, but it still hangs close to the surface, ready to burst, electrifying the air. I almost choke on the fury seeping out of his pores like noxious fumes. Malik looks at me and Dominic with an arched eyebrow. "Wanna bet that douche tries to kiss Iris in the next ten minutes?" Pouring gasoline over Kaiden's raging fire is not a good idea, but Malik doesn't care. He always finds it funny when one of us gets pissed and likes to push our buttons any chance he gets.

"I say twenty minutes." Dominic slaps a hundred-dollar bill on the table.

Malik takes his wallet out of his leather duster, which is between him and Kaiden, and matches Dominic's wager. He slides the money on the table before waggling his eyebrows at me. "Logan? What do you say, man?"

With a shake of my head, I refuse to participate in their stupid bet. Besides…I have more important things to do. Like resisting the siren call of a curvy brunette with killer thighs and eyes that could put me in a coma at a mere glance my way. Fuck. *Stop thinking about her, you idiot!*

Kaiden whirls his head toward Malik with a murderous look on his face. "She's not going to kiss him at all," he spits like he can't even conceive that as a possibility. He takes another deep cleansing breath through flared nostrils.

"Can you put a barrier spell on the table so no one can listen in?" Kaiden asks Malik after a few minutes when he finally has his power fully under control, but his eyes are back on Iris. He watches her like a hawk ready to dive and sink its talons into its prey.

Malik circles his hand above his head. A thick black fog of magic swirls into the air before it disappears as quickly as it appeared. It settles like a dome over our booth. "Done." The spell provides a barrier between us and the other patrons. They know we are at the table, but it prevents them from listening or looking our way unless we want them to.

Kaiden's eyes snap to mine. "Did you detect any scent on her?" He is referring to the woman who was found murdered earlier in the national park.

I take a sip from my beer and shake my head. A stray curl falls over my eye, and I push at it, annoyed. "Unfortunately, no. Before going to the coroner's office, the pack circled the border where she was found for hours. Nothing. It's like he's a ghost."

Malik leans forward and rests his hands on the table in front of him. "And the wounds? Was it the same MO as the other victims in the neighboring towns?"

I nod. "The same, complete with the missing heart."

"Assuming the rogue is male could be a mistake. What if it's a female behind all of the attacks?" Dominic asks from beside me, arching an eyebrow in my direction.

"The wounds looked too big and deep for a female wolf shifter to have caused them," I retort.

"Malik, what do you think? Could the rogue be working with a witch or warlock to hide its scent?" Kaiden asks after a few beats of silence, rubbing his stubbled jaw with his hand .

Malik leans back in the booth, and his eyebrows furrow as he mulls it over. "Since dark creatures don't like to work with each other outside the Conclave, I dismissed this idea when it first popped into my head, but there's no other explanation, honestly. The rogue couldn't mask its scent on its own for that long. It needs a masking spell, and that's black magic territory."

"Then I want you to go to all the covens you know personally and start asking questions about a possible dark witch helping a rogue," Kaiden tells the warlock before he turns to me. "Logan, you need to double the patrols. The rogue's killing too close to the border of your pack; we can't risk it murdering anyone under the Conclave's protection. We take care of our own. I have a feeling it's going to strike again, but I don't think it's going to move from Ashville just yet."

I suck on my teeth. "My men are tired from the endless patrols in the last two months, and until the wedding, the pack will not get stronger." I'm not happy to admit how vulnerable my pack is right now. As Alpha, I should have done better, but I will wait for her until the very last minute.

Kaiden nods, and his gaze locks with Dominic's. "Then, Dom, I want you to send some vampires from your den and replace the wolf shifters of the pack on the night shifts, not only on the full moon nights. I'll open another location for them to feed as much as they want as a reward." He raises his hand to flag the server as we finish our drinks.

After Tony comes over and takes our order, Kaiden starts speaking again, this time giving us his full attention as his eyes lock with each of us. "There's also something else I wanted to discuss with you. Malik already knows since he was with me on my last trip to Hell. The mutinies there are getting more violent by the day. Something big is coming. We need to be careful and monitor very closely all bodies of water where the veil between Hell and the human realm is more vulnerable."

Dominic crosses his arms in front of his chest, and his forehead crinkles in concern. "Do you think they will attempt to breach the veil?"

Kaiden's face is even more serious than usual as he nods. "It's a strong possibility. We knew this day would come with how widely the mutinies have stretched in recent years."

A salacious smirk spreads on Malik's face as his eyes fixate near the bar. "Homeboy is getting ballsy." We all turn to see Iris's date closing the space between them as he palms her cheek. "C'mon, you idiot, kiss her already," he says impatiently, staring at his watch.

Kaiden pierces him with a glare that could cut through skin and bone and wipes Malik's grin off his face efficiently. There is only so much he can fuck around, poking at Kaiden. He is the most patient of us, and he usually ignores Malik's antics or comments because of how much they've endured together. But Malik didn't pick a good night to talk shit when Kaiden's patience is already stretched too thin. And, after all, he is the leader of the Obsidian Conclave. There is no being more powerful than him in the human realm at this moment. Everyone thinks he is only an Elite demon, but we know the truth.

"Any news on the Kabal lately?" I ask in an attempt to break the awkward silence that has fallen between us.

Kaiden doesn't take his eyes off Iris's table as he answers me, his jaw an iron bar of tension. "I keep getting reports of more and more dark creatures being kidnapped under mysterious circumstances. I think they're building another prison for their sick experiments."

I shake my head with anger. "Fuck, I thought that shit was over when we shut down the one beneath the Vatican all those years ago. We killed almost all of their members. Do they never learn?"

Malik laughs bitterly, the sound hollow. "If there's something those sick fucks will never do is give up torturing what they consider lesser beings."

He and Kaiden know best. They both have been imprisoned and tortured by the Kabal. It's how they met. Only Kaiden had been raised as a prisoner since he was a baby under the abuse of his father, who created the organization. He'd always viewed his son as an abomination, a lesser being, and tortured him endlessly until someone broke into the prison where Kaiden and all the dark creatures were being held and set them all free.

Her intoxicating scent wraps around me like silk before she comes into view from behind Tony, the willowy server. Holding a tray with two beers, she approaches our table. *Fuck.* I tried my best until this moment not to look for her in the crowded bar, only stealing furtive glances here and there, but now my fate's been sealed and delivered on a round tray with clicking high heels. My muscles twitch with an overwhelming compulsion to stand up and approach her. Gulping, my eyes sail over her perfect curves, and I am hard again. *Dammit.* This is hardly the time or moment for that.

My gaze is riveted on her as she bends to place one of the beer bottles in front of Malik. Fuck me. The top she is wearing gives me a spectacular view of her perfect, round tits.

Suddenly, Dominic addresses her. "Ava, you work here?"

What. The. Fuck.

My blood boils. He knows *her* name. Dominic never knows a woman's name unless he is interested in fucking her or if he already fucked her. My wolf growls dangerously inside my mind. I swallow hard past the irrational pang of jealousy coiling in my chest like a venomous snake, seizing my lungs and squeezing hard.

"If I knew, I would have come here more often." The fucker winks at her, and I want to throat-punch him.

I have to bite the inside of my cheek hard until I feel the taste of copper on my tongue in order to restrain myself from pummeling Dominic into the ground with the fists currently tensed at my sides.

Why is my wolf going crazy over this woman while erasing all of my rational thinking?

Ava clears her throat. "I just started tonight. I'm sorry I didn't quite catch your name earlier," she responds, and my heart rate slows down a little because what she said denotes that they only just met and that Dominic hasn't fucked her yet. But with how he looks at her, he definitely wants to.

"It's Dominic," Malik says, and I throw daggers at him with my eyes. A Cheshire cat grin takes over his face. He saw me with Ava earlier, and he can tell I am about to fucking explode. "I'm Malik, that right there is Kaiden." He points with his thumb at Kaiden, who isn't paying any attention to us anymore as he looks at Iris. Then Malik juts his chin toward me. "And this angry furball here is Logan."

Ava turns toward me and takes the bottle from the tray. The moment she bends, she somehow trips, and before I can stabilize her, she knocks her pelvis into the table and spills the contents of the beer bottle all over my lap. "Oh my God!" she blurts in a panicked voice.

I reach for the napkins on the table, but she has already gotten ahold of them and bends over me with an "I'm so sorry" thrown my way. Then all of a sudden, her dainty hand is pressing over my hard-as-steel cock, making it twitch even with the barrier that the napkins provide. The tiny gasp she lets out when she feels me twitch obliterates every rational thought I have. *Fuck.* The smell of her arousal makes my wolf go crazy. I feel the urge to bend her over the table and pound into her pussy like I need my next breath.

Think Logan. Fucking think. Your mate. You can't betray her like this!

"Enough," I snap at her, my voice coming out harsher than I intended as I grab her wrist to stop her from touching me. If she continued, I would have pushed her to the floor and fucked her senseless, not caring that we have an audience. I let go of her wrist abruptly. I can't stand to touch her anymore. I don't know what I'll do next. I can't control myself.

She smiles sweetly at me even if I just yelled at her. "I'll bring you a fresh bottle."

"There's no need. You've done enough. Just leave," I say with as much coldness as I can muster. It physically hurts me to talk to her like that—my wolf even snarls at me to immediately apologize, but I can't. If I can't trust myself to stay away from Ava, I need her to stay away from me. Maybe if I act like a douche, then she will.

Ava winces and straightens at my tone. "I'm so sorry," she whispers. Her eyes instantly become glassy. "I'll ask Tony to bring you another, then." She turns on her heel, and I grip the table, my fingers turning white with the pressure, as I try to physically stop myself—my wolf—from going after her.

Dominic looks at me like I have grown two heads. "What the fuck is wrong with you, man? She's such a sweet girl. Why would you—"

"I swear to God, Dominic. If you don't stay away from her, I'm going to fucking stake you," I growl, wanting to bare my teeth at him.

"Sorry, he doesn't get out much," Malik yells at her disappearing back as he throws me a weird look. "What the hell, Logan?"

I snap my jaw shut as my nostrils flare, ready to tear into him. But I don't get a chance because suddenly, the tumbler in Kaiden's hand explodes into tiny shards of glass that fly everywhere, the sound like a loaded gun in the silence at our table. Malik's barrier spell hides it, though, so no one in our vicinity pays us any attention.

"What happened?" Malik asks, alarmed.

We all look at Kaiden as he stands up, his fingers clenching and unclenching at his sides. Red streaks swirl dangerously in his eyes yet again, which give over to burnished gold as his sclera becomes completely white. The ground beneath our feet trembles with his simmering rage.

I glance toward the high-top table near the bar for an answer. *Fuck.* "That asshole is kissing Iris," I say grimly.

Kaiden disappears abruptly. One second, he is standing at the table, and the next, he is gone. I am jealous of his ability to disappear and appear like that out of thin air at whim. It can be really handy sometimes.

"Where did he go?" Dominic asks as his eyebrows pull together in concern.

"Probably to blow something up," Malik replies. "It's a good thing he left. Otherwise, he would have leveled us all and killed everyone in the bar." He takes a sip from his beer. "Don't worry, if Iris is here, he'll be back in no time."

Dominic looks at the ridiculously expensive watch around his wrist, a grin spreading over his face. "Twenty minutes and not a minute later," he says. A glint of triumph shines in his eyes as he winks at Malik and pockets the money. We all have more money than we need, but the stupid fucks always like to make wagers at the most inappropriate moments.

Tony comes by and places another beer on the table, giving me a dirty look as he hands me more napkins. "You're lucky you're Emily's brother. Otherwise, I would have kneed you in the balls for being such an asshole to Ava," he huffs and walks away.

"He does have a point. You were a dick," Malik agrees with him.

Well, shit. What can I say to that? They're right, but how can I explain the visceral attraction I feel toward Ava without sounding like a creep? It's taking every drop of restraint I possess to not go after her, even as I follow her with my eyes through the bar, serving tables and smiling at customers. I want to gouge every man's eyes out just for looking at her, and if that's not insane, then I don't know what the fuck is at this point. I should probably go home, though I can't seem to make myself move.

After ten minutes, Kaiden reappears at the table Houdini-style, his eyes having returned to somewhat normal. As I search for Ava in the crowded bar again because I'm a glutton for punishment, I see Iris getting up from the bar stool, heading toward the bathroom hallway.

In the next moment, Kaiden makes Malik scoot over so he can get out of the booth. Then he slices through the crowd, people parting from his way like he is Moses or some shit, and stalks directly to the high-top table to sit down next to Iris's date. The moment the skinny guy's eyes land on Kaiden, he balks. I have to give it to him; very few people can act normal at Kaiden's sight. Aside from the fact that he looks like a mean motherfucker with his whole dark vibe and body covered in tattoos, he also has that special something that reminds people he isn't human and sits at the top of the food chain.

They shake hands, and I can hear from here the guy's bones crunching as he whimpers in pain. Kaiden just broke the hand that touched Iris's thigh. I don't know what Kaiden says to the poor guy, but he trips over his legs as he gets up from the bar stool in a hurry, almost toppling over. He scurries away like a cockroach and bolts out the door. Kaiden places a few bills on the table, probably covering what they had to drink tonight, and strides back toward our booth with a satisfied smirk on his face as Malik stands to let him back in his seat.

12

Ava

A whole week after starting at the Shabby Shotglass flies by without a hitch, and I am beginning to like it here. Moving by yourself across the country and starting a new life can be equal parts terrifying and exciting. I was nervous about being alone and meeting new people, but I enjoy working with Tony and Emily, and I think we can become good friends. Tony has already sort of adopted me, and he has such a sparkly personality that simply being in his presence is a joy.

"Ugh, I'm so happy we only have half an hour left of our shift," Tony says as he joins me at the bar, where I'm standing next to the till, printing the receipt for a table that's about to leave. "I have a hot date after this, if you know what I mean." He waggles his eyebrows as a shit-eating grin takes over his face.

"Who's the lucky guy?" I ask, turning my head to look at him.

He pulls out his phone and shows me a picture of an attractive man with russet hair and hazel eyes.

I fan myself and smile cheekily at him. "Wow. He's hot."

"He also has a monster dick," he whispers and smirks.

I narrow my eyes at him playfully. "You lucky bitch."

"Jealousy doesn't look good on you, buttercup. But yeah, I'm the luckiest bitch alive."

We both start giggling when Emily comes over from the other side of the bar and begins cleaning the sink and bar top since all her customers already left. "What are you two gossiping about?" She cranes her neck so she can look at the phone.

Tony turns the screen toward her with a smug look on his face. "About the hunk of a man I started dating. He's a doctor. Well, actually, he's going to become a doctor. He's a resident. He finishes his shift a little earlier than we do, so he's going to wait for me."

"Holy smoke show! It should be illegal for anyone to look that good in scrubs," Emily observes. "I once dated a gynecologist. Man, she really knew what she was doing. I swear she had magic fingers." She sighs and purses her full lips. "Too bad she was married, and I had no idea."

Both Tony and I grimace at her words.

"Ouch," Tony says, resting his elbows on the bar.

"We were just having fun, but it still sucked when I found out."

"I sometimes wish I was attracted to women as well. I swear some men don't even know what a clit is." William the Turd sure didn't.

Emily arches an eyebrow, a salacious smile taking over her face. "Oh, some of them know. You just haven't found the right one yet."

"Trust me, I've tried," I mutter and glance at Tony. "You can go if you want; I'll close up tonight. It's my turn anyway."

"Are you sure?" he asks, biting his lip. But he's already brimming with excitement and shuffling from foot to foot.

"Yup. There are only two tables left. Plus, Marnie's not here, and I don't think she cares anyway."

He jumps up and down and throws his arms around my neck. "You're the best, buttercup! I promise I'll be thinking of you when I have the most earth-shattering orgasm ever."

"Please don't." I laugh at his antics but cringe at the mental image because why the hell did he have to say something like that?

He disentangles from me and practically skips to the staff room as I take the check to the table of girls who are so hammered they can barely stand. After they pay, I make sure none of them intend to drive and then order a cab to take them home.

Tony comes out of the bathroom hallway near the pool tables, all ready to leave. His light gray jacket creates a stark contrast with the deep hue of his umber skin. "I'll see you guys on Wednesday." He blows us kisses and practically springs out the door.

Forty minutes later, I'm all alone, putting the chairs up so I can start sweeping the floor. As has been happening often lately, a shiver passes down my spine like I'm being watched again, so I look back toward the windows near the entrance but don't see anyone. *Goddammit, Ava, stop being so paranoid!* I roll my eyes at how stupid I'm being.

I finish sweeping the floor, and all I have left to do is take the trash outside, mop, and then I can finally go home. Lifting the trash bags that are heavier than they look, I stride to the back door of the bathroom hallway. As I exit the bar on the dingy alley where the dumpster is, my shoe sticks to something slimy on the asphalt, making me shudder. *Ew.* I try not to look at what I stepped into because when I took the trash out last week, I almost broke my neck stepping on a used condom, and I am still pretty scarred by that experience.

Please don't be a condom. Please don't be a condom. Please don't be a condom.

I decide not to look because I don't want to waste a minute longer under the flickering lamppost's creepy shadows as I grip the heavy lid of the dumpster and swing the trash bags filled to the brim over the lip of the container. The smell of Indian food from the restaurant next door mixed with that of rotting garbage and pee burns my nose and makes me queasy. I swear these heightened senses are so fucking annoying sometimes. I don't like smelling garbage or someone's body odor so easily.

The sounds of footsteps pulls my attention to my back, and I start turning around, but something jumps out of the dumpster at the same time, making me scream murder. I clutch my chest and laugh when a cat lands in front of me. It arches its back and starts hissing at me, just like Simba acted after my heart transplant. Sadness filters through me like a black fog.

The cat disappears in the shadows, and when I take a step toward the back door of the bar, the snick of an opening switchblade slashes through the air before the smell of a cloying cologne pierces a hole in my brain. The odor is so strong I can almost taste the bitterness and metallic tang on my tongue. Dread thickens the blood in my veins. I know I should run, but I turn around instead and face the three men standing a few feet away. They are all wearing black joggers and hoodies as if they prepared for this, their faces obscured by shadows.

The one in the middle holding the switchblade steps forward into the dim light, and my stomach plummets to the bottom of my feet. "Let's see how tough you are now, cunt," he spits, curling his lip in a sneer. It's the *pendejo* I punched a week ago for grabbing my ass beneath my skirt, one of the douchey frat boys. The right side of his face looks like a bruised peach, all purple and blue with yellow spots.

Holy fuck! Is all that from when I punched him?

The moment they move toward me, I waste no time and launch toward the door. I grip the handle and fling it open, flying through the corridor at high speed. Normally, I would stop and question how the fuck I'm so fast, but I'm kind of in the middle of running for my life, so I don't. Their pounding footsteps echo behind me as they get closer and closer.

Adrenaline spikes my blood, and my heart rattles hard against my rib cage.

Before I can reach the front door, a hand grabs my ponytail and tugs hard, making me yelp as I lose my balance and careen backward, almost hitting one of the high-top tables. My scalp screams in pain at the feeling of a few strands getting ripped.

I send my elbow into the ribs of my attacker, and he lets me go with a sharp curse, but the one with the knife is already in front of me. He presses the cold, sharp blade into the side of my neck as his dull brown eyes bore into mine.

"One more move, and I'll slice your throat," he snaps, venom dripping from his tone as his leering gaze rakes over my body. "We're going to teach you a well-deserved lesson, you stupid whore."

My nostrils flare as the one that grabbed my hair locks my hands behind my back. "Three men against a woman. Hardly seems fair. Were you so afraid of me that you needed backup?" I bite back with a dry laugh and struggle against the hold.

I almost manage to free myself when the third one comes closer and backhands me, sending my head flying to the side. "Shut up, bitch!"

The exploding pain lends itself to little white dots swirling all around me as the metallic taste of blood floods my mouth. When it finally hits me that I'm all alone with three dangerous men, I start trembling. Abject fear impales me with the power of a thousand rusty nails, and the copper is quickly replaced by burning bile.

"Get on your knees and beg for forgiveness," the one holding the knife commands, ill intent glimmering in his eyes as the blade bites into my skin, making me hiss, blood seeping from the superficial cut. "I'm going to shove my cock so far up your throat you'll learn to never disrespect a man like that."

I was trembling before, but now I shake violently as adrenaline seeps out of my pores. It triggers something deep within me. My skin prickles, and I swear I can feel my nails extending into claws. That's not possible, right? It's some sort of a trauma-induced hallucination. It has to be.

A vicious sound suddenly breaks through the eerie silence. It could only be described as a menacing growl, so powerful and raw it makes all the hair on my body stand on end as someone barrels through the front door. If I didn't know better, I would say a giant wolf is behind us. What is weird is my reaction to the sound. I almost find it comforting, like it's warming up my insides.

What the hell?

"Let her go before I break every single bone in your bodies and then tear out your useless spines with my bare hands," a powerful voice booms, echoing off the walls.

We all turn toward the voice that sounds incredibly familiar. Before I can make sense of what is happening, my hands are free, and the one that had me immobilized is already sprawled on the hardwood floor in a pool of blood at my feet. I can barely register the movement as the asshole with the switchblade is thrown like a rag doll through the air before he collides with the corner of a pool table. The distinct crack of his head echoes before he falls to the ground with a loud thump and a grunt and stays there.

The third one that backhanded me mutters a curse and turns, running back toward the bathroom corridor. He barely moves before Logan tackles him like a pro linebacker. I shouldn't be turned on at this moment, right? It would definitely be wrong of me, but dammit, if something deep inside of my chest doesn't bloom with pride. Logan starts pummeling the guy into the floor, and I stare at him, transfixed by how his muscles ripple with unadulterated power. If he doesn't stop, he's going to kill him, and he's going to get in trouble just because of me.

I finally manage to make my legs listen to me and close the small space between us. I place my hand on Logan's shoulder and chance a glance at my nails—not claws. *Thank God.* I must have been hallucinating earlier.

"Logan, please stop. You're going to kill him," I say in a soft voice.

Logan turns, his feral gaze slams into mine, and I don't know how to explain this otherwise, but his eyes seem to glow. They go back to normal, though, after he blinks a few times. His knuckles are bloody, but I don't think it's his blood. He stands abruptly and swears under his breath as he lifts his hand and gently touches the place where the blade cut into my skin with his thumb, a frown marring his forehead.

"Do you know where the first aid kit is? Did they do anything else to you?" he asks, his voice thick with concern as he scans me up and down as if to search for more injuries.

I swallow, his proximity making me frazzled. "I'm fine. I think it's just a superficial cut; I can clean it at home. You came just in time," I answer, breathy for no other reason than him standing so close to me. I don't even want to think about what would have happened if he hadn't come barreling through the door when he did.

Logan nods and then lifts me like I weigh nothing more than a feather, placing me on top of one of the chairs at the high-top table on my right. He takes out his phone, dials someone, and steps away from me.

"What happened? Why are you calling me at this hour?" a manly voice asks on the other end with urgency. I shouldn't be able to hear the discussion so clearly, but I do.

"Kaiden, I need your help. Some assholes attacked Ava at the Shabby Shotglass. I took care of them. Can you send someone to deal with them and clean up? I need to take Ava home."

"Are they dead?"

"No, just passed out," Logan answers.

"I'll be there in five," Kaiden says, ending the call.

13

Ava

I swear not even three minutes have passed when Kaiden walks through the front door of the bar, his strides long and purposeful as he reaches us. Like last week, he's decked in all black with a leather jacket on top, but his hair is free, touching his shoulders. Everything about him gives don't-fuck-with-me vibes. He looks at the three men who attacked me in a blatant show of disgust and then nods at Logan in acknowledgment.

How the hell did he get here so quickly? I want to ask him that, but I don't want to seem rude, so I decide not to say anything. Maybe he was in the area; it's Saturday night, after all. Well, I guess it's already Sunday since it's past three a.m. On that thought, what was Logan doing here at this hour?

"Do you know them?" Kaiden asks me, snapping me out of my thoughts.

I shake my head and take a deep breath. "No, not really. I did see them once last week outside the bar. They were drunk and acting like pervs. When I passed their group, the one with the switchblade grabbed my ass, and I turned around and punched him." I point at the *pendejo* splayed on the floor next to the pool table. "Then Dominic appeared and scared them…so I guess they wanted some kind of revenge."

Logan's nostrils flare, and his fingers clench and unclench at his sides. "I should fucking kill them," he grits out, locking his jaw with anger. He has a wild look in his eyes as he starts pacing like a wolf locked in a cage.

Kaiden places his hand on Logan's shoulder, stopping the pacing. "If you do, things will get complicated. You should go get your car and take Ava home. Malik will be here shortly."

"There's no need; I live just ten minutes away. I can wa—"

Logan cuts me off. "I'm not letting you walk home," he says, and then he approaches me. His gaze softens as it locks with mine, blanketing me like a warm hug. It creates a safe bubble where I finally feel like my lungs can fully expand since the three *cabrones* attacked me. "I'll go get my car. It's in a parking garage not far from here. I'll be back quickly. Will you be okay waiting here with Kaiden?"

"Yeah," I reply quietly. He's given me a thorough case of whiplash. He was such an asshole a week ago, and now he looks at me like I'm something precious, something he cares about. "Shouldn't we call the police?" I blurt out as I fumble with my clammy, trembling fingers in my lap.

"I know the chief personally. I'll call him after you leave. You'll probably have to go to the station to give a statement next week. There's no need for you to stay here after you were attacked," Kaiden responds as he takes out his phone and starts typing.

As Logan turns around, I stop him with a hand on his forearm. "Wait, your hands are bloody. You should wash them before you leave."

Logan's eyebrows furrow as he looks at his hands, like he didn't even realize how much blood he has on himself. Crimson splatters also cover the front of his navy Henley and the sides of his black jacket, but they're not that noticeable against the darker color. He goes behind the bar and washes his hands, then leaves quickly.

Kaiden doesn't seem like the type of person who would enjoy any type of small talk, so we just sit in uncomfortable silence, waiting for Logan to be back. I resist the urge to pick at my skin when Kaiden unexpectedly brings me a glass of water. He gives me a curt nod when I mumble a "thank you". I feel his eyes on me, but I think he's just scanning me for injuries. My shaky hands almost make me spill the water all over myself as I bring the glass to my lips and take a few sips. The three assholes that attacked me are still passed out on the hardwood floor. I don't spare them a glance, though…I can't.

Logan is back faster than I expected. Everything is a blur as he brings my jacket and purse from my locker in the staff room. He hands my set of bar keys to Kaiden to lock up, then turns toward me. In a soft voice, as if I'm breakable, he tells me Emily had already called Marnie and let her know what happened.

Before I know it, I'm in the passenger seat of Logan's truck. I inhale a lungful of his crisp, woodsy smell that wraps around me in drugging waves. He asks for directions, and I tell him where I live. The drive is relatively short so it takes him more time to park than we spent driving from the Shabby Shotglass to my apartment. I feel strangely numb, as if everything happened to someone else. I am vaguely aware that Logan has stopped the engine, but I feel like I'm having an out-of-body experience because I'm unable to move my limbs.

Logan rounding the hood and opening my door, finally snaps me out of it. Heat scorches my cheeks at the gesture as I spill out of the car. I didn't think he had it in him with how he acted last week. What now?

I should probably thank him, right?

I swallow and crane my neck to look into his honey-colored eyes. The side street he parked on is dimly lit, casting him in shadows, and enhancing the angular line of his jaw. He's so handsome it almost hurts to look at him. "Thank you for tonight."

His gaze drops to my lips. A laborious heartbeat passes. My throat rolls with a hard swallow as I wait for him to pounce on me. But he never does. Instead, something flashes in his eyes before he locks his gaze with mine again. "You don't have to thank me." His voice is rough, dripping with tension, his spine rod straight, and his muscles locked up like he is barely restraining himself.

I clear my throat loudly. "I, um, yeah…well, I guess I'll see you around." What the hell is it about this man that turns me into a blubbering mess? He probably thinks I don't have more than two working brain cells. I shake my head and turn around when I feel his palm at the small of my back, his touch burning through my clothes.

"I'm not leaving you alone right now," he says as he guides me to the entrance of my apartment building.

"I don't want to inconvenience you mo—"

"You're not inconveniencing me, Ava. I want to make sure you're okay, then I'll leave." His tone doesn't leave room for argument, so I punch in the code to my apartment building with sweat-slicked fingers. He drops the hand at the small of my back the moment we step into the elevator. Bitter disappointment thickens in my veins like syrup at the loss of his warmth.

Logan's big frame takes up almost all the cramped space of the elevator, making me feel small and dainty next to him. I gulp audibly when his hand brushes mine. The air between us sparks with energy as scorching heat unfurls in my core. It's only when the door finally opens that I feel like I can breathe again.

We both get into my small studio apartment. Fuck. The boxes. I let out a huff of relief when I remember I cleaned yesterday because I would have been so embarrassed if he saw the tornado of clothes covering the mountains of cardboard.

I flick the lights on and place my bag on the entryway table. Logan helps me take off my jacket and urges me to sit on the couch. "Where's your first aid kit?" he asks as he drapes his jacket alongside mine on one of the two bar stools.

"In the cabinet beneath the sink. I can get—"

He narrows his eyes, interrupting me. "Don't you dare move."

As Logan disappears through my bathroom door, I slump on the couch and remove the hair tie, freeing my hair from the sore ponytail. I hope I don't have any bald spots from when that asshole grabbed a fistful of my hair. My fingers tremble as I massage my scalp and slam my eyes shut in an attempt to ward off the anxiety that's creeping in the back of my throat.

But it doesn't work because a flashback of the cold blade pressing into the side of my neck passes through my mind in the darkness. An unexpected pang of fear makes my breathing ragged. *Mierda.* My heart rate kicks in overdrive, and my stomach fists as the acrid taste of bile floods my mouth with the urge to throw up. Jumping up from the couch, I immediately cut through the room and push Logan out of my way when he steps out of the bathroom, holding the first aid kit.

"What's wrong?"

I can't answer him because I'm already on the bathroom floor, hugging the toilet as I puke my guts out with violent heaves. Logan gently gathers my hair away from my face. I don't want him to see me like this, but the way he rubs my back soothes something deep inside me. Yet, it's still not enough to prevent the violent tremors, and for some reason, I can't stop the tears that blur my vision and start falling from my eyes.

Logan puts the lid on the toilet and flushes before he pulls me into his strong arms. He places me in his lap as he sits on the bathroom floor with his legs slightly bent in front of him because of the cramped space, his back resting on the glass wall of the walk-in shower. "Shh, I got you, baby," he says softly as he kisses the top of my head, and his calloused fingers wipe the tears that fall from my eyes.

I don't know how long we sit on the bathroom floor with me enveloped entirely by Logan's big body. After some time, the tears stop and I'm no longer shaking like a leaf, but Logan doesn't let me go. He keeps me wrapped in his big arms, and I've never felt safer in my entire life. It's inexplicably like finally arriving home after a hard day. Like finding something that I've been searching for my whole life. Like mending a broken part of my soul. His woodsy cologne sails over me in calming waves, and the steady beat of his heart lulls me until my eyes shut on their own accord, and tiredness pulls me under.

14

Ava

I wake with a start and squint my eyes at the bright light slanting through the window. Blinking a few times, I realize I'm in bed, and I furrow my eyebrows, confused about how I got here. Then I remember losing my shit and Logan pulling me into his arms and holding me there until I calmed down. I fell asleep while he held me, didn't I?

Fuck me.

He saw me puking, and he stayed there in the bathroom with me while I sobbed and used him like my own personal comfort pillow. He probably thinks I'm batshit crazy, aside from being the clumsiest person on Earth. Because my brain hates me, it sends me a flashback of how I spilled the beer in his lap a week ago, and I want to die inside.

Groaning, I push myself into a sitting position, but I freeze when the sound of someone breathing from the direction of the couch fills the air. Did Logan stay? Oh my God, he did stay. My heart constricts in my chest when I see his big body slumped on top of the couch through the paneled glass separating my bedroom from the rest of the studio apartment.

As I get up from the bed, I notice I'm halfway naked. He took off my jeans when he tucked me in, probably to make me more comfortable, and I cringe hard because I'm wearing the rattiest panties I own, the grandma skivvies I typically use only on my period. I didn't have time to do laundry, and the period panties were my only clean underwear.

Perfect…just perfect.

I take a pair of shorts and a tee from my dresser and tip-toe to the bathroom, but I can't help stopping in my tracks to look at Logan. He barely fits on the couch, and the bottom half of his legs hang in the air on the L portion, almost touching the TV. His head is tilted to the side with a hand thrown over his forehead, his features relaxed in slumber, and his lips parted slightly. The sun shining through the window casts his deep amber skin in a golden hue that makes him look like a sexy angel.

I realize I've been standing there like a creep for way too long, so I turn around and get into the bathroom, closing the door behind me carefully. I almost scream when I catch a glance of my reflection in the mirror. Last night's makeup is caked on my face, and streaks of black mascara are smudged around my cheeks. I honestly wonder how the fuck Logan didn't run for the hills when I look like I just stepped out of a horror movie.

Bringing my hand to my throat, I run the pads of my fingers over the bandage Logan placed over the cut and peel it off; the wound doesn't look half as bad as my makeup. I don't understand how I could sleep so deeply that I didn't feel him tending to my wound and tucking me in bed. My finger trails down to where the scar from my heart transplant surgery should be. It's so thin and faded that it doesn't even look like I had surgery.

My new doctor, the one who performed the transplant, said that there's nothing to worry about, even when I asked him if he was one hundred percent sure it's normal. I read online that the scar will never completely fade, so naturally, I had questions. He simply told me to stop doing my own research and that I should only believe him because he is my doctor. Well, what do I know? He's the one who went to med school. Shrugging, I just add that to the pile of weird things happening to me since receiving a new heart and take off my clothes.

I make quick work of washing myself, happy to scrub the bar smell off me. I let out a sharp curse when I start massaging the shampoo into my still sensitive scalp. Stepping out of the shower, I towel dry my hair, not wanting to wake up Logan, and then brush my teeth and wash last night's makeup off.

When I get out of the bathroom, Logan is still sleeping, and I don't know what to do with myself. My stomach grumbles so loudly I'm afraid I'll wake him up. Usually, Sunday is the day I bake something, do laundry, and veg out for hours on the couch watching a show or some reruns. I was planning on making some chocolate croissants from scratch today, but I don't have the time now, so I take out from the cupboard everything I need to make blueberry muffins, whisk all the ingredients, pour the batter in the tray and pop it into the oven.

Then I start whisking eggs in a bowl and take out another pan to fry bacon in it. It looks like I'm preparing a feast for six people, but with how much I've been eating lately, I will probably end up eating half of what I'm making, including the muffins.

"Mmm, it smells delicious," Logan's sleepy, gravelly voice pulls my attention toward him, and I turn around. I almost drop the pan at the image before my eyes. He's stretching, his Henley riding up with the movement, allowing me a perfect view of his delicious-looking abs and the flawlessly etched V that disappears into the waistband of his jeans. Is that a ten-pack? Does that even exist? Why does it feel like I put my face into the oven all of a sudden? I realize too late he just asked me something while I was busy ogling his magnificent body and say, "Huh?"

The corner of his lips lifts in a smirk. Ugh, I want to hit myself in the face with the pan for being so blatantly obvious. He stands up and ambles toward me, stopping near the breakfast bar, which is close enough to me that I can see a day's worth of stubble on his cheeks and a messy cloud of curls on his head. He's positively—seductively?—sleep rumpled. My hand itches with the need to sink my fingers in his hair. "How are you feeling?"

I place the pan back on the stove and turn around to answer Logan. "Better, I, um…" *Holy shit, Ava! Pull yourself together!* "Thank you for last night. I'm sorry about crying all over you…I don't know what came over me."

A serious look passes over his face. "You have nothing to worry about. It's a normal response to trauma. Plus, I got to hold a beautiful woman in my arms, so you won't hear me complain." He gives me a rueful grin that makes my heart flutter.

Heat crawls up my neck all the way to my cheeks. "I made breakfast," I say, stating the obvious and pointing like a weirdo to the pans. Not that he didn't see them already.

Ugh. Shoot me now!

He only smiles at my awkwardness. "Can I step into the bathroom real quick?"

"Yeah, sure."

As Logan makes a beeline for the bathroom, the oven's timer pings, letting me know the muffins are ready. I take out the tray and let them chill for a bit as I set plates and cutlery on the breakfast bar. Then I place a few muffins on a platter and bring it with me as I sit on one of the bar stools, waiting for Logan.

It might just be convenient timing, or perhaps it's my heart lurching every time it sees him, but the exact moment he comes out of the bathroom is when I remember I haven't taken my immunosuppressants and the other army of medications the doctor prescribed me. So, I stand and go to the entryway table to search for my pill organizer in my purse. Logan watches me closely as I swallow the five pills one after another without water. It's something I had to get used to. At first, it was a real struggle taking so many pills—I almost invariably choked them all up as soon as I swallowed—but now it's part of my daily routine.

"I don't mean to pry, but why are you taking so many pills?" he asks as he takes a seat at the breakfast bar, his forehead crinkled in concern.

I plop down on the bar stool beside him and dump some scrambled eggs onto my plate, then pass them to Logan. "I had a heart transplant almost four months ago."

"You had a heart transplant?" he asks incredulously while piling bacon on top of the eggs. "How old are you?"

I laugh because that was my first reaction, too, when I found out about my heart condition. "Twenty-one. Believe me, when I first had a heart attack, and the doctor told me I only had a few months to live, I thought the same thing. I couldn't believe something like this could happen to someone my age." Ha, look at me, sounding like a normal person again and not like a weirdo with zero brain cells. If I could, I would high-five myself.

"That must have been hard on you…"

"Yeah, it was, but I tried to make the most of what time I had left. I'm not gonna lie…I did make some stupid decisions." I take a bite of a bacon strip and munch on it. "But it all turned out for the best since I got a new heart in the end."

After a few beats of silence, Logan looks toward me. "I'm sorry for being such a dick to you a week ago," he says sheepishly, rubbing a hand over the back of his neck.

"It's fine—"

"No, it's not. No one deserves to be treated like that, and I acted like a total asshole." His eyebrows furrow and his mouth sets into a thin line.

In contrast, a small smile pulls at my own lips. "You made up for it by saving me last night, so we're all good now."

"Thank fuck because I was afraid Tony might dick punch me the next time he sees me."

I almost choke on the food I'm swallowing as a laugh belts out of me. "I'll let him know you apologized."

Logan goes for a second serving, and I do the same. He finishes the protein before me, then takes a blueberry muffin, biting into it. "Holy shit! Did you make these? I don't think I've ever tasted something as delicious in my entire life." He scarfs it down in no time and manages to eat two more before I can even blink.

Swallowing my last bite, I nod, not knowing what to say to the compliment. I'm sure my cheeks flush red.

"You'd make a lot of money selling these."

"You think?" It seems so simple, but it's the first time the idea has come up. I have no choice but to take a moment and consider it. I've always loved to bake, but I never thought I could do this for a living.

"One hundred. It's like you put crack in them or something."

I almost laugh and say, *No more crack for me.*

But I don't. Instead, I take a muffin and bit into it just to see if it turned out better than I usually make them. The texture is perfectly balanced, pillowy-soft, gooey and airy at the same time. I almost do a little dance of happiness as I stifle a moan.

Logan's eyes are like a hot brand to my face. They pull me in like a magnet. Our gazes snare when I chance a look at him. I feel like a deer in headlights stumbling onto the big bad wolf, and my lips part involuntarily on a shaky breath. Pure animalistic hunger flashes in his gaze while it roves lazily over every inch of me, like a physical caress. As though he wants to imprint every single detail onto his brain. It makes me acutely aware of how close we are to one another. My skin buzzes with the electricity sparking in the air between us.

His knee brushes mine as he turns toward me on the bar stool. "You've got something…" All the hair on my body stands on end when he brings his forefinger under my chin and then brushes his thumb gently at the corner of my lips to wipe a crumb away. He doesn't move his hand. Instead, he uses the pad of his thumb to trace my lips slowly, reverently, while his other hand settles atop my thigh. His touch burns through my skin like a hot coal. I whimper when he inches the hand upward on my inner leg, leaving a wake of shivers behind.

All of a sudden, Logan pulls me into his lap like I weigh nothing, and he swallows the whimper with his lips over mine in a scorching kiss as I straddle him. His tongue glides against mine with hot, silky strokes that turn my brain to mush. I cling to him with desperation, weaving my fingers into his hair and pulling on it. In response, Logan's fingers dig almost painfully into the sides of my thighs. A voice I don't recognize growls in my head possessively, *"Mine!"* but I don't pay it any attention. I'm too consumed by the way our tongues tangle in a fiery dance.

"Fuck, you taste better than I imagined," Logan breathes against my lips, labored like he just ran a marathon. Then his lips are on mine again as his big hands grab my ass. He jerks me into his body, causing my pulse to spike to the roof because my clit rubs onto his hard-as-steel erection in a way that fries all my nerve endings. I moan loudly into his mouth. The stimulation is making me crazy with lust.

Standing with me wrapped around his middle, Logan takes long, determined strides to the bedroom. He lowers me on top of my bed and settles in between my thighs but never allows our lips to come unfused, our tongues to cease battling for control in a mind-numbing kiss. His fingers hook into my shorts, but as he starts pulling them down, the blaring sound of a phone ringing cuts through the room.

Logan stiffens on top of me as though someone dumped a bucket of ice-cold water on his head. The spell binding us dissipates like smoke in the wind. With a sharp inhale, he pushes on his forearms and gets up from between my legs, careful not to touch me in the slightest. Like he finds me radioactive…again. He shakes his head. Somehow, it feels like he's trying to rid himself of my image. In slow increments, that feel like a thousand rusty razor blades sawing through my bones all at once, the haze of desire burning in his eyes dulls down. His Adam's apple bobs in his throat, hard. The regret shining in his eyes is like a dagger to the center of my chest as he avoids looking at me. He stalks to the coffee table, where his phone is, his movements jerky and weird.

He swears under his breath when he unlocks the screen. "I'm so sorry, but I have to go," he says roughly, picks up his jacket, and then closes the front door to my apartment swiftly behind him.

He couldn't even look at me…like he was ashamed. I know I'm being dramatic, but I can't stop the sobs that rake through my body, constricting my heart and my lungs in a vise-like grip. I don't understand why I'm so affected by him leaving, but I'm certain I've lost something vital, like the air in my lungs.

15

Logan

Blood flies as my fist connects with the jaw of one of the assholes that attacked Ava last night. The one with the switchblade that dared press it against her throat, cutting into her silky skin. I swore he would pay for that, and that's exactly what I'm doing, collecting my debt. Ava's debt.

"P-p-please," Chad begs again on a whimper as a fresh trickle of piss drips from the inside of his pants onto the cement floor, making my nose turn at the strong ammonia smell. Even his name is asshole-ish. He is tied down to a chair next to the other two dipshits that dared touch Ava. They are passed out, as I already finished with them earlier. I let out all my frustration and channel my rage as I pummel Chad until I feel Kaiden's hand on my shoulder.

"Any more, and you'll kill him," Kaiden says, his fingers flexing in an attempt to stop me.

I shake off his hand and turn my head toward Malik, sweat dotting my forehead and running down in rivulets between my shoulder blades. I've been at this for hours and still haven't gotten my fill. "Again," I rumble through clenched teeth, my breathing ragged.

Malik's gaze flits to me from his position at the long table where all the torture instruments are laid out. His finger tests the sharpness of a knife by pressing it into the blade. As if wallowing in boredom, he drops the knife, stalks forward, and pushes me out of the way. He places his hand on top of Chad's head and heals the bastard, black magic thickening the air and swirling in Malik's veins. Chad's skin pieces back together under my gaze, and the wheezing breath he lets out, probably from his ribs being cracked and piercing a lung, quiets.

Kaiden heaves out a deep sigh. "I have some things I need to take care of. You can find me in my office if you need anything. Don't let him kill any of them. I don't want to deal with that shit," he says the last part to Malik as he ambles to the door and leaves me alone with the warlock.

We're in the basement of Kaiden's building. Yeah, the fucker owns a whole damn building. Scratch that. He owns almost half the city. We normally use the basement for dark creatures that break the rules of the Obsidian Conclave, and we even have cages set up for them at my right, all empty now, like some sort of a makeshift prison. But Kaiden made an exception for me, and brought the three human douchebags here right after the attack so they can learn their lesson before we hand them over to the police. The chief won't question the state we bring them in as long as they're alive. Kaiden keeps him happy with how much money he funnels into his pockets. In return, he turns a blind eye whenever we need it.

I've been beating the shit out of them for hours, bringing them to death's door, and then letting Malik heal them so I can start all over again. I let Chad watch me take care of his friends. I'm sure watching his friends being beaten to death over and over again was a torture in its own, the anticipation of what's to come. I made sure none of them will be able to use their hands ever again for daring to lay a single finger on Ava.

Malik finishes healing Chad. He steps away, making room for me. I can't stop the sadistic smile that stretches over my face. And I don't even want to. Being a wolf shifter, especially an Alpha, is no walk in the park. But there are moments, just like now, when I can revel in my power. It took years of arduous training to fully master and control my transformation. I take advantage of that self-inflicted discipline and allow the fur to pierce the skin on my hands slowly as my nails take the shape of deadly claws. Without wasting a second, I unleash the wrath trashing beneath my skin like a hurricane on Chad. He whines and cries like a baby—music to my ears.

I slash into every sensitive spot on Chad's body without the risk of killing him. After I finish with that, I ask Malik to hand me a knife. Some would say it's an art form to cut someone's fingers while eliciting as much pain as possible. You see, the key is to put the perfect amount of pressure on the ligaments without completely severing the nerves. Oh, and to also take your time while you dig out the fingernails. I do just that. One by one, ten fingers smack the floor with a wet *thwack,* followed by bellowing screams that echo off the cavernous walls. He passes out for the hundredth time, and this time, I don't wake him. My wolf seems to have gotten his revenge.

"Are we finally done?" Malik asks, arching an eyebrow at me. "I'm hungry."

"Yeah," I respond, catching the towel he throws at me. I pat my sweaty forehead and then wipe the knife on the same cloth. I drop the knife in its spot on top of the worktable, since Kaiden can be borderline anal about this sort of thing. He likes everything neat and well-organized—even his torture chambers. Especially his torture chambers. After I chuck the dirty towel in the bin under the table, I stride to the sink near the door to wash my bloody hands. I hiss as soon as the water makes contact with the raw skin on my knuckles, but I don't mind. I'm going to heal pretty quickly—one of the other perks of being an Alpha.

Malik takes out his phone and calls someone, probably Alex, a wolf shifter from my pack that works as security for Kaiden, to come pick up the three assholes and deliver them to the police. "I thought out of all of us, you were the most level-headed. I guess I was wrong," he says, canting his head to the side. A frown mars his forehead while he studies me with newfound scrutiny, as if equally surprised and impressed by my actions. He steps next to me, pockets his phone, and flicks his gaze to my swollen knuckles. "Do you want me to heal you?"

"No," I answer without offering any explanation as to why. My wolf demands I don't let him heal me, needing the reminder of the blood spilled today.

"Did something happen between you and Ava? You took her home and came here wearing the same clothes as yesterday, so I assume you stayed the night."

I huff in annoyance. "Nothing happened."

"Cut the shit, Logan. I know when you're lying. Something must have happened. Otherwise, you wouldn't have come here with that shitty attitude, and enough bloodthirst to drain the Red Sea dry."

I narrow my eyes at him. He's worse than my sister about pestering me until I give him what he wants, which really says something. "We kissed, and I almost fucked her. If Kaiden didn't call me…"

"You feel guilty about it," he says, reading me like an open book.

I press the heels of my palms into my eyes. "Of course, I feel guilty. I fucking betrayed my fated mate. I shouldn't have stayed the night, but I wanted to make sure she was okay. It's just, from the moment I saw Ava for the first time, I've felt this gravitational force pulling me to her. Hell, I almost killed these bastards last night without a second thought of what would happen to me and my pack. And my wolf is going absolutely insane for her, but I don't understand why. She's just a human."

Malik folds his arms in front of his chest. "Are you sure she's human? From what Chad said, she only had to punch him once to destroy the whole side of his face. He looked as if he pissed off Emily, and she is almost as powerful as you."

"Of course, I'm fucking sure she's human. I would have scented her immediately and known if she wasn't. She's also had a heart transplant, for fuck's sake. I saw her take anti-rejection medication this morning. Dark creatures don't need heart transplants. Humans do."

We both exit the basement and get into the elevator after Malik does a simple spell that rids the three assholes of the ability to talk about what happened here today, but the memories will still haunt them. I would say forever, but I'm not that generous. The rules say *I* can't kill a human, but nothing is stopping me from paying off a few inmates to do it for me. Malik gets out on the ground floor, mumbling something about food and snapping me out of my thoughts. I continue riding in the elevator to the thirty-ninth floor.

Since he owns the building, Kaiden gave us each an apartment on the same floor that we can use however we like. Dominic and Malik live in them, whereas I use my house in the national park for the obvious reason of being my pack's Alpha. Still, the apartment is useful whenever I come to the city with business concerning the Conclave.

Unlocking the door and ambling to the bathroom, I stop in front of the large mirror above the marble countertops. I barely recognize myself. Blood covers every available inch of my body, my face and hair caked with it. Up until last night, I've never questioned my moral compass. Respecting the Conclave rules and not killing humans didn't seem so hard before. But the moment I saw them hurting Ava through the window of the bar, I wanted to tear their hearts out of their chests and cut them to pieces using my bare teeth.

I used to think Kaiden was crazy for following Iris everywhere, but I haven't been able to stay away since I first saw Ava at the Shabby Shotglass. I've found my way to her every night and watched her from the shadows through the bar's window, or from the side street of her apartment building, which gave me a perfect look through her bedroom window.

After patrolling our community's borders with my pack and ensuring everything was all right last night—which took longer than usual as I had to make a rotating schedule for the wolves and vampires—I drove to the city to see her. I thought I'd missed her, but then she ran inside, and the three scumbags attacked her. I almost shifted in that moment, my wolf demanding me to let him out to protect Ava. I was a second away from losing control, which hasn't happened since I was a kid. I wanted to kill them and then bathe in their blood like a sick fuck.

Peeling off the blood-soaked clothes, I step into the shower and close my eyes, letting the water rain down on me. It doesn't take long before my mind decides to torture me with the images of Ava in my lap and me feasting on her lips like a starved man. I instantly get hard when I remember the moans and tiny whimpers that escaped her luscious lips. I fist my cock and slide my fingers up and down furiously over my shaft, thinking about her creamy skin and heavenly body. I almost lost it when I saw her wearing those tiny shorts, showcasing her perfect thighs. Fuck me, those goddamn thighs haunt my every waking moment. I want to sink my teeth into them and chase the pain away with my tongue. Have them thrown over my shoulders as I worship her for hours on end. My balls tighten, and I come so fast it's embarrassing.

Raw guilt claws at my insides so viciously I bang my fist into the shower wall, leaving a deep dent in the tiles. Since I dreamed about my fated mate for the first time five years ago, I've stopped sleeping around, and I hadn't even kissed anyone until the moment I kissed Ava.

It took everything I had to walk away and leave her on top of her bed like that. To ignore the feral need to sink into her and claim her as mine. I can't believe I betrayed my fated mate. From now on, I have to stay away from Ava. I can't risk getting lost in her again. Even if I don't find my fated mate, I still have a responsibility toward my pack to give them a Luna. A *shifter* Luna, not a human. That's something my pack would never accept. The decision burns through me like acid, but the memory of betraying my fated mate steels my resolve.

I just hope I'll be strong enough to stay away.

16

Ava

"Well, that was fast," Tony tells me as we step out of the precinct.

A gust of cold air slams into my face and ruffles my hair. "Yeah," I say and zip up my jacket. Tony opens his umbrella, and we huddle under it as we make our way to where I parked my car earlier. It rained all morning, but it seems we can't catch a break because it's drizzling again as the sun hides behind the thick canopy of dark, dreary clouds.

Tony offered to accompany me and be my emotional support when I told him an officer had called and asked me to come by the station to give my statement of the attack. It was much easier than I thought it would be. As soon as I gave them my name, they immediately ushered me into a private room to take my statement and show me photos of the three men who attacked me so I could confirm it was them. I thought I would have to identify them in a lineup, but they said it wasn't necessary. I was glad I didn't have to see their faces again. The last three nights since the attack, I've been having terrible nightmares. Only, Logan never shows up to save me in them. This morning, I woke up all sweaty and so sick to my stomach that I threw up.

We sidestep a puddle at the same time, and Tony turns his head slightly to look at me. "Are you still planning on coming to work tonight?"

I nod. "Marnie told me I can take as much time off as I need, but honestly, I don't want to be alone. I think working will help keep my mind off it."

"I would take the time off if I were you, buttercup. But you do you."

We stop at a red light before crossing the street. "So, how are things with McDreamy, or should I say McSteamy?" I ask, a salacious smile spreading on my face.

Tony makes a gesture with his hand in the air. "Oh, we broke it off."

My eyes widen in surprise. "That fast?"

"Well, this bitch needs to be entertained. He was always busy studying, and he had long shifts. Plus, I can't do monogamy. It's so boring."

I laugh at his response. "How long were you together?"

"Like two weeks, and trust me, it was enough." He shudders like he is appalled by his brief monogamous rebellion. "Are you hungry? There's this Mexican restaurant a block from here. It's a hole-in-the-wall, so don't expect anything fancy, but I swear they have the best tacos in all of Ashville."

"I love tacos," I tell him, grateful that I don't have to be alone after being forced to remember every single detail of the night I was attacked.

Tu Tía Loca is exactly as Tony said, a hole-in-the-wall with only four small tables. Still, the inside is cozy and charming, with colorful walls decorated in intricate *Día de los Muertos* murals, a different skull on each wall, my favorite being the one on my right with a gorgeous crown of blue-purple flowers. We place our orders at the small counter and sit at the only available wooden table next to the foggy window. The place smells incredible, and I can't wait to stuff my face with the tacos *al pastor* I ordered. Murmured conversations fill the air, along with the sound of pots and pans being used in the kitchen.

Tony clinks his cocktail glass with mine. "So, what are you doing for Halloween?"

I shrug and take a sip out of my virgin margarita. "I honestly haven't thought about it since it's a month away."

"What do you normally do?"

"Well, before finding out about my heart condition, I never partied at all because my mom would have a conniption every time I mentioned I wanted to go with Chloe, my best friend, to one, so…I would just stay home and give candy to the kids, and that's about it."

Tony gasps at my words, bringing a hand to his chest like he is personally offended by my uneventful youth. "That's it, you're coming with me at the bonfire on the shore of Shadow Lake. It's going to be amazing. It's a yearly Halloween tradition in Ashville, and you'll get to meet a lot of my friends. Maybe hook up with someone." He waggles his eyebrows at me.

My first instinct is to refuse him, the old Ava rearing her head, and then I berate myself for falling into the same patterns as before. I'm finally out of my mother's reach, and I promised myself that I would live and experience as much as I could now that I know what it's like to have my days numbered. I smile warmly at Tony. "I would love that."

"I've already planned out my costume. I'm going as Freddy Mercury. I have a fabulous pair of golden sequined pants, and I bought a fake mustache and a wig. I'm going to look incredible."

Gnawing on my bottom lip, I say, "I don't have any ideas for a costume, and I can't afford to spend too much."

"Something slutty always works." He takes a hearty sip of his margarita, then his eyes widen. "Buckle up, buttercup, 'cause I just had the most brilliant idea. You're Latina, right? We could both go as singers. I have this purple jumpsuit we can adjust, and then you can go as Selena Quintanilla. I even have a spare microphone I can give you."

"That's such a good idea. I loved Selena when I was little."

An old lady with silver braided hair wearing a beautiful violet ample skirt and a flowery peasant blouse comes out of the kitchen and brings us our food. She has these deep lines etched into her face, the kind at the outer corners of her eyes that say she's had a full life of smiling with abandon.

"*¡Buen provec*ho*!¡Que disfrute*n*!*" she tells us as she slides the plates filled with tacos onto the table.

I return the smile. "*¡Gracias, señor*a*!*" She reminds me so much of my *Abuelita* on my mother's side. My dear *Abuelita*, who told me to believe in myself and to follow my dreams. Unfortunately, I didn't get to spend much time with her since she still lived in Mexico, but I visited her as much as I could in the summer. She was the one who taught me how to bake. We used to spend hours in the kitchen together. It was our thing. She sadly got sick a few years ago and died of lung cancer. I still miss her terribly.

She left me a hefty inheritance I could access when I turned twenty. That's how I could afford to live (or die) on my own, and then I still had some money left to buy my car and rent the apartment here in Ashville.

Tony takes a bite of one of his tacos at the same time as me. "Holy smokes! I think I died and went to heaven," I say through a mouthful, my eyes widening. I do a little shimmy with my shoulders as I take another bite.

He smirks at me. "Told ya."

We don't talk as we eat and make a mess out of our hands. There's something so satisfying about being able to enjoy a meal without concerning yourself with decorum or what the other person thinks.

Tony wipes his hands, and his gaze flits to me. "So, Logan drove you home, huh?"

"Yeah, he also insisted on making sure I was okay. So I let him into my apartment, and then I freaked out big time. He held my hair while I threw up for what seemed like forever, and then I used him like some sort of comfort pillow and cried all over him." I cringe at the memory.

"Are we talking about the same asshole that treated you like shit on your first day working at the bar?" Tony asks, jaw slack. "I mean, he is fine as hell, and I would be all over him if he wasn't straight, but I wanted to knee him in the balls that night. I seriously considered it. He's lucky he's Emily's brother," he scoffs.

"I promised Logan I would tell you he apologized. He was afraid you would castrate him the next time you saw him." I laugh, and then my smile dies on my lips the moment I remember how he left in a hurry after he kissed me.

"Uh-oh. What was that look?"

I purse my lips. "What look?"

"Oh, c'mon, buttercup. Do you think I was born yesterday?" He arches an ebony eyebrow in my direction.

"I'll tell you if you promise you won't mention anything about it to Emily. I don't want things to get awkward at work."

Tony makes an X sign with his finger over his heart, then mimics zipping up his lips and throwing the key as if to say, "My lips are sealed."

Sighing deeply, I let the words pour out of me, "Okay, so after I cried all over Logan on my bathroom floor, I fell asleep, and then I woke up the next morning with him still there, sleeping on my couch. Long story short, I made him breakfast, and then he kissed me. We were about to do more, but his phone rang, and then he looked at me with this deep shame and regret I'll never erase from my mind. He got his phone and took off faster than a bat out of hell. I know I'm not the most beautiful or your average size-zero girl, but it still stung like a bitch."

Tony clucks his tongue, throwing me a scathing glare. "I'm going to stop you right there, buttercup. I may be gay, but I know when I'm looking at a beautiful woman and you, baby girl, are hot as fuck. Have you looked at yourself? So many women would die to have your curves. So what if you're not a stick? Fuck him. We'll find you someone you can hook up with at the party."

He holds his cocktail glass up in the air between us. I meet him halfway, clinking my glass to his, and by the time we both finish our margaritas, I'm already feeling better about the whole Logan situation.

17
Ava

Busy with work, the days melt into each other, time passes in a blur, and before I know it, Halloween is already knocking at the door. It was a bit strange to be back at the bar after the attack, Wednesday night being the hardest, but Tony and Emily helped me keep my mind off it, and we fell into our routine.

Logan hasn't shown his face since he left my apartment in a haste, which doesn't lessen the blow I suffered to my ego. I hoped he would at least give me a reason for acting like that. I guess I don't deserve an explanation.

Well, fuck him.

The sound of my phone ringing pulls me out of my thoughts. I lift it from the coffee table and let out a deep breath at the caller's name on the screen. Tucking my legs under me on the couch, I pause the show I zoned out on and tap to accept the call, my stomach a ball of restless energy.

"*Hola, Mamá,*" I say dryly.

"*Ya te olvidaste de tu madre,* Ava. I was expecting more from you," she huffs in my ear, and I can already picture my mother pinching her lips in displeasure. It's been two months since I left home to move across the country, and I haven't spoken to her since.

"What were your exact words? Oh yeah…'You're dead to me. Don't bother calling me or coming back home because I don't want to see you ever again. You're a disgrace. My biggest disappointment.' So, I was just respecting your wishes." My tone is clipped, but it's nothing compared to the scalding tongue lashing my mother gave me when I said goodbye. I knew our relationship changed the moment I started taking control of my life, but still, hearing those words from my mother cut deeper than I would like to admit.

"*Ay, qué dramática eres,*" she scoffs.

Oh, so I'm being dramatic now? I just repeated her exact words.

"When are you going to stop this nonsense and come back home? I talked to your professors, and they told me you can go back if you —"

My jaw ticks as I cut her off. "Please don't start again, *Mamá*. I'm not going home or back to law school. I'm happy here. *This* is my home now."

"Well, your inheritance will dwindle to nothing eventually, and then you won't be able to afford rent. You can't expect me to send you money —"

"When did I ever ask you for money? Besides, I have a job. I can pay my own rent."

"What job?" she asks, surprise evident in her tone.

I roll my eyes in preparation for her reaction before I answer her. "Server at a bar."

Here it goes…

"*¡Ay, Dios mio, qué vergüenza!* Are you out of your mind, Ava? I busted my ass after your deadbeat father left us for you to have a hot meal on the table and be able to attend college, and this is how you repay me? By leaving law school, moving across the country, and working at a bar *como una puta?*" she screeches and ends the call abruptly.

Grinding my teeth, I inhale a calming breath despite my fingers tightening on my phone. I barely stop myself from hurling it at the TV as I let out a frustrated scream. After a few moments, my heart rate goes back to normal, and I shake my head in disappointment. Until now, I felt guilty for not reaching out to my mother for two months, but honestly, I was expecting this sort of reaction from her, especially after I started working at the Shabby Shotglass.

She didn't even ask how I'm feeling. I mean, I did have a heart transplant four months ago. I get up, stride to the kitchen, and pull out all the ingredients I need to bake a chocolate cake. I was planning on being a couch potato until Tony came over so we could get ready together for the Halloween party. But my mother's phone call left me with a bitter taste in my mouth and a pang in my chest that just won't go away, so I'll bake something in an attempt to make myself feel better. I hope it works.

"Oʜ ᴍʏ Gᴏᴅ, you made this?" Tony says a few hours later, his voice traveling through the crack in the bathroom door.

"Do you like it?" I ask as I pull on the purple jumpsuit he brought over for me, trying to stick it to the tape on my boobs as best as I can. I definitely cannot wear a bra under it. Hopefully, the tape will be strong enough, and I won't flash anyone at the party.

"Do I like it? It's like an orgasm but in my mouth. Girl, you've got mad talent. It's the best cake I've eaten in my entire life. If my mamma would hear me right now, she would whoop my ass, but damn, I dare say it's better than sex." He pauses, seemingly considering what he just said. "Okay, maybe not better, but a close second."

"Well, I'm happy you love it so much," I chuckle out as I get out of the bathroom. "You can have as much as you want, and I'll bake you another whenever; just let me know," I say. My gaze flits to Tony, who's sitting on my couch. He looks amazing in his full Freddy Mercury costume while stuffing his face with the chocolate cake I served him a few minutes ago.

He makes a circle with his finger in the air, urging me to turn around as he chews and then swallows. I do a pirouette and pose like a model on a runway with a fierce stare. "So, what do you think?"

"Shit, you look hot, buttercup. If only I were straight," he jests with mock aggravation.

We both laugh. "Can you help me with my wig? I never wore one before."

"Oh, sweet innocent child, of course, I'll help you." He takes the last spoonful of cake from the plate, brings it into the kitchen, and places it in the sink. Then, Tony fusses over me in the bathroom for a good while, making sure my wig will stay in place. He even takes the time to trim the bangs so they look exactly like Selena's.

The sun rays filtering through the windshield reflect in the golden sequins of Tony's pants, creating a disco ball effect in my car's interior. We take full advantage of our makeshift nightclub and sing off-key at the top of our lungs to "I Want to Break Free" by Queen. Tony connected his phone to the speakers and has been playing Queen since we left my apartment.

"To properly get into character," he said earlier, winking at me.

Children in costumes accompanied by their parents crowd the

streets in the residential area of Ashville on their way to trick-or-treating. Most of the mansions in this neighborhood are decorated, and it brings the Halloween spirit to life. I almost do a double take at the massive skeleton that looks like it's escaping one of the houses, the bony hand splayed on the lawn bigger than my car. As I take in the macabre ornaments, memories of Chloe and me going trick-or-treating together when we were kids flash through my mind. We've been best friends since kindergarten. I feel her absence like a missing limb. I hope I'll get to see her soon.

By the time we manage to find a free parking spot, the sun is already disappearing in the horizon, the sky darkening with every second that passes, now a fiery copper with violet streaks as it gives way to dusk.

The icy air prickles my cheeks as we make our way on the forest trail. The worst part about this is that we unfortunately have to walk about half an hour until we reach Shadow Lake. The part of me that is stuck in the past worries about the exertion, about passing out, and I have to remind myself that I am not half dead anymore. Unlike I would have been four months ago, I'm not out of breath at all, and being here in the forest, surrounded by the smell of damp earth and pine trees, fills me with energy, a sense of all-encompassing belonging. The blanket of rusty leaves that covers the forest floor crunches with our every step, and Tony keeps me entertained with awkward stories from when he was a teenager and still in the closet.

As we reach the clearing near Shadow Lake, the party is already in full swing. Music blasts from two ginormous speakers, and more than a hundred people in costumes surround the massive bonfire in groups, holding red Solo cups. Everyone is talking and laughing, and some are even dancing to the music.

The full moon casts a silvery glow over the thick canopy of trees and on the rippling water, making the lake appear translucent, like a burnished steel mirror. Restlessness overtakes me as I feel static energy skitter over my entire body. I clench and unclench my fingers, trying to shake off the weird feeling.

"C'mon, buttercup. I spotted some of my friends," Tony squeaks as he grabs my hand and pulls me toward the bonfire to a group of people.

He hugs each of them, and then he comes back to my side. "Everyone, this is Ava. Ava, everyone." He pauses and gives me a devilish wink. "Ava here is single and ready to mingle," he proclaims to the whole group of ten people.

They all droll out some sort of "Hey" in my direction, and I wave awkwardly, heat spreading from my chest all the way to my ears for being put in the spotlight like that. Tony steps away and engages in a conversation with one of the guys in the group.

"Oh, I love your costume," the redhead girl wearing iridescent fairy wings and a silky emerald billowing dress says to me from my right. She looks like I would imagine a real sylph would. The light cast by the bonfire gives a warm glow to the side of her face, making the rhinestones above her eyebrows twinkle.

"Credit goes to Tony. It's his jumpsuit; I only bought the wig. And I love your costume, too. The wings are incredible."

"Thanks, I made them myself. I'm Olivia, by the way." I shake her hand when she thrusts it in my direction. She proceeds to tell me everyone's name in their group, but I'm terrible at remembering names. As soon as she finishes, I have already forgotten them.

Tony saunters toward me, accompanied by a guy wearing a Joker costume. "Ava, this is Ethan."

Ethan smiles as his gaze flits to me, tilting his chin since he already said hello earlier. He's wearing a Joker costume, complete with the face paint. He has a boyish charm, his wavy blond hair curling slightly at his ears, and he is a bit taller than Tony. Not as tall as Logan, though. I clench my jaw and push the errant thought away.

Ocean-blue eyes rake my body appreciatively. "Do you want to get something to drink?" Ethan asks.

"Sure," I reply and look at Tony. "Are you coming too?"

"No, you lovebirds go without me. But you can bring me some beer."

Ethan falls into step with me as we start walking toward the keg that's placed on the ground near a log serving as a makeshift table a few feet away, close to the tree line. "So, how do you know Tony?"

"I work at the same bar as he does, the Shabby Shotglass, in the Raven district."

"Really? I go there all the time but haven't seen you before. I can't believe I didn't notice someone as beautiful as you."

"I started working there recently, a month and a half ago. I just moved to Ashville."

"Ah. I've been busy with a school project the past two months, so I haven't gotten out much. But I would love to show you the city. If you want, of course."

Sawing my lip between my teeth, I ponder his offer. Even if Logan was such a dick to me, our kiss inevitably pops into my mind. It's as though something inside me refuses to move on. *Ugh, stop thinking about him, Ava. He doesn't deserve to occupy space in your head.* I shake Logan's ghost off my shoulders, and tell him, "Yeah, sure, I would like that."

We finally reach the keg but have to wait in a line to actually get our drinks. "Cool, it's a date." He winks and gives me a rueful smile that looks downright sinister with the makeup he has on, sweetened slightly by the boyish dimple.

"What do you study?" I ask after a few beats of silence.

"Architecture," he responds and takes three red solo cups. "Do you want beer? I think there's also some Vodka and OJ in the coolers."

"Um, I can't drink alcohol."

"I got you, no worries," he says, then starts searching through the drinks in the cooler. He throws me a look over his shoulder. "So you got two options, orange juice or alcohol-free cider."

"Cider, please."

He hands me the cider after he opens the bottle using his keys. He then pours two beers for himself and Tony, and we fall into an easy conversation as we stride back to the group. It doesn't take long before I'm jumping to the music alongside Tony and Olivia. I laugh as Tony twirls me and bumps his hips with mine. He then excuses himself to talk to a guy dressed as a firefighter who's been ogling him since we arrived. Olivia takes his place, and we start grinding to the music. I think the last time I had so much fun was when I went to the Deadly Sins concert with Chloe. Well, before I decided to snort cocaine like a dumbass and trigger my second heart attack, of course.

About an hour later, and after two more drinks supplied by Ethan, I realize I haven't seen Tony since he went to talk to that guy. "Have you seen Tony?" I ask Olivia.

"When I last saw him, he was pulling the firefighter with him through those trees." Her eyes are glazed by alcohol when she points with her finger at the tree line on our right. "He's probably getting some action, if you know what I mean," she tells me with a smirk, slurring the words.

"I think maybe you should drink some water," I say, a bit worried that she's going to get sick soon.

She hiccups. "Yeah, that's probably a good idea."

"I'll take her," Ethan offers as he returns from his bathroom break. "Do you want another cider?"

"Yeah, thanks."

They both leave, and at this point, I have to shuffle on my feet a bit and press my thighs together because my bladder is so full I feel like it's going to burst any minute now. The idea that I have to go squat behind a tree where anyone can see me is not appealing at all, but at the end of the day, the only other option I have is peeing myself. So, I decide to put on my big girl pants and go take care of my business.

I make it past the tree line on my right when it dawns on me. I'm wearing a freakin' jumpsuit. *Mierda.* I haven't thought this through. So, if someone accidentally passes by me, they will get a full damn show. At least I'm wearing my jacket on top, but still. I pinch the bridge of my nose during the second it takes me to gather my courage, and when I think I finally made it far enough and start taking off my jumpsuit, a heaving noise pulls my attention to a guy dressed as Batman puking his guts out only two meters behind me. I hastily retie back my jumpsuit around my neck as the disgusting smell burns my nostrils, making me gag. I step away from him as fast as possible and decide to go further into the woods.

After walking for about fifteen more minutes, I look around and listen, but there's no one here, only the wind rustling the branches of the pine trees and the lonely hoot of an owl in the distance. I take care of my business with a happy sigh, and when I finally finish sticking the cleavage portion of the jumpsuit back to the tape, a blood-curdling scream cuts through the air.

My stomach drops to the bottom of my feet. Another scream follows. It sounds exactly like Tony. The screech saws through my bones like a serrated knife, and my body reacts instantly. I have to do something to help him. My legs propel me forward at lightning speed.

Icy pine-scented air fills my lungs and burns the back of my throat with every hurried inhale, and I don't think I've ever run this fast in my entire life. The forest is nothing more than a hazy blob around me. The speed ends up being a curse, though, because soon the unmistakable stench of copper is filling my nose so potently I can almost taste it on my tongue.

I skid to a halt behind a tree when I come face to face with a golden, sequined-clad leg twitching on the ground. Ice shards fill my veins the moment I step to the side, and my eyes take in the horror scene before me.

Nonononononononono! It, it can't be.

I'm dreaming. I have to be dreaming. This can't be real. My body is frozen in place, and I can't hear anything over the ringing in my ears and the pounding in my chest.

Everything seems to move in slow motion as the biggest wolf I have ever seen claws Tony's heart out of his chest.

He's not alone; a mangled body sits in a pool of blood next to Tony. The firefighter guy is barely recognizable, with his limbs all wrong and his chest slashed open savagely.

I muffle a scream and take a trembling step back—right onto a branch. The crack slices through the eerie silence, and the wolf turns its head back toward me, baring its teeth menacingly. A deep growl leaves its chest as it steps in my direction.

Oh, God. What do I do? What do I do?

It pins me in place with its icy-blue eyes, and they look so human it's jarring. So jarring that a weird tingling starts at the bottom of my feet, spreading all over my body in seconds. Then, all I feel is agony. It's like my skin is being pulled too tight over my bones, and someone is pouring boiling water over me at the same time.

I bite my tongue and all I taste is blood when I feel a bone cracking and then another and another until I'm writhing on the cold, damp forest floor. I'm blinded by red-hot pain as my gums burn and my nails extend into sharp claws. Thick fur pierces my skin, and my mouth is filled, all of a sudden, with razor-sharp teeth.

What is happening to me?

This is what dying must feel like.

Am I, am I turning into a wolf?

No, no, no.

¡Despiértate, Ava!

Wake the fuck up!

The problem is…I can't wake up. The nightmare continues.

Blinking a few times, I turn my gaze toward the wolf that looks at me with its too-human eyes as if surprised, its head cocked to the side, auburn fur glittering in the moonlight. It's all a blur as someone wearing a dark cloak steps next to the mangled bodies, collects the two hearts from the forest floor, and then disappears through the trees. The wolf takes another step toward me, but before I can panic, it stops. It lifts its snout in the air, sniffs, and changes its mind, turning around and running after the person wearing the cloak.

A very canine whimper leaves my chest as I step carefully toward Tony on all fours. The gruesome picture before me will forever be seared into my brain. I'm sure I'll have nightmares to remember this cursed night by for many years to come. If not my whole life. That motherfucking wolf made a mockery of my dear friend's body. His face is frozen in a terrified wail, unmoving eyes staring at the star-studded sky. The neck is nothing more than a threadbare piece of meat. And the chest…God…the chest is the worst. Only a cavernous hole, from which the insides spill like a gurgling river of blood, painting the ground in violence. Still, I press my snout into his side.

C'mon, Tony. Please, please wake up!

Realistically, I know it's impossible. He doesn't even have a heart anymore, but my mind doesn't seem to register that as I press my paw into what's left of his arm, jolting his lifeless body.

A deep, powerful growl rumbles behind me, and I turn around just in time to see yet another gigantic wolf charging at me, fury flashing in its human-like honey eyes. Those eyes…I, I think I recognize them. I think this might be the wolf I've been dreaming about for the last four months.

Instinct takes over, and before I realize what I'm doing, I'm already running away at warp speed through the thick canopy of trees with the wolf at my back. My muscles scream in pain with the sheer effort; he's so damn fast. It already feels like he's been chasing me for an eternity, and I don't know how much longer I can keep running.

Why is he doing this?

"You killed them," someone growls back in my mind. It's a voice I recognize, and I'm so shocked by it that I stop for a second before I realize my mistake and start running again.

Only it's too late. The wolf barrels into my side, and we are a flurry of snapping jaws and flying limbs as we fall into a ravine, rolling and rolling until the back of my head smashes into something solid. Blackness takes over my vision.

18

Logan

A month. A fucking month since I last saw Ava, and I feel like an addict going through withdrawal. She's the first thing I think about when I wake up in the morning and the last thing on my mind when I go to sleep at night. Guilt is a living, breathing entity inside of me. It festers, eats at me, and claws at my mind. She's gotten under my skin and imprinted herself in my brain. Every single day this past month, I've gotten into my car and sped to the city, only to return with my tail between my legs once I realized I promised myself I couldn't walk that path again. I'm afraid that the moment I lay my eyes on her, I won't be able to stop myself, and then everything I worked for my entire life will go up in flames. The clock is ticking, taunting me with its cruelty. I only have one more month to find my fated mate, but all I can think about is Ava.

Not to mention that the dreams are back, and my mind is fucking with me. Last night, I dreamed of my fated mate for the first time in four months. The sense of complete and utter peace encompassed me, but then I woke up and realized the wolf I'd dreamed about wasn't my mate. I dreamed of dark mocha fur with a tawny underbelly instead of golden. Pale topaz green eyes instead of sparkling azure. And now, I don't know what's real anymore and what's not.

"Mornin', sunshine." My sister's voice travels through the hallway before she saunters into my kitchen, stopping at the table where I'm sitting with a half-empty bottle of vodka in front of me since I woke up a few hours ago. Her perfectly arched eyebrows furrow when she takes in my disheveled state. "It's a bit early for hard liquor, don't you think?" Her tone is condescending, judging.

"Hey, sis," I mutter. "Nice to see you too." I take another swig from the tumbler, welcoming the burn that comes with it. The warmth pools in my stomach and muddles my brain a little bit more. The dream fucked me up so good I needed something to dull the guilt polluting my mind. Only it didn't work; I still feel her beneath my skin, so I'll drink until I forget. I eventually have to, right?

Emily pulls out the chair across from me and plops down on it. "You do realize today is Halloween, right? You know how important this day is for the kids who haven't been touched by the weakness yet. You have to show your face for trick-or-treating. And it's a full moon tonight. You're the Alpha—"

"Do you think I don't know I'm the Alpha?" I bellow as I push up from the table abruptly, causing the chair to almost topple over as the glass smashes on its side and spills on the table. I grab my hair in fistfuls and pull at it in frustration. "Do you think I can ever forget, Em? I'm reminded of it every fucking second of my life. It's easy to judge me when the weight of the world is not pressing on your shoulders," I snap. "You don't know what it's like to have so much responsibility you're drowning in it."

"Fuck. I'm sorry," she murmurs, voice laced with regret. She stands and comes to me, throwing her arms around my big frame and pulling me into a hug.

I sink into her as needles stab the back of my eyes.

"Honestly, I don't know what I would do in your place. Probably lose my fucking mind," she admits. She pulls back, locks her eyes with mine, and grips my shoulders. "Something is eating at you. I can feel it. You've been acting strange for more than a month, and as much as you try to put up a front, I can see through it. C'mon, Lo, talk to me. You haven't talked to me in so long. Not really. I'm still your person. You know that, right?"

I clear my throat and swallow, stepping back from her hold. The vodka finally hits me hard, so I sway slightly on my feet when I reply. "It's just the same shit, Em. Everything that's been going on with the weakness. The kids falling into the deep sleep. What's going to happen a month from now on my birthday. The rogue—"

She cuts me off as she crosses her arms in front of her chest. "Bullshit. There's something else. Something you're not telling me."

My nostrils flare, and I shake my head. "I'm going to sleep this off," I grumble, my words more slurred than I would like. I push by her to get out of the kitchen.

"Is it Ava?"

Her words are like a blow to my solar plexus, stopping me in my tracks and turning me around. "What?"

"Something happened with Ava last month, right? I figured as much, but I was waiting for you to tell me."

A muscle jumps in my taut jaw. "Nothing happened."

She arches an eyebrow at me. "C'mon, Lo. Don't insult me. I'm not that stupid. You didn't come home after she was attacked, and then when you did, your knuckles were so swollen you looked like you'd been fighting a brick wall for hours. And you smelled like you'd bathed in blood."

"Let it go. Nothing happened," I grit out.

She huffs and sucks on her teeth. "Do you think I haven't felt you outside the bar? At first, I didn't understand why you would leave in such a haste every night, and then I smelled you outside the Shabby Shotglass after my shifts. The fact that you wouldn't even come inside puzzled me. Then Ava got attacked, and you started acting all weird. Not to mention, you were conveniently there that night. What the fuck is happening?"

"That's a fun little story you just made up. Maybe you should write a book," I deadpan. "I'm going to sleep. I'll see you later." I turn on my heel, and with hurried steps, I try to put as much distance as I can between us.

"Oh, fuck you. I know I'm right," she screams at my disappearing back as the front door slams behind her.

THE FULL MOON beckons me like a siren, perched high in the indigo sky on a backdrop of glittering stars, singing an ancient tune as the animalistic part of my brain takes over completely. Everything is simpler in wolf form. The crisp, pine-scented air fills my snout and ruffles my fur. My paws sink rhythmically into the forest floor while I lead the pack toward the herd of deer we caught wind of one hour ago.

We work together in perfect synchrony, like a well-oiled machine, as we take into consideration the speed of the wind and its direction so we don't scare off the prey before the perfect moment for an ambush arises. The herd leads us past the border of our lands, near Shadow

Lake, when I feel it. The jolt of electricity down the center of my chest as if lightning struck me. And I know it without a doubt. It's her. It's my mate. She's near.

"*Take the lead,*" I order Emily with urgency, using the mental link that allows us to speak to each other when we're in wolf form.

"*What?*" she asks, confused. "*Why? Did something happen?*"

I turn my head toward her slightly. Being my Beta, she is closest to me in formation. "*Take the lead, Emily. I need to check something.*"

"*I'll come with you.*"

"*No, you won't. You're taking the lead. It's an order,*" I growl in warning.

She immediately complies and comes to my side, ears drawn back in submission as her tail tucks between her legs. She doesn't have a choice. An order given by the Alpha of the pack is irrefutable. Even if she wants to, she can't disobey me. "*Don't come after me when you finish with the hunt. If I don't return, you'll lead the pack home. Understood?*"

"*Yes, Alpha,*" she responds, but her tone is tense, and I can feel her frustration pouring across our mental link.

I lower my head toward my Beta, give her a very human-like nod, and then turn around and run like my life depends on it. I scent her: vanilla and caramel, violets, and something musky, earthy, and animalistic. Shock ripples through me.

I know that smell; it's imprinted in my mind and the very fabric of my soul.

My wolf knows it, too. "*Mine!*"

My paws pound the forest floor, and I'm almost flying through the air in my desperation to reach her. I'm so close. So close. Only a few more seconds, and then I'll finally have her. "*Mine!*" Coming out of the cluster of pine trees, my eyes settle on the wolf in front of me. Dark mocha fur with a tawny underbelly.

No, it can't be.

I almost trip on my own legs when I finally look *past* my mate, to the two horribly mangled bodies lying on the forest floor, seeping blood, the ground a gruesome crimson.

Dominic's words invade my mind. *"Assuming the rogue is male could be a mistake. What if it's a female behind all of the attacks?"*

Then Malik's. *"Are you sure she's human?"*

They ring in my head over and over as realization dawns like a knife impaling me in my gut. It's Ava. She's the rogue. She tricked us, played the innocent human all along, and caught me in her web of lies. A mournful whimper leaves me at the sting of betrayal, the pain so intense I almost keel over.

It's a struggle to keep the fury at the forefront while warring with my wolf and the mating bond singing in my chest, wanting nothing more than to claim her at this moment.

"Mine!"

No!

I win the battle in the end, and fury comes blazing in, flowing in my veins and steeling my resolve as I advance toward her in a run, growling with all my menace.

19

Ava

When I come to, the first thing I notice is the smell of freshly chopped wood, earthy and musky with a hint of pine. It's quickly overpowered by a dull throbbing in the back of my head, and the muscles in my arms are screaming in pain, my wrists raw as if there's something digging painfully into them. My throat is as dry as the Sahara desert, and my eyelids weigh a thousand pounds. After a few seconds, the effort pays off, and I'm finally able to open my eyes.

I'm in some sort of a basement. The space is small and rudimentary. The walls are all wooden, and there's only one narrow rectangular window placed high on the wall on my right. It's covered by snow, and fiery orange light slants through a small hole. It must be either sunrise or sundown; I can't make much of it other than that. On the wall in front of me hangs a display of hunting knives, and under them sits the only piece of furniture, a scruffy-looking oak table.

I look up and realize why my muscles are in so much agony. My wrists are tied together, and I'm dangling from a hook in the ceiling like in some mobster movie, my toes barely touching the cement floor. I'm naked. But why? How? Who would do this to me?

And then it hits me. The Halloween party. *Oh God…Tony. Poor Tony.* He's dead. Torn to pieces by that wolf. My heart cracks down the middle when the images start playing on a loop like a broken record in my mind.

A sob escapes my throat, and then the dam breaks. I can't stop the overflowing current of emotions that rake through my body as my tears start flowing freely, blurring my vision and wetting my cheeks, cascading down on my naked chest.

Heavy footsteps and a creaking sound pull my attention toward the wooden stairs on my left. I blink a few times in order to clear the blurriness caused by the onslaught of tears. Honey eyes lock with mine as Logan descends the last two steps, and his fingers flick over a light switch. The sudden burst of light blinds me momentarily, but it's a short moment, and it doesn't stop my heart from fluttering in my chest at the sight of him. I haven't seen Logan in a month, and I feel as if I've been starved for the sight of him. My eyes drink him in ravenously, and the strange attraction I feel for him hits me full force.

"L-logan? Please, help me." My voice comes out raspy, like I haven't spoken a word in days.

A cruel smirk tugs at the corner of his lips as he saunters toward me with a predatory gait, all clean lines and taut, sinewy muscles under his gray tee and dark denim. "You can drop the act, Ava. Or is your real name even Ava?"

My eyebrows pull together in confusion. "Of course it is. What are you talking about?"

He reaches me, and then one hand comes up, cruel, punishing fingers grabbing the sides of my face and pressing into my cheeks. "I must admit, you've put on a good show, playing all innocent and tempting.

You're a good actress. Maybe you should look into Hollywood. If you survive, that is."

Logan's touch burns through my skin, even if it brings me pain. The air between us crackles with energy, and all of a sudden, I'm aware of the fact that I'm stark naked and at his mercy. The room is stifling; it feels like I'm inhaling the air coming out of a hot oven.

"What show? What are you talking about? I don't understand—"

"Cut the act! You can't fool me anymore. Where's my real fated mate? What did you do to her?" His upper lip curls, baring his teeth while his fingers bite into my cheeks, and I wince in pain. He looks feral, almost like a wolf.

An image from the woods, being chased by the giant wolf with ash-brown fur and amber eyes, flashes through my mind. My stomach takes a nosedive straight to the bottom of my feet. It's *him*. Logan is the wolf I've been dreaming about. But unlike my dreams…he's here to hurt me.

The temperature in the room continues to rise. A drop of sweat rolls down my spine, and my hair sticks to my sweaty forehead. "Please, Logan. Please. I don't know what you're talking about."

His jaw locks with anger as he dips down and crowds me, his nose pressing into mine. "Did you do some kind of spell on me? Are you working with a witch?"

A laugh bubbles out of me before I can stop it. "A witch?" His nostrils flare in response, and I realize he's being serious. Are witches real?

¡Mierda! What else is out there?

His hand releases my jaw, but he lowers it and circles my throat in a punishing grip, cutting off my air supply and making me sputter. "Stop playing with me," he seethes.

In that moment, something weird happens to my body; my nipples stand up at attention, and desire pools at my core. Despite hanging in a literal dungeon. Logan finally releases me when I feel like I'm going to faint. I gasp for air, and it's impossible to form a thought with the haze of lust muddling my brain.

His gaze roves over me lazily, a glint of hunger shining in his eyes, and then, as if he can't stop himself, he palms my breast, brushing an electrifying thumb over my taut nipple. I can't stop the moan that escapes my mouth.

What is happening to me?

It's so hot in here it feels like I have descended into the pits of Hell. Perspiration coats my entire body, and I'm so wet between my legs that I'm dripping down my thighs.

Logan's chest moves rapidly with every inhale, and his nostrils flare as if he is scenting the air. In the next second, his eyes narrow. A muscle jumps in his taut jaw. When he steps into me, my nipples rub onto his chest, sending ripples of desire down the ladder of my spine. I have to bite my lip hard to stifle another moan. "Answer me! Where is my fated mate?"

I close my eyes and swallow, my throat raw. "I don't know what you're talking about," I rasp as my eyes snap open. There's something wrong. "Please," I whisper, but I don't know what I'm begging for. "I feel weird. I need, I need…" I press my thighs together in a failed attempt to stop the searing fire that's taken over my body. Looking down, I see the massive erection tenting the front of Logan's jeans, and I whimper with need.

Logan tilts his head, and something flashes in his eyes as his eyebrows shoot up in surprise. "You're in heat," he says in disbelief.

I don't understand what being in heat means, but somehow, it's exactly how I'm feeling. Only heat is too mild of a word. I'm being scorched from the inside out.

Logan circles me, and then I feel him at my back. "Why are you killing humans?"

"I didn't kill anyone—"

"Liar!" He fists my hair, and his other hand palms my right ass cheek before it comes down in a punishing blow that I feel right in the center of my pussy.

Tears spring to my eyes with the sting, but more in shame because I'm so turned on I can barely see straight.

"What do you need their hearts for?"

"Logan, you have to listen to me, I didn't do any—"

"Liar!"

Thwack!

"How did you manage to hide your scent for so long?"

"I don't under—"

Thwack!

My eyes roll in the back of my head as every slap brings a new surge of pleasure.

"Are you working with a witch?"

"Plea—"

Thwack!

Logan surprises me in the next moment by caressing the smarting skin. "Look at you, dripping for me. You like this, don't you? Being at my mercy," he drawls, his voice like gravel, thickened by his desire. He angles my head before I feel his breath fanning the side of my neck, sending shivers all over my skin. Then his thumb brushes over my engorged clit in one swift motion.

I catch fire.

I can't stop the loud moan that tumbles out of my mouth. He dips a thick, long finger inside me and pumps it in and out, making me crazy. I would normally be embarrassed by the sounds I'm making, but I'm past the point of caring. Pleasure singes me. My blood bubbles inside my veins. I'm so close. So close. As if sensing I'm about to reach the high I so desperately crave, Logan takes out his finger. My cry of frustration almost sounds like a feral growl.

"Open your mouth!" he commands. It feels like he's the master puppeteer, pulling my strings. And without thinking, I obey. He pushes the dripping finger inside my mouth, pressing it against my tongue. "Suck."

The moment my lips close around his digit, a violent tremor goes through Logan. Our gazes snare and hold as I suck on it, tasting myself. A deep growl leaves his chest. It makes me vibrate with need. He drops the hand holding my hair, and then he pinches my nipple. Hard. I cry out at the assault on my nerve endings.

He slides his finger out of my mouth, which I let go with a loud pop. Using the pads of his pointer fingers, Logan circles my areolas slowly, but not near enough my nipples where I need him. His left hand bands around my waist, plastering my back to his front. I feel every inch of his hard-as-steel cock pressing into my back.

"P-please," I beg.

Logan laughs, the sound cruel. He glides his free hand down my body until he reaches my inner thighs, his movements slow, maddening. His fingers inch up and brush over my outer lips, but he still doesn't give me what I want.

"Please, Logan," I sputter, blinded by the lust coursing in my veins like molten lava. Tears escape my eyes and roll down my cheeks out of sheer frustration. He's playing with me like a cat with a mouse, and I fell into his trap. I have no other choice; the haze of desire is too strong. I need him inside of me like I need my next breath.

"Do you want to come?" he taunts.

"Y-yes," I mumble on a breathy whisper.

"Then tell me the truth, and maybe I'll consider letting you come." His breath fans the side of my face, and his delicious, woodsy, spicy scent envelops me, coating my skin like molasses.

"I told you the truth. I'm telling you the truth. Please, Logan. Please.

You have to believe me. I didn't do anything," I try to plead with him, my tone coaxing.

Logan abruptly lets me go, so my full weight yanks down on the rope around my wrists and the hook. My muscles scream in agony, and I'm reminded that I'm hanging from the ceiling. At this point, I can't even feel my hands anymore. I chance a look up. My fingers are starting to turn blue from the lack of blood circulation.

My fingers quickly become the least of my worries. A cold barrel of a gun is pressed in the center of my forehead.

"Stop fucking lying to me!" he sneers, a crazy look in his eyes, his lips curled in disgust. "These are not regular bullets, Ava. They're made out of silver and dipped in aconite." He smirks like I'm supposed to know what that means. "So you better start telling the truth."

I can't take it anymore, the craziness of it all, the fire blazing through my body.

I snap.

"I don't know what that means, you stupid fucking bastard!" I scream at the top of my lungs. Logan doesn't react to my outburst; he just narrows his eyes and tilts his head. "I didn't do anything. I didn't kill anyone. I don't even know what a fated mate is, and honestly, I don't even fucking care. I was at a Halloween bonfire party near the lake. I needed to pee, so I went by myself into the woods, and then I heard a scream. It sounded like Tony, so I ran to him." I take a deep breath in. "I reached him, but it was too late." My voice cracks, and my lower lip trembles with my admission.

"Tony, he…he was being mauled by a big wolf with auburn fur. It clawed out his heart. Then I realized I was in danger, but when I decided to get out of there, I stepped on a branch. When the wolf noticed me, something happened to me. All the bones in my body started to break, and I felt like I was dying." I shudder at the memory of the intense pain.

It takes a few seconds for me to be able to continue.

"It sounds insane, I know, but I think I transformed into a wolf. When my vision cleared, I saw someone wearing a dark cloak, collecting the hearts from the forest floor. The wolf then disappeared with that cloaked person through the trees and left me there. As if that wasn't crazy enough, before I could even catch my fucking breath, another wolf came charging at me. I guess that wolf was you because, apparently, people transforming into wolves is a thing now. Next thing I know, I wake up here. That's it. That's my truth. That's all I know. I keep thinking that maybe, *maybe*, I'll wake up from this fucking nightmare. But I'm not going to, am I? This is all real."

A deep belly laugh belts out of me, and I sound just like a crazy person. It dies as abruptly as it came out. I throw Logan a scathing glare. "So shoot me, you oaf! Fucking shoot me and get it over with," I seethe.

His lips twist in a wry smile. "Did you just call me an oaf?"

My jaw locks with anger. "Oh, I can do better than that: motherfucker, egotistical bastard, dickhead, *pendejo, hijo de put—*"

Logan cuts me off. "Okay, I think I got the gist of it," he says dryly. He lowers his gun and sits for a minute with everything I said as he starts pacing the small space. Then he turns to me. "So what, I'm supposed to believe you shifted for the first time last night?"

"Is that what it's called? Shifting? Yeah, I did, and trust me, it was a fucking shock, to say the least."

"So you were bitten, then. Where's your sire?"

My eyebrows scrunch in confusion. "My what?"

He widens his stance and crosses his arms in front of his chest. "Your sire, Ava. Stop playing stupid."

I let out a frustrated groan. "I'm not playing stupid. I don't know what that is. No one fucking bit me. All I know is that my life was normal until I discovered I was going to die a few months ago. Then my heart stopped. I had a transplant, and all of these weird things started happening to me."

He arches an eyebrow at me. "Where's your scar?"

"What?"

"If you had heart transplant surgery, then why don't you have a scar?"

"It healed, okay? I know it's weird, especially since I had the surgery four months ago. But my doctor said not to worry about it. It's just one of the weird things that happened after."

"What are the others? Enlighten me," he deadpans.

I swallow and close my eyes briefly, trying to stay in the present, but it's getting harder by the minute with how badly my skin is burning. I feel like someone threw me into a furnace. "Like dreaming about a wolf with a coat of ash-brown fur and honey eyes almost every night, becoming weirdly strong—like breaking things without trying—smelling and hearing someone before they walk into a room…"

Taking a deep breath in, I open my eyes. My vision is slightly blurry, and beads of sweat are now coursing freely from my hairline over my face. "And then there's Hope, the girl I received the heart from. A girl who was in a cult in this weird little town, Devil's Creek. They did satanic rituals wearing the skin of wolves. At least, that's what my private investigator told me. So my best guess is that the heart I received is cursed or some shit. Just my luck to receive another chance at life and then get a freakin' curse," I mumble the last part to myself.

A laugh bursts out of Logan, and then he doubles over and continues laughing like he just heard the most amusing joke ever. He comes up for air after what seems like forever and wipes at the corner of his eyes. "That has to be the funniest shit I've heard in my entire life. You really expect me to believe you?"

"Glad you found it entertaining, *pendejo*," I snark. "Yes, I do because I told you the truth. She also disappeared when she was fifteen years old and then reappeared the night she died in a car accident. It's real; her disappearance was even broadcasted on the news eight years ago. There are articles online."

"I don't know if you're crazy or delusional enough to believe that story, but what you're telling me is impossible. Wolf shifters are either born or sired by a bite. When you get bitten, there is a ninety percent chance you'll turn feral and go crazy. But you already know all this, so stop stalling with your bullshit and tell me where my fated mate is," he demands with a sneer and points the gun at me again.

I don't say anything else as I glare at him, my breath coming out in short pants. I'm grinding my teeth so hard I'm surprised they don't turn to dust. I don't have it in me to continue this crazy conversation. I have tried every single thing to reason with him, and he won't hear it, so why should I waste my breath anymore when he's not going to believe me anyway?

Something inside of me is going feral. I keep hearing in my brain, *"Mine!"* over and over again, and all I want to do is climb Logan like a tree and fuck his brains out, but at the same time, I hate him so much for doing this to me, for not believing me. He hung me like an animal, and I still want him so damn much it hurts. Every inch of my skin is weeping for his touch, and I'm so mad at myself for feeling this way, but I can't stop it. I don't know how.

Anger is rolling off Logan in waves as he stares me down, waiting for an answer. Well, we'll be here forever at this rate because I have nothing else to give him, so he can as well shoot me and get it over with. This doesn't fucking scare me. I already looked death in the face twice. The way I see it, I was supposed to give my last breath in that tour van …. At least I got the wings I so desperately craved.

"Fine," he spews and lowers the gun when he finally realizes I'm not going to say anything. "Have it your way then. We'll talk in a few hours. Maybe you'll change your mind by then." He turns and leaves me there in the basement, but I don't miss the way his muscles lock his movements like it's physically hurting him to walk away from me.

20

Logan

The icy air cracks across my cheeks like a whip, and the flurries of snow blind me as I trek in the middle of a blizzard on the narrow forest path, on my way to try and get some cell service so I can call Kaiden with the phone I keep in case of emergencies at my cabin. Seventy inches of the white powder have fallen from the sky in the last two hours. Since the cabin is so high up in the mountains, the wind is unforgiving, and I can barely see in front of me. If the storm doesn't let out by tonight, all the roads will be blocked. Even in wolf form, it's almost impossible to travel in seventy inches of snow.

The trek is made even harder by my wolf demanding I go back to Ava and complete the mating bond. He's been fighting me tooth and nail since he laid eyes on her wolf for the very first time. It would have been so easy to lose myself in her earlier. Hell, it's physically painful for me not to touch her, to hold back.

Her curvy, sinful body is perfection, almost as if it was made for me.

The scent of her arousal nearly threw me off the deep end. All I wanted to do was kneel before her and eat her pussy like a starved man, then sink into her and claim her as mine for hours on end.

Ava being in heat confuses me. A female wolf shifter goes into heat when she is ready to complete the mating bond, but I know this can't be true because she's not my real mate. There's some kind of spell in the middle of this. She did something to my real fated mate, and after I find out what, I'm going to kill Ava. My wolf growls at me for daring to think like that about his mate and demands that I go back to her again.

"That's not our real mate," I seethe at him in my mind for the umpteenth time. Sweat dots my forehead and drips down my spine, my muscles straining with the sheer effort I'm making to get away from Ava. Only the burn of betrayal keeps me placing one step in front of the other.

The moment I brought Ava to my cabin after she passed out in the ravine not far from here, I made the same trek to call Kaiden and tell him everything that happened. But then Ava wasn't in heat, and even if I struggled with it, the trek was much easier. Now, it seems almost physically impossible to do. But Kaiden, Malik, and Dominic are investigating Ava and the two bodies I had to leave behind in the forest. I have to know what they found out.

After thirty more minutes, I finally get one bar, and my phone pings with a slew of incoming messages. I briefly go through them and see they're all from Emily. I choose to ignore them until I get a better understanding of the situation. I know she got quite close to Ava in the short period they've known each other, and I don't want to hurt her until we know everything that's been going on. Finding out about Tony will gut her, and then adding Ava's betrayal on top of it will surely destroy her. I messaged her last night and told her I'm on Conclave business and that she will need to take care of the pack in my absence.

I dial Kaiden. As soon as he picks up, he puts me on speaker.

"What did you find out?" I ask with impatience.

"She's clean, man. I was at her apartment earlier, and there's no residual magic," Malik responds. "If she ever worked with a witch, they must have met somewhere else."

"We also found her phone in what was left of her clothes after she shifted in the forest. It's also clean," Kaiden intervenes.

"And it's true, she did have a heart transplant four months ago," Dominic juts in. "Our hacker managed to find her medical history. She didn't lie about that."

"We did find something interesting at her apartment, though, and in one of her emails, a file. She hired a private investigator to look into her heart's donor. She received her heart from a girl who disappeared mysteriously eight years ago from a small mountain town, Devil's Creek. Her name was Hope Moore. When I saw the name, it gnawed at me because I knew I've heard it before. She was on our list of possible Kabal kidnappings, along with other dark creatures that year. She was a wolf shifter. I'll send you the file so you can take a look," Kaiden says, and my phone rattles against my ear with the incoming email.

It takes me some time before I can finally grasp the information Kaiden relayed. Of course, I heard a part of it from Ava. But then I thought she was just spinning another story full of lies to deceive me. Is it possible she was telling the truth? I tell them everything Ava did earlier, my heart pounding so fast it feels like it's going to claw its way out of my chest.

We're all quiet as they process my words.

"What if she did turn for the first time last night, triggered by her friend getting mauled to death?" Dominic asks after some time. "You know, like the kids shifting the very first time. You said a strong emotion always causes their first shift."

"If the Kabal had a hand in this, then it might be true," Malik says grimly. "When they imprisoned Kaiden and me, we witnessed all kinds of sick experiments on dark creatures. We already know what they're capable of, and we know of the mysterious dark creatures' disappearances over the years. Maybe we didn't stop them like we thought."

Shit.

Why is everything they're saying making sense all of a sudden?

Kaiden's voice breaks through my thoughts. "Also, don't you think it was too easy for you to find her last night? How could she expertly evade us for months on end, covering her scent and even leaving a dead body at the border of your territory with the constant patrolling, and then get caught so easily? It doesn't add up."

I end the call, telling them to let me know if they find anything else, and open the email sent by Kaiden. The moment I see Hope's photo, a sinking feeling of desperation overtakes me. Her golden hair and vivid blue eyes, like the azure water in the Caribbean. The eyes I've been dreaming about for five years.

Hope Moore was my fated mate and now Ava has her heart.

I can't believe I was so blind and refused to listen to my wolf when it tried to tell me countless times that Ava belongs to us.

If Ava has Hope's heart, does it mean she is now my fated mate?

It has to. Otherwise, she wouldn't be in heat right now.

Fuck.

What have I done?

21

Ava

I don't know how much time has passed from the moment Logan left, but I'm in some kind of special version of hell right now. His distance is physically painful to me in a way I never thought possible, and the feeling that I'm being burned to a crisp from the inside out has taken over my body completely. I can't think beyond the need to be fucked and the need for Logan to touch me. Which is funny; I wouldn't have thought I was the kind of girl who goes stupid over a man. And yet here I am.

Despite many attempts that ended in failure, I try to pull my hands out of the rope again as forcefully as I can. But I only manage to make my headache worse and the rope tear into the raw skin of my wrists viciously as I dangle like a fish from a hook.

"Motherfucker!" I scream in frustration as tears stream down my face, mixing with the beads of sweat. I feel disgusting, and my bladder is so full that it's going to explode any minute now. I could just pee myself.

I mean, what's one more humiliating thing to add to the list, right? I bet he won't even be able to tell with the sweat puddle at my feet.

"*Pinche pendejo de mierda,*" I mumble under my breath.

"I think I like oaf more," Logan says with a sheepish smile as he descends the stairs in a hurry, holding a bottle of water. My heart, the traitorous bitch, does a somersault at the sight of him.

"What do you want?" I seethe.

He doesn't say anything as he stalks toward me with long strides. He stops a couple inches away, and his Adam's apple bobs in his throat, his eyebrows furrow, and something flashes in his eyes. It almost looks like regret. Ha, what a joke. I'm pretty sure he is a psychopath.

"Here, I brought you some water." He uncaps the bottle and lifts it to my mouth, but I press my lips together, refusing to drink.

"How do I know it's not poisoned?" I ask in a clipped tone.

"It's not poisoned," he sighs.

I huff. "Yeah, sure. Like I'm gonna take your word for it, *cabron*."

Logan rolls his eyes at me and takes a big swig. When he brings the bottle to my lips the second time, I gulp the water greedily. He discards the empty bottle on the scruffy oak table and turns back to me, eyebrows pinched. Taking a step closer, he extends his hand toward the side of my face as if he wants to brush his knuckles over my cheek, but I jerk my head and pull back as much as my position allows me.

"Don't fucking touch me," I snap, but my whole body is vibrating with the need to feel his skin against mine.

"I'm so sorry, Ava," he says so softly I almost think I imagined it. Then he starts untying the rope around my wrists.

"What's happening?" I ask, bewildered. And then every kidnapper movie I've ever seen flashes through my mind, and I'm suddenly sure he's about to kill me.

Before I fall to the cement floor, he catches me in his arms, and the contact with his hard body sends me into a frenzy, making me moan. Jesus, I'm about to be brutally murdered, but instead you would think I'm the horniest person on planet Earth with the sounds I'm making. Well, it kind of feels like I am. He sweeps me up like a bride, with his forearm supporting the back of my knees and the other my back.

"Let me go!" I demand and push at his chest. "I don't want you near me."

"Stop struggling. I can't let you go. If I do, you won't be able to stand in the state you're in. Just let me bring you somewhere where you can sit first."

My eyebrows knit in confusion. "Why are you being nice to me all of a sudden? What changed?" A thousand needles prick my arms and fingers as the blood starts circulating again in my extremities.

"Everything," he answers cryptically, climbing the stairs with me in his arms.

Just the fact that he's holding me to his chest alleviates somewhat the scorching need that's taken over my body completely, and I don't even feel bad that I'm drenching his clothes with my sweat. My head rests over his chest, and my nose presses, on its own accord, to his skin. Closing my eyes, I inhale his delicious, woodsy, spicy scent. Why does he have to smell so good, dammit? I desperately want to hate him, but I can't. Somehow, there's something inside of me that wants him beyond everything that he has done to me.

Logan opens the door at the top of the stairs and steps into a mountain cabin with high beams, wood-paneled walls, and a lit stone fireplace. It's almost idyllic. You know, if he didn't kidnap me and tie me up in the basement like a serial killer.

"Can you bring me to a bathroom, please? I need to pee," I say and try to hold it in a bit longer.

He cuts through the open space, bypasses the living room with the incredible wall made only out of floor-to-ceiling windows with a spectacular view of the snow-capped mountain peaks, and enters a bathroom. He places me on a toilet but doesn't leave; he just stares at me with a weird look on his face.

"I need some privacy," I tell him, and he snaps out of it, leaving me alone in the room with a "sorry" mumbled under his breath. When I finally start peeing, I feel so relieved I almost burst into tears. I need to come up with some sort of an escape plan, but my body is weakened by the fever, and I'm so freakin' turned on, I don't know how I'll manage that. I feel like I can't even stand on my own legs.

And besides, there's a blizzard outside. I saw it briefly through the floor-to-ceiling windows. And let's not forget about the fact that I'm still naked. If I somehow manage to jump out a window, I'm not surviving ten minutes in that snow.

A knock on the door pulls me out of my thoughts. "Done?"

"Yeah," I respond, and a wave of scorching heat hits me hard, making me double over. I think I lose consciousness for a few moments.

"Ava? Shit, you're burning up," Logan says with aggravation, but I can't open my eyes. I black out.

My eyes snap open at the feeling of ice-cold water pouring down on me, and I realize Logan's holding me against his body beneath a spray of water in the walk-in shower, one of his hands under my ass, supporting my whole weight and the other cradling my neck as my front is melded completely to his, my thighs on either side of him. He's fully clothed, and the material of his wet clothes against my feverish skin makes my nipples harden into diamond-hard tips and my breathing ragged.

I can feel every single drop of water the moment it makes contact with my skin. Liquid fire blazes through me. The air between us thickens, and tiny electric shocks make my pussy clench with a need so potent it's like a ravaging wildfire obliterating everything in its path, consuming my every thought.

"I can't take it anymore," I cry out. My hips start gyrating as they seek much-needed friction. "Please, Logan," I beg with desperation.

"Shh, I got you, little wolf," he says in a soothing tone. Next thing I know, I'm gently positioned on the floor. The wet, cold tiles dig into my back. His breath is hot on the side of my neck as he sucks on my ear lobe, sending chills down my spine. He trails soft kisses from the column of my neck all the way to the apex of my thighs, and it feels too damn slow and torturous, so I mumble something in protest to hurry him.

Logan chuckles in response. The sound vanishes into thin air as he buries his head between my thighs. The moment his lips latch onto my clit, my back arches off the floor while my fingers bury into his hair, pulling on his curls.

"Oh, oh God! It feels so good. Don't stop, Logan. Please, don't stop!" I moan loudly. In response, a guttural groan rattles from Logan's chest, the sound so animalistic and powerful it vibrates against my heated flesh. He alternates between sucking, licking, and little nips, dragging his teeth across my clit, but it's not enough. "I need more!" I cry out.

He plunges two thick fingers inside me and pumps them furiously, massaging my inner walls while crisscrossing them against my G-spot. That, combined with the maddening assault on my clit makes me detonate in a blinding orgasm that leaves me panting on the shower floor.

But Logan doesn't stop; he continues to eat my pussy like a man possessed as my walls spasm around his fingers until another orgasm crashes into me in violent waves of pleasure.

"Fuck, baby. You taste so sweet. Better than I could ever imagine," he growls against my gushing pussy before he licks me clean, pushing his tongue inside me, fucking me with it. He palms my breast while he presses the pad of his thumb against my taut nipple and makes delicious circles with it. Then he pinches it hard as he bites into my clit at the same time. The pain mixing with pleasure surges through me like an electrical bolt and sends me over the cliff again, panting loudly his name and every curse word out there while my thighs start shaking violently around his head and shoulders.

Still, Logan doesn't move from between my legs. He continues to eat me out relentlessly as he fucks me with his fingers. After the fifth orgasm, I pass out, and I vaguely feel Logan turning the water to warm, washing me slowly, almost reverently, before he picks me up in his arms. I lose my grip on reality again when he starts drying me with a fluffy towel.

22

Ava

I wake up draped across Logan's naked chest, my head in the crook of his neck, nose pressed against the side of his throat like I sought out his smell unconsciously, one of his arms at the small of my back and the other at the nape of my neck. I'm still completely naked, and my wrists are bandaged.

Logan's skin feels amazing against mine, his intoxicating scent wrapping around me in waves, settling something deep inside of me. I know I should run for the hills. I should try to slip from his hold as quietly as I can, grab some clothes, and run. But I can't. The scorching fire of need is still blazing, though settled slightly by the multiple orgasms Logan gave me earlier when he ate my pussy with the hunger of a prisoner on death row receiving his last meal.

Images of us on the shower floor flash through my mind, and I'm suddenly aware of the hardness pressing into my belly. I instantly get wet.

Logan is sleeping beneath me. I blink a few times, taking him in:

smooth brown skin rippling with muscles, the perfectly etched V, and the trail of slightly curly hair disappearing in the waistband of his gray sweats. Without thinking, I trace the tattoo on his right bicep with my fingers and glide my hand down his torso until I reach the waistband of his sweats and let a finger slip inside. I'm instantly met with the head of his cock. I swallow hard. Should I? Fuck, I can't stop myself from circling the silky tip with my finger. A bead of precum comes out. My mouth waters with the need to taste it as I spread it around.

I know I shouldn't, but yet again, it doesn't feel like I have much choice. Before I can even grasp the repercussions of what I'm about to do, my body makes the decision for me as my hand inches down. I wrap my fingers around his shaft, the heated skin like velvet against the palm of my hand. I gulp at the sheer size of it, so long and thick, with veins bulging along the sides. I pump my hand up and down, and it twitches with a spasm against my palm.

Suddenly, a large hand grabs my wrist, halting my movement. "I can't believe I'm saying this, but if you don't want me to flip you over and fuck you, then you need to stop," Logan rumbles beneath me in a deep, sleepy voice that stokes the fire inside of me even more. "I won't be able to restrain myself if you keep touching me."

"Maybe that's exactly what I want," I blurt out and lift my head to look at him, gulping at the intensity in his half-lidded stare as our eyes collide. There's so much hunger in them. His lips look so pillowy and soft. All I want is to kiss him and sink onto his cock.

His Adam's apple bobs in his throat. "We can't. We need to talk first. I have to explain everything to you. There's no excuse for what I have done, but I hope you'll eventually find it within yourself to forgive me. I'm so, so sorry, Ava. For everything…"

His words bring me back to reality like a bucket of ice-cold water thrown at my face. I immediately disentangle myself from him, even if

I feel like dying for putting space between us. I shouldn't feel like this, not after everything he did to me.

"I want to leave. Please take me home." I feel too exposed all of a sudden. I take the sheet thrown haphazardly on the side of the bed and wrap it around me as I stand.

Logan pushes up from the bed and stands on the other side. "I can't do that, even if I wanted to, we are snowed in…we can't leave. Besides, you're in heat. You're going to start burning up again soon."

My fingers clench, fisting the sheet. "I don't care. I want to go home."

"You don't understand. You're going to start feeling worse by the minute, and your wolf will eventually take control of your body." He runs a hand through his curls, a pained look passing over his face. "It's because we're fated mates. You're going to be in heat until the mating bond is completed."

"What?" I ask in a high-pitched voice. "An hour ago you thought I killed your mate, but now you've changed your mind? We're fated mates now? What the fuck is this crazy shit? What does mate even mean?"

"Fated mates are like halves of a splintered soul, endlessly searching for each other and destined to be together for eternity. Don't you feel it, Ava? The sense of rightness when we are near. The longing, the scorching need?"

This is exactly how I feel, but I don't tell him that. "You're delusional," I mutter instead and take a step back.

"Listen to me, please. Fuck. I don't even know where to start." He presses the heels of his palms into his eyes and then looks at me. "Hope Moore, the woman you received your heart from…*she* was my fated mate. I have dreamed about her for five years until the dreams stopped abruptly four months ago."

He takes a deep breath in and continues, "I didn't understand why she didn't come to me as she was supposed to, but now I do.

She couldn't because she was kidnapped, and then she died, and you received her heart. I don't know how, but receiving Hope's heart somehow transformed you into my fated mate, into a wolf shifter. I felt this magnetic attraction to you from the first moment I saw you at the Shabby Shotglass, and I know you felt it, too. All I wanted to do was claim you right then and there. I fought it because I thought I was betraying my mate. I didn't…I didn't know what happened to Hope."

"So what, I'm like a pity fuck delivered to you by destiny? Should I feel honored or something?" I scoff, trying to mask the way my voice trembles as my heart bleeds inside my chest, the caustic sting of jealousy ravaging my insides.

"It's nothing like that, Ava. Fated mates are sacred. You're everything to me." He shakes his head, a curl falling over his forehead with the movement. My hand itches with the need to push it back and caress his gorgeous face.

Stupid, Ava. Stupid.

I arch an eyebrow at him. "Oh, I'm sorry, was I everything to you when you tied me up and then hung me on a hook like Jeffrey Dahmer Jr.? Or when you pointed a gun at my head and wanted to shoot me?" My tone drips with venom.

He winces like I've hit him and sinks to his knees in front of me. My eyebrows shoot up in surprise.

"Please, Ava. Please, you have to forgive me. I can't even express how sorry I am for doing those things to you. My fury blinded me. There's this rogue wolf shifter that's been on a killing spree for months. You probably saw it on the news, all the animal attacks happening recently. The rogue's responsible for all of them. It's been evading us all this time, hiding its scent somehow. When I saw you next to the two bodies in the woods, I lost it. I thought you were the rogue."

I think of Tony's body, mangled on the blood-soaked ground. "Tony was my friend, *pendejo*. He was such a good person. How could you ever think I could do something like that to him?" A tear crests over my eyelashes and falls, rolling over my cheek. I wipe at it furiously.

Logan stands and takes a tentative step toward me. At that, I step back, and he stops. A sorrowful expression takes over his face. Eyes filled with regret meet mine as his shoulders slump. "I'm sorry. I didn't know you were my fated mate. I just…Fuck." He grabs his hair in fistfuls and pulls at it. "I'm so stupid. So fucking stupid. Please, Ava, you have to forgive me."

"I don't know if I can," I whisper. Despite myself, a wave of fire passes through my body, making me sway slightly on my feet. I suddenly feel lightheaded. "How do I stop this…this inferno that burns me from the inside out? I want it to stop. I don't think I can take any more of this."

"You can't. The only way to stop it is to complete the mating bond."

"What does that even mean?"

"It means the moment we have sex, our souls will be forever intertwined. You will be mine, and I will be yours for all eternity. It's a sacred union, even more so than marriage, because you can never divorce out of a mating bond. It's for life and beyond."

"Yeah, I'll pass. There must be another way."

"Trust me, there isn't."

"So what? If I refuse to complete it, I'll just burn until I die? Because it feels like I'm dying with every second you're not touching me. I hate it. I don't want to feel this way anymore." The tears start falling freely now, and I know I must look like an emotional wreck, but it's so difficult having Logan in front of me and not giving myself to him fully. It literally hurts, like being gutted with a rusty knife.

"I don't know, honestly. I have never heard of a fated mate refusing to bond once the female is in heat. And I'm hurting too, Ava. It takes everything

I have in me not to bend you over and fuck you into oblivion. I don't know how much longer I can control myself. I can smell your arousal from here, and it's making my wolf crazy. You're not the only one struggling."

Gulping at his words, my gaze roves over his body. Sweat dots his hairline, his muscles are locked up, and his fingers clench and unclench at his sides as if he is barely restraining himself. I inhale deeply, but it's like I'm in the bowels of Hell again.

"I need a moment to process all of this," I mumble weakly, but when I want to turn around, I can't. It's like someone else shoves me into the back seat of my mind so all I can do is watch everything unfold in front of my eyes as my legs eat up the space between me and Logan.

I practically tackle him to the bed, and my lips fuse with his in a mind-numbing kiss. There's nothing slow or tender about the way our lips and tongues move against each other. It's all-consuming and raw, like jumping from the edge of a cliff and falling into the abyss. Logan's fingers bite savagely into my hips as I gyrate on top of him, the friction making me see stars.

I succumb to the feeling and let it consume me completely.

23

Logan

Ava's eyes glow with animalistic hunger as her wolf takes over. She steps toward me purposefully and drops the sheet to the floor. Since the moment she woke up, she was a ticking time bomb, and I knew this would happen eventually, but I at least wanted to try to explain my reasoning and apologize. I just hope she'll be able to forgive me at some point. I'll do anything to regain her trust. The moment her lips touch mine, I'm a goner. My wolf pushes me aside, a spectator in my own mind as the mating bond begins.

A groan rumbles from deep within my chest as Ava pulls down the waistband of my sweats and frees my throbbing cock, sinking on top of me inch by agonizing inch with a tantalizing moan. Blazing topaz-green eyes lock with mine, and I almost black out the moment I feel her silky heat wrapped around me. *Fuck*. She looks like a goddess on top of me, perfect heart-shaped face, bee-stung lips, pupils blown to the max, and rosy taut nipples that beg to be sucked.

Before she can sink all the way to the hilt, I grab her hips and maneuver her onto her belly with her plump ass in the air. I love her ass. I love her body. I love everything about her. I take my sweats off quickly, and I can't stop myself from marking her thighs with my teeth before I dip and taste her as my tongue pushes through her slick folds, licking her slowly from clit to the back hole a few times. She tastes like sin and heaven wrapped into one perfect curvy package.

I fist her hair and pull at the same time I enter her, thrusting in one swift motion. Her whole body shakes as she lets out a mewl. Her tight pussy takes me so beautifully. I let her adjust to the size for a few seconds before I start hammering into her like a man possessed. The sound of our bodies slapping together alongside our ragged breaths and pleasured moans fills the air.

Dropping the silky strands, I band my arm around her waist and lift her torso. A low hiss leaves my lips when her back fuses completely with my front. It's fucking bliss. I use my hand wrapped around her delicate jaw to guide her head to the side so I can capture her lips with mine. Greedily, I swallow her loud moans and whimpers. My balls tighten in response to the delicious shivers she sends down my spine as her nails score my scalp. I palm her perfect breast and pinch her nipple before I let my hand skate downward toward her mound. The moment the pad of my middle finger finds her clit, her hips buck.

I kiss her deeply one last time before I sink my teeth into the side of her neck and thrust into her like a piston, finally claiming Ava as my mate. In the next moment, her pussy spasms violently around me as it traps my cock in a vise-like grip.

A tsunami of white-hot pleasure slams into me, making my vision blurry. We both fall over the edge together, me with a loud groan, her with a shrill cry. I feel the very fabric of my soul disintegrate and then be completely rebuilt as the mating bond fuses us. It's like my world has shifted on its axis and been blown apart at the same time into tiny little atoms, all coming together into a cosmic explosion. It's like finally arriving home. Ava is my home now, for all eternity. Mine to cherish and protect. My Luna. My everything.

With the mating bond completed, I regain control of my body. We collapse on the bed together. The moment we just shared is somehow not enough; I need her skin on mine, so I pull Ava into my arms. I'll never let her go.

We are both breathing as if we just finished running a marathon, and I flit my gaze to Ava, searching for any sign that she is upset by what just happened. It's like I'm trapped in a dream. Because she doesn't seem real. Face flushed, parted swollen lips, eyes glazed over with post-orgasmic bliss. I almost pinch myself just to be sure. *Fuck me.* She is so arrestingly beautiful it hurts to look at her.

"God, I can't believe I attacked you like that," Ava says in a sexy, low, raspy voice after a few beats of silence.

"There's nothing you could have done. Our wolves took over. I just wish I had more time to explain that to you before it happened." My heart kicks up in my chest, beating so hard I can hear it pounding its way out of my throat. I loathe to admit it, but I know it to be the fear of rejection. "How are you feeling?" My hand trembles as my knuckles brush the side of her gorgeous face, and I wait with bated breath for her response.

"Honestly, I know I should be furious with you. I still am in some way, but somehow, I feel like I finally found something I've been searching for my entire life. Like my heart is whole again. I finally feel at peace. I don't know how else to explain it."

I let out a shaky breath of relief. "I know what you mean. I feel exactly the same."

She starts making circles on my chest with her index finger, and I drink in her casual touch as if I'm dying of thirst. "You know…I've never had an orgasm before. Well, not like ever, but with someone else. Now, I finally understand what the fuss is all about. It was…I don't even have words to describe it. Not a single word can do it justice."

Male pride filters through my veins at her words, and I want to kiss her so fucking badly, but I don't want to do something to ruin the moment.

"It's a good thing I have an IUD because we didn't use protection. Is there something I should be worried about?"

I twirl a silky mocha strand on my finger. "I'm clean; I haven't had sex since I started dreaming about my fated mate five years ago. I haven't even kissed anyone in these five years…until you." I cringe at the mention of Hope and swallow hard.

Her hand stills, and she looks at me, a frown etched on her forehead. "That's why you ran away from my apartment like your ass was on fire. You were trying to be faithful to your mate."

I nod. "Yeah…I was so confused. I didn't understand why I felt like I couldn't stay away from you when I knew I had a fated mate. My wolf knew who you were before I did. That our hearts were meant to find each other. But I didn't listen to him. How could I? It made me fucking miserable. I've never felt that sort of war inside me before. My heart ached for you, but at the same time, I felt like I was cheating on my fated mate."

Sympathy fills her eyes. "That must have been so hard."

"It was like being trapped in Hell." I swallow hard and inhale a shallow breath. "And then, the night before Halloween, I dreamed about your wolf for the first time. It fucked with my head. You have to understand, for almost five years straight, I have been dreaming only about golden fur and azure eyes. I thought something was wrong with me. Then, the next day, my pack and I were hunting a herd of deer near Shadow Lake, and I caught a scent. I knew it in the very fabric of my being that it was my fated mate. But then I saw your wolf over the dead bodies, and in that moment, my heart splintered. I let my fury take over.

I thought you were the rogue and had cast some kind of spell to deceive me. That you did something to my mate—"

"You do believe me now, right? That I had nothing to do with it."

"Of course, Ava. I'm so sorry for everything. I have no excuse…" My chest is filled with lead.

Her eyes narrow playfully. "I'm still mad at you, but I no longer feel like throat-punching you, so I guess it's a start."

"Thank God. I'll take anything that I can get, and I'm not above using dirty tricks to make you forgive me." I flip Ava onto her back and settle between her thighs. She gasps in surprise, and I take a moment to admire how stunning she looks. Her soft body beneath mine cast in the warm glow of the sunset light streaming through the window. Creamy bronzed skin and satiny just-fucked hair fanned on the pillow, lust-filled mesmerizing eyes, perfectly etched fuckable lips, and a constellation of freckles smattering the bridge of her upturned nose and cheeks. She is pure perfection; my wet dream come to life. My throat burns with the realization she is finally mine. Euphoria, like no other, makes my insides pitch as my heart beats like a jackhammer against my ribcage.

"You're so fucking beautiful," I tell her.

Her eyes soften. "Ditto. Too bad you're an oaf," she says, and the little smirk curving her plump lips drives me crazy.

"Your oaf." I can't stop myself from dipping down to taste it. I lick the seam of her lips slowly before spreading them with my tongue and stealing her breath. Biting her lower lip with just enough pressure so I don't draw blood, I take my time to savor her lips properly, moving my tongue against hers in a slow, tantalizing dance. I start tracing kisses all over her face and continue downward, mapping the column of her throat with my tongue as I begin sliding my cock slowly over her clit, using our cum to create mind-numbing friction.

My hands glide across her body, desperate to feel her skin against mine.

It doesn't take long before Ava turns into a writhing mess beneath me. I breathe against her taut nipple before I circle it with my tongue and suck on it greedily. The other begs for my attention, so I pop it into my mouth next.

"Oh God," Ava whimpers, and her fingers weave through my hair, pumping more blood to my cock. *"I need you, Logan."*

I don't think she even realized she spoke to me through the mental link only fated mates have. *"What do you need, little wolf?"*

"I need you inside me."

"Do you need me to fill that pretty pussy?" I rumble against her heated flesh as I continue the assault on her sensitive nipples.

"Yes," she pants. "Please! I can't take it anymore."

Fulfilling one of my many fantasies, I part her thighs further and hike her legs on my shoulders. My eyes don't leave Ava's while I push the head of my cock through her drenched entrance. It takes everything in me not to slam into her. My muscles tremble with the sheer effort. I want to savor this moment since earlier, we were too consumed by the lust-induced frenzy. So, I use every ounce of willpower I possess to slowly sink into her tight heat. In stark contrast, our chests move in unison with rapid heaves. I grab her chin and thumb her lower lip before pushing it into her mouth. Her cheeks hollow as she sucks on my thumb as if she is sucking my cock. Fuck me. This woman. I almost bust my load like an angsty teenager.

"Look how your perfect pussy is stretching around my cock," I rasp. Fiery topaz greens lower at our joined bodies. I pull out fully, and with a snap of my hips, my balls slap into her ass. Intense pleasure surges through my veins, zapping my nerve endings. Her eyes roll to the back of her head with a loud moan, and the moment her eyelids shutter, I slide my thumb out of her mouth and circle her throat with my hand, applying slight pressure. "Eyes on me, baby!" I command, and when she obeys, I slide out again fully before I ram into her.

I apply a little more pressure on her throat, watching closely for any sign that she might not like what I'm doing, but her already blown-out pupils stretch further, and her body starts trembling beneath me. "You like being at my mercy, don't you, little wolf? My hand wrapped around your throat as your pretty pussy takes my cock."

"Yes! More, I want more," she pants and inhales deeply when I slightly relax the hold on her throat.

"Use your hand to tap me if it becomes too much or if you feel like you're going to pass out," I tell her and wait for her nod of approval before I squeeze. Her walls tighten around me the moment I steal her breath. I use it as my cue to nail her to the bed with rapid thrusts. "That's my good girl." My other hand brushes over her curves to where our bodies are joined. I press the pad of my thumb into her clit. Sliding it up and down, then moving it in circles, I use Ava's tiny whimpers like a map to guide me in finding the type of touch she likes best.

It doesn't take long before we crest together in a blinding orgasm. The reverb of our cries a sweet, sinful melody as we tumble over the edge and wave after wave of pleasure slams into me.

24

Ava

"So, what you're saying is that witches, demons, and vampires are real?" I ask before swallowing a piece of perfectly done steak Logan cooked for us after he fucked me slowly against the shower wall and then washed me and wrapped me in a fluffy towel. We're now sitting at the rustic dining table nestled between the kitchen nook and the couch. The blizzard finally stopped about an hour ago, and the night sky has started to clear, the moon halfway visible in the canopy of dark clouds.

I know I should still be mad at him, but hearing his side of things made me understand the confusion and the conundrum he was faced with. I don't know what I would have done in his position. And then there's the mating bond and the mind-boggling fact that he is my fated mate. I can't even explain the connection I feel to him; it's like our souls have intertwined, and we are an extension of each other.

With the mating bond completed, I feel so attuned to Logan, to his soul, to the very fabric of his being that I know without a doubt he is a good person through and through.

There was a moment I thought I was nothing more than a replacement for Hope. That it wasn't *me* Logan was attracted to, but Hope's heart. However, as soon as the mating bond snapped into place, I no longer felt jealous. I am simply thankful that Hope has given me another chance at life. And even if it's not close to what I imagined, becoming a wolf shifter and being someone's fated mate, I'm still grateful for it.

"Yeah, and other creatures, too," Logan replies as he cuts a piece from his steak. He's already told me all about what being a wolf shifter entails, him being Alpha, the pack dynamic, and his responsibilities within the Obsidian Conclave. To say my mind is blown is an understatement.

"I can't believe this whole world that humans have no idea about exists. That I had no idea existed."

Swallowing, he puts his fork down and looks at me. "Well, there's a lot of folklore surrounding dark creatures, so it's not like they don't have an idea. A lot of books and movies, too, but with the advancement in technology, it was easier for them to believe that dark creatures were no more than the result of the overactive imagination of the medieval human. That made it simpler for us to slip into the shadows and not get hunted anymore."

"Will I have to get a tattoo like yours and Emily's too?" I pop a crispy potato wedge into my mouth and chew slowly.

"It's pretty much mandatory. If you don't, then it will mean you don't want to abide by the rules of not killing human beings and not biting them, in our case. And that you won't accept the protection given by the Obsidian Conclave. Hellseekers will be able to kill you."

"Hellseekers are the demon hunters, the ones in the Order of Sariel, right?"

Logan slumps back in his chair. "Yeah. Back in the day, before the Celestial Treaty was signed and the Obsidian Conclave was created, hellseekers hunted dark creatures alongside demons. They aren't allowed to get involved in Conclave business now, though. The Obsidian Conclave deals with all things regarding dark creatures, even punishing them whenever they step out of line. Still, hellseekers don't always care about the rules, and there have been instances of them abusing their power, even if a dark creature was under the protection of the Conclave. They think of us as lesser beings." His jaw ticks, and I don't miss the way his fingers tighten around his fork.

My eyebrows draw together as I take a swig of water from my glass and place it back on the table. "Well, that sucks. Especially since they're supposed to be the good guys with their bloodline sanctified by the archangels. God, I can't believe archangels and demons are real," I mumble the last part to myself and shake my head incredulously. "So, that's why catching the rogue is your responsibility, because he is a dark creature, and he broke the number one rule of not killing humans, right?"

He nods and stabs the last piece of steak left on his plate, chewing it thoughtfully and then swallowing before replying. "It would not be the first rogue we've had to kill. There have been many over the years, even working in groups to form packs, biting humans, and turning them into feral wolves. It wasn't pretty, but we eventually managed to stop them. This one, though, has managed to evade us for months by hiding its scent. That's why we believe it's working with a witch."

"I think that person I saw in the dark cloak collecting the hearts might have been the witch. I didn't see a face, though, or anything that could help me identify it, but the wolf had auburn fur and icy blue eyes, and it was definitely male. And you're right, besides Tony and the other guy's blood, I couldn't smell anything else." Everything I have eaten threatens to make a reappearance. With a few tears, I drop the fork and the knife I'm holding on top of my plate. They clatter loudly in the silence.

Logan pulls me onto his lap like I weigh nothing more than a feather. His woodsy smell and the warmth radiating from his glorious body are like a safety blanket, enveloping me in calming waves. "I'm so sorry about Tony," he says softly, his fingers caressing the side of my face.

"Me too," I choke out, and I can't stop the tears from flowing. "I haven't known him for long, but he was such a good person, so bright, and he kind of took me under his wing from the moment we met. In the short time we have known each other, he was such a good friend to me."

He thumbs my tear-streaked cheeks. "Emily loved him too. She used to talk about him all the time."

"He didn't deserve to die like that. You have to find the rogue and make him pay for it," I say with venom in my voice, and I mean it. I hope the Conclave will give him a painstakingly slow death. I know it won't bring Tony back, but the rogue deserves the worst kind of torture for murdering so many innocent people. My wolf growls in my head in agreement, which in itself is a shock. Logan told me that with my wolf awakened, I will be able to feel her more and more.

"We will. I'll make sure of it."

"C'MON, TRY AGAIN," Logan encourages me.

Sweat dots my forehead, and my whole body shakes with the effort. "I can't, Logan. I just can't," I grit out in frustration.

Logan's trying to teach me how to control my shift, and so far, in the two hours we've been at it, I've only managed to make a fool of myself and sweat. That's it. At least I have something nice to look at. Logan's incredible body is on full display, making me all hot and bothered as he demonstrates yet another shift. It takes him just a few seconds to go through it and for his wolf to make an appearance.

He stalks toward me, making clicking sounds with his gigantic paws on the hardwood floor. I let my fingers run through his soft, ash-brown fur as he brushes his massive body against my side. He's so tall his head reaches my chest. I bend slightly to scratch behind his ears, earning a happy rumble from his throat.

"I don't think I'll ever get used to how freakin' majestic you are," I say. He licks my face before taking his place in front of me in the middle of the living room area that we cleared earlier to make space for us to shift inside the cabin.

Logan reappears in his human form faster than I can blink. "You're thinking too much about it. You have to push past the mental block. It was a very traumatic experience for you, and not knowing it was going to happen made it all worse. It only hurts that bad the first time. By the fifth shift, you won't even be able to feel it anymore. I promise."

I huff in annoyance and cross my arms in front of my naked chest. "Easy for you to say. You're an expert on it."

"I've had years to practice. It gets easier, trust me."

"Yeah, I don't know about that. It kinda felt like I was dying a slow, painful death. Just the thought of going through that again is enough to make me wanna throw up. I mean…it was even worse than getting a heart attack. And that sucked. Big time."

"C'mon, just one more time. Try not to think too much about it."

I roll my eyes at him. "Fine, but this is the last try. I'm tired and sweaty," I grumble, refusing to admit how childlike I sound.

"Let's try something different. Close your eyes. Concentrate on that ball of energy in the center of your chest. That's your wolf, Ava. Let her come out."

I do as Logan says and bring my palm to the center of my chest, where I feel a spark.

"Imagine all your insecurities and fears coming together in the form of a brick wall inside your mind."

I visualize the wall in my head, and it looks downright impenetrable.

"Now climb it, get on the other side."

My jaw ticks. "I can't. It's too tall."

"It's your mind, Ava. You make the rules; don't ever forget that. Make the wall shorter. Throw a bomb at it. Pulverize it. Whatever it takes." Logan's tone is soft, coaxing.

The moment I imagine myself throwing a bomb at the wall, I feel it crumbling. In the next second, a weird tingling sensation engulfs me, from the bottom of my feet to the tips of my hair. My muscles spasm, and my skin feels like it's being pulled too tight over my bones. I double over when I feel every bone in my body snapping into tiny, jagged pieces. There's a second when I think it's all done. But then, whatever reprieve I thought I gained crumbles to ashes the moment my ligaments fracture one by one. *Pop. Pop. Pop.* White-hot pain scorches me as my fur pierces my skin. Almost as soon as it started, the pain is gone, and I'm standing on four legs.

"Fuck yeah! That's my girl," Logan hollers in excitement and hurries to the front door, opening it and letting the cold morning air filter into the cabin. "Let's go for a run," he says before shifting and prancing outside.

I follow on his tail and descend the wooden stairs. The sun is cresting over the mountain peaks, its warm rays filtering through the pine trees, making the blanket of snow gleam as if made from tiny little diamonds. Before I realize what's happening, Logan's wolf slams playfully into my side. The momentum sends us rolling in the pristine white powder a few feet back. On top of me, he nudges his snout against mine and licks my muzzle. In response to his attack, I sink my canines in his neck, but only with a soft nip. He lets me go with a wolfish smile.

"Oh, you're gonna pay for that," I tell him through our mental link as I stand and shake the snow from my fur with a low growl. It's still mind-boggling to me that we can do that, and it came so naturally, like speaking.

"Only if you can catch me," he says with a chuckle and darts through the trees. He digs a trail through the mountain of snow, only his ears visible.

I quickly follow after him, and I don't think I have ever felt freer than in this moment. It feels like flying. I bask in this newfound freedom, in letting my wolf take over completely and running at high speed through the piles of snow, the icy wind filling my snout and ruffling my fur as I follow Logan's scent through the trail he made in front of us.

25

Ava

"Favorite color?" I ask and take another sip from the steaming mug of hot chocolate.

"Green," Logan answers, pressing his thumb in the arch of my foot.

I let out a happy sigh at how good it feels. After spending hours outside, we came back and took a nap. Then Logan cooked us lunch from his freezer stash, and now we're sitting on the fluffy carpet in front of the fireplace. My back is resting on the armchair, perpendicular to Logan with my feet in his lap while he massages them. The sounds and the smell of the burning wood fill the air. I'm wearing one of Logan's T-shirts that's more of a dress on me, and him, a pair of low-slung sweats. His perfectly etched chest and corded amber muscles are on display under the soft glow of the lit fire.

Everything feels so perfect I don't ever want to leave this little bubble we have immersed ourselves into. I know it won't be long until we have to go back to reality, though. The last time I took my immunosuppressants was two days ago. I honestly don't know if I still have to take them. Logan said wolf shifters don't experience the same illnesses as humans. There's also the fact that I don't feel any side effects yet. Still, we don't know what might happen, so we don't want to risk it. We agreed to leave the cabin tomorrow morning since the snow has already started to melt. My job at the Shabby Shotglass is also waiting for me.

"Ha. You're only saying that because that's my eye color." I nudge him with my foot. "I want real answers, buddy."

"Your eyes are my favorite color."

I roll my eyes at him. "'Kay, Mr. Smooth Talker. Mine is red. I look really good in red."

"I bet you do," he purrs in a husky voice, and that's all it takes for my breath to catch as the air sparks between us. I press my thighs together, trying to relieve some of the ache that's making my clit throb with need, but I only manage to make it worse. Logan doesn't miss that, and a smirk curves his plump lips. His eyelids droop as his gaze rakes over my body with undisguised hunger.

I swallow hard and clear my throat. "Favorite movie?"

"*The Notebook.*"

My eyebrows shoot up all the way to my hairline, and I let out an incredulous laugh. Then I narrow my eyes at him. "Stop making fun of me. C'mon, Logan, I'm serious; what's your favorite movie?"

He pops a shoulder. "*The Notebook.*"

"I can't tell if you're being sincere or if you're messing with me."

His cheeks take a reddish hue. "I'm serious. What Allie and Noah had was raw and real, and it's something I always wished for, a love that surpasses everything."

"For real? But that's such a chick flick. I was expecting you to say something action-packed…*John Wick* or something. Anything but *the Notebook*. So, my mate is a closeted romantic." A Cheshire cat grin spreads over my face.

"But don't tell anyone that, especially my sister or Malik," he blurts out. "I'm never going to hear the end of it. They're going to make fun of me until the day I die."

"Don't worry, *bebé*. Your secret is safe with me." I smile cheekily and wink at him.

"What's yours?"

Biting my lip, I ponder my options because I love old movies, and there are some great ones to pick from. "*The Shawshank Redemption*," I say finally and take the last sip of hot chocolate, placing the mug on the floor beside me. "Favorite food?"

"Steak, medium rare."

"Such a simple man," I quip.

He arches an eyebrow at me. With a wicked gleam in his eyes, he unexpectedly grabs my legs and pulls me under him in one swift motion. A squeak of surprise leaves me as he traps me under his massive body. He dips down, burrows his nose in my hair, inhales deeply, and then exhales against the side of my neck before his teeth nip my earlobe. I shiver in response.

"You know what I love to eat more than steak? More than anything in the world," he rumbles in my ear as his hands glide upward on my thighs.

My heart comes alive and skips a beat as my nipples draw into hard tips, rubbing on the thin material of the T-shirt I'm wearing. "What?" I breathe. I'm already dripping, and it only took him a few seconds to get me there.

"You," he purrs, cupping my bare pussy with his big hand while sneaking the other beneath my T-shirt. He palms my breast and rubs the taut nipple between his fingers. Spikes of pleasure ripple through my entire body as he runs his middle finger along my soaked slit. "Mmm, is this all for me, little wolf?" he asks in a low, raspy voice when he dips it inside me.

I release a shaky breath as blood thickens inside my veins like syrup.

After he pumps it a few times, he brings his hand to his mouth, and with his eyes focused on mine, he licks the soaked finger with a guttural sound of pleasure from deep within his chest as if I'm the best thing he has ever tasted. In the next second, he tears the T-shirt I'm wearing with his bare hands and exposes me to him completely. His eyes are liquid fire as he roves them lazily over my body. "You're the most beautiful thing I have ever seen." His voice is dripping sex, wrapping around me like warm honey. When he bends and takes my nipple into his mouth, my body bows off the floor. He starts sucking. Hard. The loud moan that leaves my parted lips bounces off the walls.

"And you're all mine," he breathes against my other nipple before he assaults it with maddening tongue circles. *"Who do you belong to, Ava?"* His voice breaks through the haze of desire only for a moment as I realize he just spoke to me in my mind.

"You, Logan! Only you."

His answer is a deep throaty groan as he sucks and nips a trail with his delicious sinful mouth from my breasts to my pussy, his breath fanning over my clit before his tongue flattens against it.

"Logan," I pant. "So good…please don't stop!"

Next thing I know, Logan's arms band around my waist. I'm lifted in the air and placed over his face at the same time he lies down beneath me, my center hovering over his mouth and my knees on either side of his cheeks.

"Um…what—"

"I want you to ride my face, baby," he cuts me off by replying in my mind, a wicked gleam shining in his eyes.

I swallow and bite my lower lip, my hands turning clammy. *"I don't know how to. I've never done this before."* What if I suffocate him? If I put my weight on him with the size of my thighs…I know it's not my best moment, but William the Turd's words flash through my head. *You're a fat bitch.* With them ringing in my ears, I try to get up, but Logan stops me swiftly, locking my hips over his face as his fingers bite into my skin.

"*Ava, look at me! And don't you dare move!*"

Our gazes lock.

"*I've been dreaming about this from the very first moment I saw you. So, grab the damn couch and use it for leverage as you slide over my mouth.*"

"'Kay," I say, still a bit unsure, and place my hands on the couch before I start grinding on his lips. His stubbled cheeks rub into my sensitive skin as he laps at my clit greedily, sending sparks of electricity through my every nerve ending. The angle is incredible, and Logan's big hands are everywhere. Touching. Exploring. Guiding my hips, cupping my breasts, rubbing my nipples.

"*I wish you could see yourself. You look like a goddess riding my face. My goddess. Give it all to me, baby. Suffocate me with your perfect thighs and come all over my mouth. I want to swallow every last drop.*"

"Oh, God," I cry out when the pleasure becomes almost too much to bear, blurring my vision, making my hips buck and my pussy spasm. Logan spears his tongue and fucks me with it as I break at the seams. A huge wave of ecstasy slams into me, and I cry out Logan's name like a prayer.

My limbs turn to mush while Logan licks me clean to the last drop. I slump to the side and try to catch my breath when Logan pushes up from the floor and lifts me in his arms, wrapping my legs around his middle. I lock my hands behind his neck and press a kiss to the hollow of his throat.

"Fuck, baby. That was the hottest thing I have ever seen, you riding my face and coming all over it," he says gutturally before he crushes his lips to mine in a fervent kiss. I taste myself on his tongue as he licks at my mouth with overt desperation. His dick is rock hard between us, tenting the front of his sweats, and I whimper when I feel it twitching against my center.

He continues kissing me while he strides to the table. I slide down his front inch by agonizing inch. The moment my bare feet touch the hardwood floor, he twirls me around and bends me over the table.

Logan palms my ass, caresses it, and then slaps my right ass cheek hard. I yelp at the unexpected pain that is followed by a jolt of pleasure, like a bolt of lightning going straight to my clit. He wrestles his sweats off him before he nudges my legs apart and rocks against me, rubbing the crown of his cock into my slit before slamming into me from behind with a sharp hiss.

He bottoms out and stills. "You feel so good, baby. So goddamn tight." He starts pounding into me over and over in a maddening rhythm, nailing me to the table, a hand fisted in my hair and the other bruising my hip. He is fucking me so hard that the table lurches with every thrust beneath me.

"*Mierda*," I cry out. The sound comes out all garbled from my face being smooshed against the table. "I'm so close. I'm, I'm gonna—"

"Come, Ava," Logan commands and slaps my ass cheek again.

Pleasure surges through me, so intense my whole body starts shaking. My sex ripples and spasms around Logan's cock violently. I bite my tongue hard. I think I even black out for a few seconds. Logan fucks me through my orgasm, chasing his own, his balls slapping against my ass cheeks. Not before long, he reaches his high with a sexy roar. We both fight to catch our breaths as he collapses on top of me on the table.

"Holy fuck," Logan mumbles in my hair and puts his weight on his forearms, placing a kiss on my shoulder.

"Mmhm," is the only response I can manage. I think he fucked my brain matter out of me because I can't seem to form another thought or word at the moment.

Logan picks me up effortlessly from the table and cuts through the room until he enters the bathroom with me in his arms. I love how easy it is for him to carry me around like I weigh nothing. It makes me feel precious and cared for. He sits me on the bathroom counter and wraps a hand around the back of my neck, the other angling my chin as his plush lips slant over mine. He kisses me slowly, reverently before his tongue sneaks out and licks at the seam of my lips. I open up for him, and he pushes his tongue inside my mouth, swirling it against mine, stealing my breath and my goddamn soul. I don't know how much time passes, but I don't want him to ever stop.

"I could do this all day," Logan says. But after a while, he reluctantly steps away to turn on the shower, his hair ruffled by my wandering hands and his pupils blown out to the max.

I laugh huskily. "Me too."

After he checks the temperature with his fingers, he takes me again in his arms and places me under the hot spray. Logan doesn't even let me wash my own hair. When we finish our shower, I'm so relaxed I feel boneless. As we step out of the bathroom, the sound of a car approaching in the distance reaches my ears. It's foreign in the calm that surrounds the cabin.

"Did you hear that?" I ask Logan.

Logan tosses me the clean tee he brought from the bedroom and quickly stabs his legs through his sweats. "Yeah," he replies, his eyebrows furrowing.

As I finish putting the T-shirt on, someone pounds on the door impatiently. "Are you fucking serious, Logan? You hole up in here on the night of your engagement party and leave me to deal with everything? Everyone's waiting for you at home, and Mom wants to kill you," Emily's pissed-out voice travels through the door before she barges into the cabin with a murderous look on her face.

Surely, I didn't hear her right. The words engagement party ring in my ears over and over again, like terrifying echo chamber.

The room spins with me as I look at Logan, waiting for him to tell me that this is just a joke. I'm only met with a deafening silence. He tenses, and his Adam's apple bobs hard in his throat as he swallows audibly.

"Logan," I whisper on a trembling breath. He still doesn't say anything, but I don't miss the look of utter guilt passing over his features as his eyes flit to mine with panic.

Something breaks inside of me. I can't believe I was so stupid… so gullible.

A keening wail leaves me as I shift, still painfully, in less than a second, ripping the T-shirt to pieces, and fly by Emily through the front door and into the night. I run like my life depends on it, and I don't look back.

26

Logan

Fuck, fuck, fuck, fuck, fuck.

A weighted silence fills the air after my sister's sudden appearance. With everything that happened and then the mating bond snapping into place, I got completely lost in Ava, and I totally forgot about the fact that I was supposed to get engaged to Grace today. I haven't seen Grace since the ball, but my mother convinced me she would be perfect as my chosen mate. I promised I would marry Grace on my twenty-fifth birthday and get engaged to her a month prior to that. My mother has been organizing the engagement party and the wedding for weeks. Even if I felt like I was betraying my fated mate, I went along with it because it was the only solution I had to strengthen the pack. For the children to wake up, I had to do my duty as Alpha.

I'm such a fucking idiot.

I swallow hard when Ava whispers my name. The saliva goes down my throat like a boulder, sinking to the bottom of my stomach. Even though I know I should say something…anything, I can't utter a single word. I don't even know how to start explaining this to her. What a fool I've been, thinking I had more time. I'm sure she feels like the rug has been pulled from under her.

The moment the words register in Ava's head is clearly written on her face. I can feel her heart breaking as if her pain is my own. It slashes through me like a serrated blade. "Ava, I can explain. Please hear me out," I tell her softly, but I don't think she hears me because, in the next second, a sound so full of sorrow leaves her chest it almost brings me to my knees. Before I can react, she's already out the front door in her wolf form.

Emily's eyes widen in shock. "What in the actual fuck? Was that Ava?" she shrieks, but I don't pay her any attention as I shift and start running after her.

"Ava, please! Stop running; I can explain," I say through our mental link, following her scent through the pine trees, my paws sinking in the melting snow.

"Go to hell, Logan! And stay there," she snaps venomously, and then I feel her through our bond getting further and further away. How the hell is she running so fast?

"Care to explain what that was, Lo?" my sister asks, following right behind me.

"Not right now. Help me find Ava first, and then I'll tell you everything."

"Fine," she grumbles. I feel she wants to ask more questions, but she doesn't push me. Not now. Not when she hears the desperation in my tone.

Only, we don't find Ava. We follow the scent trail until it ends abruptly near a creek. We circle the perimeter over and over again for hours, but nothing. Somehow, without training, she managed to mask her scent and block me mentally. The absence is an all-consuming void inside me, cleaving my heart in two and filling my chest with lead.

"We have to go," Emily says as the indigo sky gives way to purple

and the cottony clouds get drenched in pink.

"I can't leave her here, Em, what the fuck?"

"We've been at this for almost seven hours, Lo. She might have already left the national park for what we know. She clearly found a way to mask her scent, and we need to smooth things over with the pack. I haven't even had the chance to tell you the good news."

"Just give me half an hour more to search for her, please, and you can tell me later. I need to concentrate on finding her."

"'Kay," she relents. "But after that, we need to go and sort things out."

One hour later, we are fully dressed, and we get into my truck without Ava. This time, Emily doesn't insist on driving, probably sensing how on edge I am. The responsibility toward my pack wraps around my lungs like barbed wire as the desperate need to find my mate twists my insides into painful knots. I feel trapped between a rock and a hard place.

I can't believe how quickly everything crumbled. With a sharp curse, I punch the steering wheel. It doesn't lessen the anger bubbling under my skin, ready to seep out of my pores and consume me. I could blame Emily, of course, for barging in with no filter on her mouth and ruining everything, but I know it's only my fault I'm in this position because I didn't tell Ava everything about me.

"The kids woke up," Emily says, looking at me from the passenger seat with a bashing grin. "That's what I was trying to tell you earlier."

My eyes widen. For a few seconds, I forget about Ava completely. "What?"

"The children touched by the weakness all woke up Monday night. I tried to contact you, but you were out of reach. It was the weirdest thing. They just opened their eyes and started calling for their parents. They're all good. It's like nothing happened to them."

Of course, they woke up. I found my fated mate, and we completed the mating bond. The pack is at full strength again. I just haven't thought about this at all; everything and everyone seemed to disappear when I was with Ava. "It's because I have found my fated mate, Em."

This time, it's her turn to look at me like I've grown two heads. "What? But who?" She tilts her head, and a weird expression takes over her face. "No…don't tell me…"

"Yeah, it's her. Ava's my fated mate."

An incredulous laugh bubbles out of her. "You're joking, right?"

I shake my head and sigh. "No, I'm not joking."

"But, I don't understand. How the fuck is that even possible? I'm so confused…she wasn't a wolf shifter when I met her. I would have smelled her immediately. And then I saw her shift right before my eyes. What the hell is going on, Lo?"

I tell Emily everything that has happened since I left her in charge of the pack Sunday night, and her emotions change from devastated to completely shocked.

"I can't believe Tony is gone. He was my favorite person to work with, and he was such a good friend," she sniffles and wipes at her tear-streaked cheeks. "What a clusterfuck. I'm sorry for barging in, Lo, but you got us so worried. You left abruptly when we were hunting, and you only texted me once to tell me you'll be off with some Conclave business. That's so not like you. Then you wouldn't answer any of my calls. I had to hunt down Malik to tell me where you were, and he refused to let me know what was happening. He said it wasn't his place."

She pauses, biting her lip. "And Mom was going crazy, then the party started, and everyone arrived but you. Conrad almost blew a fuse when Mom told him we don't know where you are. Half of his pack arrived yesterday for the engagement party, and they are still here. Mom managed to calm him down eventually, telling him that the Conclave business is of utmost importance and that you wouldn't miss your engagement party if something major didn't happen. Mom said we'll just resume the celebration when you get back. What are you going to do?"

I roll my neck until it cracks, trying to get rid of the tension that accumulated in my muscles since Ava ran off. "I'm going to tell them the truth, that I have found my fated mate and can't get engaged to someone else. Then I'm going to get Ava back."

I TAP MY foot on the hardwood floor of my study, grinding my teeth as I look for the thousandth time at my watch and start to pace the room like a caged animal. Conrad was supposed to be here an hour ago. He is surely punishing me for missing the engagement party. Fuck diplomacy and pack politics. I'm about to lose my shit because every single minute I spend not looking for Ava deepens the gaping hollow in my chest. Even if Emily and the pack are scouring the national park looking for her, it's not enough. I need to be there. Being separated from her cuts me deep, like someone ripping my heart from my chest with their bare hands. If Conrad doesn't show up in the next five minutes, I'm going to wring his fucking neck.

The sound of the front door closing and three sets of footsteps coming in the direction of the study echoes through the quiet of the house. I heave out a deep sigh, ready for this meeting to be over already. My mother enters the study first, her disapproving gaze settling on me as her lips draw into a thin line. It's clearly written on her face that my absence has angered her. Grace follows quickly behind my mother with her father at her back. Her ocean-blue eyes glimmer with hope when they meet mine. I lower my gaze and gulp nervously because I know I'm going to break her heart, and she seems to be such a sweet girl. Even if I never felt an ounce of attraction to her, she still doesn't deserve to have her hopes and dreams crushed.

"You better have a good motive for missing the engagement party and making fools out of me and my daughter in front of both our packs," Conrad grits out, and a muscle feathers in his jaw.

My mother's nostrils flare as her head whips toward Conrad at her back. "Now, now, Conrad. I told you my son would never miss such an important event if not for a good reason." Her tone is short, clipped. She might be mad at me, but she will always put me and Emily above anything else.

"He's here now, Father. That's what matters most," Grace says softly, trying to placate Conrad. "We can get engaged tonight, right, Logan?"

Clearing my throat, I gesture for them to sit, guilt coiling in my gut when Grace smiles sweetly at me. She's wearing a flowery sundress, and with the halo of blond hair on her head and ocean-blue eyes, she looks downright angelic, but my heart beats only for Ava. "There's something that we need to discuss. If you could please take a seat."

Grace's eyebrows draw together. My mother sighs deeply and takes a seat in front of my desk at the same time as Grace. I'm still standing, waiting for Conrad to sit, but he simply stalks forward, embedding his fingers in the back of Grace's chair, white-knuckled.

"What is it now?" Conrad snaps, looking at me through narrowed eyes.

I choose to stand since I don't want to give him the opportunity to look down on me. I'm still the Alpha of my pack and the representative of the wolf shifters within the Obsidian Conclave. Conrad shouldn't forget that. Still, I go for pleasantries because my mother raised me and Emily well, and honestly, I don't have time to get into a fight with the Alpha of the Ironclaw pack at this moment. With how unstable I'm feeling, I'm afraid I might kill him and start a war.

"I'm deeply sorry for not announcing my absence and for putting you and Grace in such a dire position, Alpha Conrad. But there is a very good reason I couldn't attend the engagement party." I pause and then look at Grace. Even if I don't want to see the hurt on her face, she deserves the respect of being looked at in the eyes when she hears the news. I suck in a deep breath and say, "I have found my fated mate."

Grace's eyes widen, and when the realization kicks in fully, her lower lip starts trembling, a silent tear going down her cheek. She tucks her chin into her chest and gingerly wipes at her damp cheek. *Fuck.* I didn't want to hurt her, but what could I have done? She needed to know the truth.

"I don't give a shit!" Conrad bellows, making Grace flinch. "I promised my daughter to you, and you will marry her and take her as your mate."

"Careful, Conrad. Did you forget fated mates are sacred?" my mother says, and her tone drips with venom.

My wolf rages at him. I have to suck in a sharp breath in order to settle the anger simmering in my veins before it boils over, prompting me to do something I'll surely regret after the dust settles. I keep my tone as steady as I can when I say, "That's not possible. We already completed the mating bond."

"What?" Conrad's fingers are fisted at his sides, and spit flies from his mouth with every word that comes out. "You better do as I say, boy, or I will challenge your Alpha position and take your pack from under you. You're a disgrace. You don't deserve to be Alpha. You put your fated before the wellbeing of your pack for years, and now you're going to humiliate us further after I made my daughter wait for months to get married to you?"

"Enough!" my mother snaps and sits up straight, her shoulders squared and her posture regal as she turns toward the Alpha of the Ironclaw pack. If looks could kill, Conrad would already be a pile of bones on the floor. "My son is a much better Alpha than you will ever be, Conrad. How dare you act so high and mighty when the only reason you are so desperate to marry Grace to my son is your gambling addiction and the debt you owe to the demons you took money from to fuel it."

Conrad sputters and turns ghostly white, his mouth gaping like a fish.

My mother arches a perfectly trimmed ebony eyebrow at him. "What, did you think I wouldn't find out eventually?" She laughs, but it's all jagged teeth and sharp edges. "I suggest stopping these foolish idle threats if you don't want every single wolf shifter in the country to find out about the money you owe. You will lose your Alpha position at the snap of my fingers."

Grace stands up on trembling legs. Anger flashes in her eyes like lightning as she turns toward her father. "Is that true?"

Conrad's shoulders slump, his anger leaving him like a deflating balloon. "Please, they're going to take my daughter from me if I don't pay them by the end of next month."

Anger slithers through me at his words. I ball my hands into fists at my sides so I don't pummel him into the ground. "You promised me your daughter's hand even though you knew they would come for her?"

He shrugs nonchalantly. "Well, you would have had no choice but to give them the money when they came. You couldn't let them take your Luna, now could you?"

"You piece of shit," I spit out and see red. The only thing holding me back from throttling him is his daughter standing in between us.

Grace looks like she's about to faint. "You sold me to demons?" Her voice trembles as she presses a hand in the center of her chest.

I take a deep breath through my nose. Looking at Grace, I make my decision. She had her heart broken, and her world tilted on its axis on the same day, and even if I think her father is a piece of shit, I can't let her be taken by demons. She doesn't deserve that. "I'll give you the money to cover your debt. But don't be mistaken, Conrad. I'm only doing this for Grace and for the fact that she waited months to be my fiancé. I can't mate her anymore, but I won't let your mistakes ruin her life," I grit out. "There will be conditions, though. I will draft a binding document, and you will sign it. You will relinquish your Alpha position, and if I catch you gambling again and putting your family at risk, I'll let Kaiden Black deal with you. Do you understand?"

The vein on the side of his neck looks like it's about to burst. "Fine. I'll sign your contract. Just give me the money," Conrad says with disdain.

I shove my hands into my pockets. Another attempt at resisting the urge to strangle the scumbag. "You'll have it by the end of the week. After you sign it, I'll wire you the money."

He nods stiffly and turns on his heel. "Let's go, Grace. There's nothing left for us here." He walks out the door hastily, not waiting for his daughter.

Grace surprises me when, instead of following her father, she rounds my desk and envelops me in a warm hug, her lithe body dwarfed by my big frame. I hug her back. "Thank you so much, Logan. I will find a way to repay you, I had no—"

I swallow hard and step back, cutting her off. "You don't have to repay me, Grace. Consider this a consolation gift. I'm sorry about everything. I never meant to hurt you."

She tilts her head, and a soft, bitter smile tugs at her lips. Then, her forehead crinkles with anguish. "I didn't know my father intended to use you for your money. If I had known, I would have never accepted the engagement." Her eyes glisten with unshed tears. "I'm happy for you, Logan. Finding your fated mate must feel like a dream come true. She is a lucky woman. I wish you both all the happiness in the world." She gives me one last smile before leaving the study.

I stare at her disappearing back.

My mother's voice breaks through my thoughts and the guilt that claws at my gut. "So, you finally found her."

"I did…and then I lost her," I tell my mother. The raw pain of being separated from Ava hits me like a ton of bricks, suffocating me.

"Then go get her back, son. The pack needs its Luna."

27

Ava

Hiding in an animal carcass is not how I envisioned spending my night…yet here I am. I was becoming tired, and Logan was gaining speed on me, so I submerged myself in the creek to keep him off my scent. I swam downstream until I saw a small cave and hid in it. Thank God for thick wolf shifter fur; otherwise, I would suffer from a bout of horrible hypothermia.

In the back of the cave was a humongous bear carcass, and I hid inside it. I guess being a loser and watching nature documentaries for so many years instead of going to parties paid off in the end. I once saw that wolves sometimes do this to keep their scent hidden from other predators, and it stuck with me. In my desperation, I had to try it. Well, I guess it worked because he hasn't found me yet.

It took everything in me to shut Logan out from my mind and our bond, but the thought of him with someone else and the burn of his betrayal kept me going even when I thought I couldn't anymore. Now, though, after hours of much-needed reflection, I feel stupid for letting my emotions run rampant and get the best of me. Logan said that with my wolf being awakened, I would feel everything in a heightened state, and boy, he wasn't kidding.

God, I acted so recklessly. You would think I was still a teenager for the way I ran off.

Don't get me wrong, I'm still mad, and my heart feels as though someone stomped all over it and then stabbed it with a fiery knife for good measure, but I regret not letting Logan explain like he wanted to. And in the aftermath of my rashness, I'm faced with a decision; go back to the cabin or make my way home. Because I sure can't stay here inside of a rotting carcass forever. At the cabin, I'd have to face Logan, my wounded pride, and the possibility of rejection. At home, I'd be simply running from my problems and avoiding closure.

In the end, I decide to go home and then maybe call Logan and ask him to meet me somewhere so we can talk. However, I'm not sure how I'll do that since I'll need my phone to call him, and from what I remember, my phone is still in the woods along with my Halloween costume, where I shifted for the first time.

Dawn breaks, and golden rays of sunshine illuminate the mouth of the cave, but I still don't move. I'll wait for the full day light; I don't know where this cave is located, and I need the light to find my way back home through the dense forest. Ugh. I just want to curl up in bed and stay there for the foreseeable future. Some more time passes before I get out and let my wolf take over completely as I start running, the icy air filling my lungs with each inhale. I don't know where the national park ends, but I trust my wolf will take me there.

At least two hours pass until I finally find my way down to Shadow Lake. If it snowed here, it surely wasn't more than a light dusting, and it has already melted. The ground is muddy beneath my paws, and the damp, chilly air fills my snout. It smells musty, like decomposing leaves, pine sap, and wet bark.

There's a house in the distance I spotted from a few miles back. I creep closer, using the tree trunks as my cover. My hope is I can sneak in and find some clothes and a shower in the house. Perhaps the theft will be a smudge on my moral punch card, but I can't exactly shift and then go out into the world buck naked. Getting arrested for public indecency is not on my to-do list for the day. Or maybe I could get lucky and the smell of dead bear carcass wafting out of me like a pungent cologne will make the police pass out fast enough for me to escape. Just kidding.

Still hiding in the tree line, I watch a family of four leave in a minivan and listen closely to ensure no one else is inside the house. When I don't hear anything aside from the rustling of the wind in the leaves, I approach the wooden front porch and round the corner, shifting when I reach the back door.

I say a prayer and turn the knob. *¡Chingada madre! Pinche puerta.* The door is locked, but I use some of my newfound strength to jingle it a bit left and right. After a few moments, it breaks, and the door opens with a soft creak. I quickly enter the kitchen and amble through the narrow hallway, searching for a bathroom. Pushing the door to my right, I find it, but there's only a toilet and a sink, and I desperately need a shower, so I get out.

They already have the Christmas tree out in the living room, the lights flickering softly as I make my way to the staircase. The stairs to the second floor are lined with numerous framed photos of the couple on their wedding day and the kids at different stages in life. The house is small but well cared for, and guilt twists my stomach into knots for invading their home. I don't have another option, though. I just hope they won't notice someone was here.

Entering what seems to be a master bedroom, I slip into the en suite bathroom and immediately hop in the shower. I try my best not to throw up as I wash the disgusting scent off me. I have to wash and rinse about five times before I don't feel like heaving anymore.

After I dry myself, I make a beeline for the closet and rifle through the woman's clothes to find something to wear. Her hips are much narrower than mine, so I have to take a pair of sweats from her husband's wardrobe, a tee and a hoodie from hers, and a pair of old-looking sneakers that I don't think she'll miss too much. The shoes are a number too big, but I can manage walking in them. Before I exit the bedroom, I also grab a light jacket.

As soon as I'm dressed, I get out of there and try to remember the way to the parking lot where I left my car before the Halloween party. Not like I have my keys or anything, but from there, maybe I can try and get a cab.

I don't know how long it takes me to get to the parking lot, but it's definitely longer than the half hour Tony and I walked to the Halloween party. Luckily, once I get there, a girl is ambling toward her car, and I ask her to call a cab for me. She offers to drive me to the city, saying she's on her way to the Raven district anyway after her run.

As we coast through the morning traffic, it turns out she has a bit of a motor mouth. Once she starts talking, she doesn't stop even for a second. She tells me all about her toxic ex and how he manipulated her. *Ha, me and you, sister.* At least I don't even have to talk. I space out and nod when I feel it's appropriate. Not before long, she drops me off at my apartment building. I thank her and get out with a heavy sigh.

Punching in the code for the front door, I enter the building and go straight to the super's office on the first floor. I rap my knuckles against the door and wait for him to answer. Exaggerated, almost cartoonish moans and the distinct sound of skin slapping together travel through the door. He's either having sex in there, or he is watching porn. I think it's the latter, though.

"Just a minute," he bellows, panic lacing his tone. He takes his sweet time to answer the door, and when he finally opens it, his face and neck are beet red, and I don't miss his laptop and the mountain of used tissues on his desk. He's a short man with a balding head that shines brightly in the overhead neon light, an aquiline nose that points slightly to the right, and a beer belly that's spilling over his belt. There's a wet stain on the crotch of his brown pants, and I do not want to think about where that came from. "What can I do for you, Miss Perez?" he asks, wiping at the beads of sweat accumulating on his receding hairline with the back of his hand.

"I lost my keys and can't get into my apartment. Can I borrow the extra key you have?"

"S-sure," he stammers and goes to the wall where all the keys are hung. "You're renting 7C, right?"

"Yup," I answer, popping the *p*.

"Just make a copy when you can and bring it back to me, please," he says, handing me the key with the hand he most likely didn't wash after jerking off.

I take it between my thumb and forefinger and try to suppress the disgusted shudder that passes through my body. *Ugh.* He closes the door in my face hastily after I thank him. Before I get to the elevator, he is already resuming his morning activities, the exaggerated moans reverberating in my ears and making me cringe.

The elevator doors slide open with a ping, and I shuffle inside. A weighted sigh leaves my lungs while I rest my head on the back wall. I'm so fucking tired. Of everything. Despite my best efforts, just like Sisyphus, I roll back down the hill as my thoughts, yet again, wander off to Logan. He's imprinted himself so far beneath my skin that I still feel his touch in every cell, every nerve ending. To make matters worse, I'm still sore after he nailed me to the table and fucked me like it was the last time.

A snort that quickly morphs into a whimper escapes me at the irony of that…because it really was the last time. Damn him and his lies. The back of my throat burns with unshed tears. I try my best not to break into heaving sobs at the mental image of him at the altar with another woman. It's honestly a miracle I managed to keep my shit together as long as I did with the way I feel my chest caving in and my battered heart hemorrhaging all over.

C'mon, Ava, just a few steps, and then you can lose it once you're inside.

As I step into the hallway, it takes me a few seconds to register that Chloe, my best friend that it feels like I haven't spoken to in months, is sitting on the floor next to my door, her knees drawn to her chest and her back resting on the wall. It's as if God himself took pity on me and sent my best friend as divine intervention to help me glue my broken pieces back together. My knees almost buckle under me in relief. She sips from a take-out coffee and scrolls on her phone as loud music plays in her earbuds, oblivious to the bloody war slashing my insides to ribbons.

The hallway is a blur as I start running toward her like my life depends on it. She lifts her head when I almost reach her, her eyes widening, probably more in shock at my speed than at seeing me. But like all humans do when faced with the supernatural, she quickly brushes it off. With a loud squeal, she throws herself at me, enveloping me in a tight hug. Even though her peach scent is way too strong for my new wolfish nose, I inhale it deeply. I missed her so damn much.

"Oh my God, Ave! I'm so happy that you're okay, but I'm pretty sure you're breaking my ribs," she yells in my ear. The sound is so loud to me that a sharp pain pierces my brain and makes my jaw clench. I resist the urge to press my fingers into my temples as I relax my hold, hoping I didn't do any real damage. I'm still adjusting to the fact that I'm not human anymore. That I'm not as breakable as I once was. Well, physically speaking, because my insides are raw, like an open wound left under the blistering desert sun.

She pulls back. When she sees my expression, she cringes. "Oops, sorry. I yelled, didn't I?" she whispers exaggeratedly after taking the earbuds out and pocketing them.

I shake my head incredulously, smiling so largely my cheeks hurt. "What are you doing here, Chlo?"

In stark contrast, Chloe's eyebrows drop in a deep frown as she gives me a withering glare. She flaps her hands in disbelief before folding them in front of her chest. "First off, I want to strangle you, you bitch. Did you throw your phone off a cliff or something? Because, truly, I can't explain otherwise how in the world you could ignore all my calls and messages for days on end. You made me sick with worry."

She lets out a cleansing breath. "I'm here because the next stretch of the tour is in the US, and the band's playing at a club in the Raven district Friday night. I thought Knox would surely push me off the plane if I was going to mention you one more time on the way here." The death stare quickly transforms into guilt as she rambles, "We arrived last night, and I came to see you. You weren't home, though. So, um, don't be mad at me, please, but I called your Mom and told her I can't get ahold of you. I didn't know what else to do. Ben traced your phone and said you're supposed to be at your apartment. Clearly, you weren't, so I decided to come back today and wait for however long was necessary until you showed up. I was planning a trip to the police station, to be honest."

As if the fog of fury finally lifts from her vision, her beautiful onyx eyes travel from my toes all the way to my face, and a glint of worry shines in them when she takes in my disheveled appearance. "What the heck are you wearing? You kind of look like shit, Ave. Are you okay?"

"I kind of do, don't I?" The admission is effective in wiping away my smile completely. The moment Chloe hugs me again, I finally lose it and start ugly crying with whole-body sobs and snot going down my face. I try to talk, but the words come out all warped through my hiccups.

"Where's your key?"

I drop it in her extended palm, still unable to form a word. After she opens the door, she grabs my hand and, like a mother hen, she fusses over me, urging me to sit before she ambles to the kitchen. She returns with a glass of water that she places on top of the coffee table. In the next second, I'm wrapped in her arms again. It takes me ten full minutes to compose myself, and I finally notice my phone and keys on top of my coffee table, where I always keep them. I pull back with a frown.

Who the hell brought over my things from the woods?

Chloe takes my hands in hers, her eyes locking with mine. "Talk to me. I need to know who we're murdering tonight because I have never seen you like this, not even after finding out you only had a few months to live."

"I don't even know where the fuck to start," I say, sniffling, my voice nasally and scratchy. Of course, I can't exactly tell her I'm a freakin' wolf now and that I shifted for the first time when I witnessed Tony getting mauled by a rogue at the Halloween party. And then there's the fact that I have a fated mate. *Had Ava, you had a fated mate.* If that part was even true. It felt true, though…like I finally found the missing part of my soul. Raw pain rattles my insides like an earthquake when all the moments I shared with Logan flash through my mind for what feels like the umpteenth time today.

I free one of my hands from Chloe's hold and take a few sips of water, trying to swallow the tears that burn the back of my throat. Inhaling a calming breath, I tell her what happened between me and Logan while leaving out all the weird supernatural parts and Tony's death. So, I basically had to lie a lot.

"Well, at least there's a bright side," Chloe deadpans, lifting a shoulder after I finish my story. "You finally found someone that knows what a clit is."

A laugh bubbles out of me, but it quickly turns bitter. "Yeah…too bad he's got a fiancé, and he's getting married."

Her upper lip curls, and she rolls her eyes, crossing her arms in front of her chest. "Ugh, I hate men with a passion. They are the absolute worst."

I arch an eyebrow at her. "Except for Knox, right?"

She sticks her tongue out at me. "He doesn't count; he's a sweetheart."

I nod, agreeing with her. "I know. I also hate all men besides Knox. How is he, by the way?"

"They have rehearsals all day at the venue they're playing Friday night. You wanna go? Listen to some of their new songs?"

"Yeah…I don't know about that. To be honest, I don't feel like seeing Jude right now."

"C'mon, it will be fun, and I don't think sitting here and moping will do you any good."

"I'm not in the mood."

"Fine, then we'll do something else," Chloe says, standing and striding toward my closet. "I'm kidnapping you to my hotel. They have the most amazing spa. We can spend all day there, and then you can sleep with me tonight. Knox won't mind. We're renting the penthouse suite."

I turn sideways on the couch to see what Chloe's doing. "I can't. I'm supposed to be working tonight."

She looks at me over her shoulder, then goes back to rifling through my wardrobe and stuffing some of my clothes in my overnight bag. "Can't you call in sick or something?"

"No, we're already understaffed," I choke out, remembering Tony. "Besides, I think I should call Logan and ask him to meet me. I want to hear his side of the story."

Chloe sighs. "'Kay, call him, and after you guys meet up, we can spend the rest of the day at the spa, and you'll leave for your shift when you have to. Then I'll grab Knox, and we'll come to your bar when it opens. When you finish your shift, I'll take you to my hotel. Do you have a bathing suit in here?"

"Check the underwear drawer. Take the red one; it's my favorite," I tell her as I pick up my phone. "And Chlo?"

"What?"

"I love you, and I'm so happy you're here."

"Aw, I love you too. You know you're my favorite person in the whole world." She blows me a kiss and saunters to the bathroom, probably to get my toiletries.

I know I have to mentally prepare myself to speak to Logan or else I will have my third heart attack of the year, so I take a deep breath in and let it out through my nose, hoping it will be enough. With trembling fingers, I dial Emily's number since I don't even have Logan's. My stomach bottoms out when Logan picks up instead.

"Ava, baby, thank fuck. Where are you? We've been looking everywhere for you."

"I, um…" Turns out the breathing wasn't enough. Clearing my throat, I try again. "I'm home…I managed to find my way home."

"Listen to me, baby, please. I fucked up bad. I should have told you everything, but I got caught up in what was happening between us. I know I don't have any excuse, but I want to explain everything to you. It's not what you think."

And I hate my simpering whimpering little heart, but hope filters strongly through my veins at hearing his words. "It's not?" I breathe.

"I'll tell you everything. I need to see you. I've been going crazy since you ran off."

"That's why I called, so we can talk. Can we meet somewhere?"

"I'll come to your place. This is not a discussion we can have in a public place where anyone can overhear."

"'Kay."

"I'll be there in half an hour."

"See you then," I say and hang up as Chloe comes back from the bathroom and dumps all my toiletries in my overnight bag.

"What did he say?" she asks as she strides to the couch and plops down beside me.

"He's coming here to talk."

"Oh, then I'll probably need to make myself scarce. I kind of want to meet him, though, and dick-punch him for making you cry. I can stay and glower at him while you guys talk. You know, like one of those dads with the shotguns in the movies. Make him uncomfortable as fuck."

I laugh out loud at the mental image of Chloe trying to intimidate someone Logan's size and built like a tank. "I'll be fine, Chlo. I'm a big girl. I can handle him."

"Fine. I need to get something to wear for the concert anyway. Knox gave me his credit card and said to get whatever I want as long as he can rip it off my body after the concert. He's always horny as fuck after he plays. But I can just go to the café where I picked out my coffee earlier and wait until you guys finish your talk if you want to go shopping with me afterward."

"It's okay. I'm not in the mood to go shopping, so you can do your thing, and then we can meet back here or tell me the hotel's name, and we can meet there instead."

"I'll come get you. I even have a driver and bodyguard now," she says, hugging me and standing. "Please change your clothes and go wash your face. You know I love you, but you look like you crawled out of a Goodwill box, and you can't let the dickbag see you like this."

"Yes, Mom, I'll change."

"That's my girl." She pats my head and winks. "Now, can you please tell me where I can find clothes that are rock star girlfriend-worthy? I need something sexy and edgy."

"You can try that fancy neighborhood in the southern part of Ashville. I've never been there, but I heard the stores are super high-end, and you can only find designer stuff. If Knox is treating you, then you should take full advantage."

"Oh, I definitely will. 'Kay, I'll see you later. Text me when you guys are done." She takes her jacket from the hanger near the door and blows me a kiss before leaving.

Heaving out a deep sigh, I make a beeline for the bathroom, deciding to take another shower. If I can still smell the stench of dead animal on my skin, Logan will, too.

28

Ava

As I put my jeans on, a weird feeling seizes my chest. I'm nervous as fuck about seeing Logan, but it's not that. It's something different, as if the mating bond is alerting me of Logan's presence. It vibrates and makes my skin tingle as goosebumps spread all over my body. Then a loud knock comes from the front door, and I stride toward it, my stomach fisting into a ball of restless energy. My palm is so sweaty that my hand slips when I grab the handle.

Before I can open the door fully, Logan barrels inside and pulls me into his big arms. A shudder passes through him as he bands an arm across my middle, and brings the other to the nape of my neck, holding me possessively while he buries his nose into my hair and closes the door with his heel at the same time.

His woodsy smell envelops me like a cloud, and my heart slams into my ribcage so hard I'm surprised my ribs are still intact. The mating bond purrs between my ribs as my wolf finally settles for the first time in hours. A sense of complete peace encompasses me. I'd like to say I'm allotting myself a few more seconds of pure bliss before I pull back, but the truth is I physically can't move; my wolf is not allowing me to. She's locking my muscles while she basks in the warmth rolling off Logan and sinking deep into my bones.

"Fuck, baby. Don't ever run away from me again. I went crazy looking for you," he says roughly.

"I'm sorry," I whisper and swallow hard. "But seeing that look of utter guilt on your face, Logan, it nearly destroyed me. I felt as though someone clawed my heart right out of my chest. I know I acted irrationally…letting my emotions get the best of me, but at that moment, all I wanted to do was get away from you."

"I know, baby. I know." Logan pulls back. His gaze zeros in on my lips. A long heartbeat passes before he frames my jaw with his big hand, tracing my lower lip with his thumb, his touch, and the way his body feels against mine, igniting my blood and soaking my panties. "I'm dying to kiss you. Can I kiss you?"

There's nothing I want more. However, I don't tell him that. I slip out of his hold and look down, my fingers clenching at my sides as my teeth sink into my lower lip. "What about your fiancé?" That black hole in my chest is cracked wide open again, threatening to swallow me whole.

He runs a hand over his face. "I was never engaged. I was supposed to get engaged yesterday."

I shake my head and finally lift my eyes to his, my eyebrows pinching in confusion. "I don't understand."

"Let's take a seat, and I'll explain everything," he says, urging me to sit on the couch. He takes off his jacket, drapes it on the back of the couch, and heaves out a deep sigh as he plops down next to me. I can't stop roving my eyes over the entire length of his body. He looks incredible in jeans and a baby blue tee that stretches over his muscles like second skin and makes his amber skin pop.

"As an Alpha to the pack, I am obligated to take a mate before the age of twenty-five; otherwise, the pack was going to be weakened. But I knew I had a fated mate out there somewhere, and I couldn't just settle for a chosen mate. I waited and waited and never lost my hope that my fated mate would eventually come to me."

He pauses, swallows, and then continues, "Then the children of my pack got touched by the weakness and fell into an endless sleep. I suddenly found myself between a rock and a hard place. I did a lot of research in the hopes of finding a cure, but not even Malik was able to bring them back past a certain point. It was just going to get worse and worse from there. The weakness would eventually spread to the whole pack. So, I promised to get engaged to Grace, a wolf from a neighboring pack, a month before my twenty-fifth birthday and marry a chosen mate the day I turned twenty-five. I have never even kissed Grace. Hell, I've only met her once. That's it. I was going to marry her and make her my mate because I had to."

"Wait. Um, so you didn't get engaged to her after all?" I interrupt, fumbling with my fingers in my lap because I suddenly don't know what to do with my hands.

"No, Ava. That's what I'm trying to tell you. I didn't. She went home. Her father, the Alpha of the Ironclaw pack, was not happy about it when I told them I had found my fated mate, even if fated mates are sacred to our kind. Turns out he was a piece of shit and only wanted to marry Grace to me because of his gambling debts. Anyway, when the truth came out, I offered to pay off his debt as a consolation gift for Grace, and they eventually left."

"But what about the kids?"

"They woke up the moment we completed the mating bond. That was the only thing needed to cure the children and then strengthen the pack; the wedding was just a formality."

I take a moment to sit with what he just told me. "Why didn't you tell me? When we were at the cabin, you could have said something."

His shoulders slump. "Honestly…I was ashamed and afraid of your reaction. The days I spent with you at the cabin were the best days of my life. I have never known such happiness, such peace."

His Adam's apple bobs in his throat, and he places a warm hand over mine before continuing. "And deep down, I knew I had to tell you, but I was afraid you would think I betrayed you somehow, that I accepted to take a chosen mate when all I ever wanted was my fated. And I got so lost in you, that I completely forgot about my responsibilities as an Alpha and the engagement party. It felt good not to have the weight of the world pressing down on my shoulders for a weekend."

"I can understand that, Logan…that you were in a difficult position. I just wish you would have told me."

"I was going to. I know it sounds like I'm just saying this right now, but I never meant to hurt you. I need you so much, baby. I can't live without you. You're everything to me. Please forgive me."

I look down, slip my hand from under Logan's big one, and scoot over with the intention of standing up. "I don't know, Logan. I need some time to thin—"

Before I can finish my sentence or stand, Logan pulls me in his lap in one smooth motion. His fingers bite into my hips as he maneuvers me on top of him so my knees are on either side of his muscular thighs, his huge erection pressing right at my center. His lips crash to mine, and his silken tongue invades my mouth, rendering me stupid. Desire surges in my veins as Logan kisses me so thoroughly he steals the breath in my lungs along with any rational thought I might have.

Logan gets up with me wrapped around his body, and with long strides, he ambles to the bed and throws me on top of it. His hand slips inside my shirt and cups my breast as his finger brushes over my taut nipple, eliciting a desperate whimper from my mouth. His other hand unbuttons my jeans and unzips them with hurried movements before his fingers glide into my panties and find my soaked slit.

"Your pussy is dripping for me, baby," he rasps through our mental link and shoves two fingers inside me, pumping them in a maddening rhythm as the heel of his palm rubs into my clit. He continues to kiss me ravenously as he moves his fingers, and feral sounds that I don't even recognize leap from deep within my chest.

"Aaaah…so good, Logan. I'm so close!"

He suddenly pulls back.

My eyebrows furrow. "Why did you stop?"

We're both breathing hard, our chests heaving as he brings the fingers that were inside me to his mouth and licks them clean. His tongue darts out, tracing his lips like he doesn't want to waste even a drop of my arousal before saying, "I need to be inside you. And, baby, you can take as much time as you want to think, but I told you before, I'm not above playing dirty, and I'll use every trick in my arsenal to keep you because you're my fated mate, and I will never let you go."

With rapid movements, Logan peels off my jeans along with my lacy thong that he brings to his nose, inhaling the scrap of material deeply before pocketing it with a wink. When he opens his zipper, his massive cock juts out. He enters me with a hiss as our eyes lock. Golden fire sends my pulse into overdrive, and a loud moan tumbles free from my lips.

His nostrils flare as his hips start moving painstakingly slow, so slow I feel every inch of his cock deliciously ravaging my insides.

"You wreck me, Ava." *Thrust.* "You're all I fucking think about every second of every goddamn day, and if you think you can run away from me again, you are sorely mistaken, because. You. Are. Mine." *Thrust.*

"You're all I see." *Thrust.*

"You're running through my veins." *Thrust.*

"You're the breath in my lungs." *Thrust.*

"The tether to my soul." *Thrust.*

"Mine!" *Thrust.*

"I'll chase you to the end of the Earth and beyond if I have to."

As soon as he finishes saying that, he picks up the rhythm, and soon, pleasure zips through me like a lightning storm. My pussy spasms violently around Logan's cock and triggers his own release. He comes with a deafening roar and rolls over, draping me over his chest.

"Fuck. I needed that," he says with a gentle kiss on my forehead.

"Me too," I whisper through a yawn. The orgasm has left me boneless, and soon enough, exhaustion starts pulling at my eyelids, the steady rhythm of Logan's heartbeat and the warmth emanating from his body lulling me to sleep.

The peace is only momentary. The sound of a phone ringing slices through the air and startles me awake.

Logan groans as his arms tighten around me. "Ignore it."

The phone starts ringing again.

"Maybe you should answer. It might be something important."

"Nothing is more important than being with you right now."

His phone rings again, and he growls in frustration, finally sliding out from under me gently and pushing up from the bed. He takes it out of his jeans and stabs at the screen before bringing it to his ear. "What?" he clips out, annoyance dripping from his tone. "You better have a good reason for interrupting me, Em."

"Logan, something happened." Emily's concerned voice reaches my ears.

I don't intend to listen to their conversation, but I can't help it.

Emily swallows audibly before saying, "Josh is dead."

All the color drenches from Logan's face, his expression crestfallen. "What?" he asks with urgency. "What happened?"

"It was the rogue. Josh was on patrol on the eastern border. He was killed so close to our community, Lo."

Bile surges in my throat at Emily's words, and I'm suddenly reminded that just a few days ago, Tony was murdered, too. I push the harrowing memory of how he died away as I bend and take my jeans from the floor, then pull them on. Logan needs me right now.

"Motherfucking fuck!" Logan bellows and slams his eyes shut as his fingers fist at his side. His whole body is shaking, fury emanating from him like plumes of fog from dry ice. "Does Layla know? Ryan?"

"Not yet. We just found him. And, Lo…there's something else. The rogue left a note. It's addressed to you."

"I'll be there. Don't let anyone else know, and don't move his body. I have to be the one that gives Layla the news." He opens his eyes and rakes his hand through his curls in frustration. "Fuck! I'm going to blow up her entire world."

"It's not your fault."

"I know…But they just got their son back. Ryan only got to spend a few hours with his dad, and now Josh is dead. That poor kid."

"Is Ava with you?"

"Yeah, I'm at her place."

"The rogue, he…You need to keep her safe. The rogue might be after her."

"What do you mean?"

"You'll understand once you see the note. Just come back home."

"Okay. Wait for me," Logan says grimly. He slides his phone back into the pocket of his jeans, but he doesn't move. Rather, he's paralyzed by tension and twitching fingers as his eyes turn glassy.

Standing and closing the small space between us, I envelop Logan in a tight hug. His arms come around me like steel bands, and he clings to me with desperation as though I'm both his lifeline and the only thing that's tethering him to sanity. Raw pain mixed with sadness and white-hot fury filters through my veins until my wolf goes crazy. My eyebrows knit in confusion at the foreign emotions sieging me. Then, a gasp tumbles free from my mouth when I realize I can feel what Logan is feeling at this moment through our bond. The pain is debilitating, like a black hole of despair cleaving me in two. I can't stop the tears that stab at the back of my eyes from falling and rolling over my cheeks.

I don't know how long we stand here, clinging to each other. It might be minutes or hours. After a while, Logan pulls back. He gently thumbs away the tears from my damp cheeks before clearing his throat. His voice comes out rough and scratchy as he says, "I need to go back to our community in the national park. There are a lot of things that I need to take care of. Will you come with me? I won't be able to concentrate on anything if I don't have eyes on you at all times."

Sighing, I say, "My best friend Chloe is visiting. I don't want to upset you even more, but she's only staying a few days...I want to spend some time with her. I missed her like crazy. She wants me to stay at her hotel until she leaves. Plus, I'm working tonight. I can't blow off work."

Logan's nostrils flare. "I don't think it's a good idea. Emily said something about the rogue...that he might come after you. I can't risk you getting hurt, baby. I just can't."

I step back from his arms and fold my lower lip between my teeth, gnawing on it. "I can't live my life in fear. Besides, you will be busy with pack matters, and I don't think me interfering or meeting everyone at a time like this is a good idea. And Chloe's boyfriend is a famous musician. He's got an army of bodyguards following him and Chloe everywhere. I'll be safe staying with them, and then when she leaves, I'll come stay with you, or we can work something else out until you find the rogue."

He sucks on his teeth and mulls over what I said. The muscle feathering in his jaw clearly indicates that he's not exactly happy, but he reluctantly agrees. "Fine. You'll stay with your friend, and I'll go inform the pack and plan Josh's funeral. But I'll assign a security detail from my pack to watch the hotel and accompany you to the bar. Just promise me you won't leave the hotel, okay?"

I nod. "Promise."

Logan strides to the kitchen area and paces the room while making a few calls, letting Kaiden know about Josh's death, and arranging the security detail. In the meantime, I text Chloe and tell her I'm ready to go. After twenty minutes, my phone vibrates with a text message.

> **Chloe: I'm waiting outside in the car. Blacked-out Escalade. Xx**

> **Me: K. See you in five. X**

"Chloe's here. She's waiting for me in the car downstairs, " I tell Logan. After he grabs my overnight bag, we both get out of my apartment and stride toward the elevator. Unexpectedly, Logan reaches for my hand before entwining his fingers with mine. My pulse hiccups at how my palm fits in his big one. I know we're just holding hands and that he just fucked me three ways to Sunday, but I can't help feeling giddy at the small gesture.

The blacked-out Escalade is idling in front of the building. Before I can say anything, Logan drops my hand and pulls me to him, his lips slanting over mine in a soul-scorching kiss. He takes his time as he languidly explores my mouth until everything around us fades into a blurry background. When he pulls back, I'm flushed all over. You wouldn't think, that after the way he fucked me earlier, I would get turned on so easily, but here we are, ladies and gentlemen. I'm dripping. Again.

Logan smirks, dipping down to whisper in the shell of my ear. "The smell of your arousal is making me crazy, little wolf. All I want is to strip you naked and sink my cock into that perfect pussy again. I can't wait to have you in my bed. I'm going to worship your body for hours."

I whimper in response and melt in his arms like butter on warm toast, his hot breath eliciting tingles all over my body. His lips find mine again, but as we start kissing fervently, we're interrupted by Chloe opening the door of the SUV and clearing her throat with cartoonish exaggeration.

"You're going to get arrested for public indecency if you keep going like that. I think you gave a granny on the sidewalk a heart attack," she chuckles out as she exits the car, slams the door shut, and closes the space between us. "So, I guess it's safe to say you two made up." She thrusts her right hand in Logan's direction, and they shake hands. "I'm Chloe."

"Logan. It's nice meeting you, Chloe."

She narrows her eyes at him. "I'm not so sure if it's nice meeting you, too, Logan," she drawls. With a saccharine smile, she says, "If you make my bestie cry ever again, I'll cut up your balls in your sleep."

Logan's lips twist in amusement. "Don't worry. If that ever happens again, I'll cut up my own balls, and then I'll gift you the knife to cut off my dick, too."

"Deal," Chloe says, folding her arms in front of her chest. She reaches for the overnight bag in Logan's hand. "I'll take this."

The driver quickly exits the car, all flustered. "Miss Lim, let me get that for you." He takes the bag from Logan before Chloe can reach it and places it in the trunk.

"Thanks, Allan. And I told you a hundred times before, call me Chloe, please."

I lift an eyebrow and snort a laugh. "Oh, I'm sorry, Miss Lim. We wouldn't want you to break a precious nail," I drawl with mock aggravation.

She rolls her eyes and then gives me a dirty look. "Oh, shut up. Can we go? Knox is waiting for us. They just finished rehearsal."

"Yeah," I say.

Logan gives me one last hug and kisses the top of my head. "I'll call you. Be safe." He shoves his hands in his pockets and watches us get into the SUV. Allan puts the car into drive and glides smoothly into the traffic as I say hello to the hunky bodyguard in the passenger seat.

"Dude, you didn't tell me how fucking hot he is," Chloe says as she fans herself. "Jesus fucking Christ, that man is fine as hell, and he's so goddamn tall and muscly. So, is he engaged or not? Because if he's stringing you along, I swear to God, Ave, I'll slash his tires and set his house on fire. I don't care how hot he is."

"He's not. It was all a misunderstanding." Just as I finish telling Chloe this, my phone starts ringing. I pull it out from the pocket of my jacket. Marnie's name appears on the screen, and I answer, sinking into the buttery soft leather of the seat. "Hey, Marnie."

"Hey, Ava." She sighs and takes a few seconds to blow her nose. I can tell she's been crying. "I think you already heard the news about Tony."

"Yeah, Emily told me," I blurt out and then have a mini panic attack because I don't know if she has spoken to Emily yet.

"What happened to him is so sad. He was such a kind soul and so young…he didn't deserve to go like that. Anyway, I wanted to let you know that I'll be closing the bar this week, possibly next week, too. It just doesn't feel right to entertain people while we're mourning. His mom was a very good friend of mine. I saw Tony grow up and become a wonderful man." She heaves out another weighted sigh. "I'll be helping her with everything she might need. I'll let you know when the funeral is; maybe you'll want to come."

"Thanks for letting me know. Of course, I want to come. Tony has become a very good friend in the short time I've known him." My voice breaks, and I bite my lip, sniffling, a fresh curtain of tears blurring my vision. "Please let me know if you need any help."

"There's no need, we'll handle it. I'll let you know about the funeral. Bye, Ava."

"'Kay, Marnie. Bye."

A mournful sob leaves me as I press my trembling hand to the center of my heaving chest. I close my eyes and take deep breaths, but it only makes it worse because in the darkness, I see the rogue tearing into Tony again and again in vivid detail, his helpless body torn to pieces on the blood-soaked ground. I was so wrapped up in Logan I pushed Tony's horrible death into a corner of my mind and then labeled it 'Later.' It was deliberate, of course. I just couldn't deal with it, so I thought that maybe if I kept it there, it wouldn't hurt as much…later, but now I feel as if my lungs are collapsing and my already shattered heart is being stomped all over by an elephant.

The dam breaks, and I start ugly crying again for the umpteenth time today. I thought I had a broken heart before the transplant, but it's nothing compared to how I'm feeling right now.

"What the fuck? Who was that? Why are you crying again?" Chloe asks, alarmed, from beside me.

"My f-friend T-tony. H-he's…he's dead."

She hugs me tightly. "Holy shit, Ave, I'm so sorry." She tightens her hold, placing a kiss atop my head. After I calm down, she pulls back and looks into my eyes. "We'll hole up in my room and order everything they have on the menu for room service. We'll pig out and do a movie marathon. How does that sound?"

I wipe at my tear-streaked cheeks and offer her a half-smile that I bet looks more like a grimace. "Like heaven."

29

Ava

Two days later, hunched over the bathroom counter and looking into the mirror, which I'm sure cost more than the entire sum of furniture in my small apartment, I line my waterline with a waterproof black kohl and then do the sharpest wing I can manage with my puffy eyes. Even with the thick layer of makeup, I still look like I've been crying for two days straight. Well, at least I tried.

Chloe convinced me to go to the band's show tonight, and we were supposed to get ready together, but Knox came into the room asking if he could speak to her privately an hour ago, and judging by the loud moans and grunts that I'm currently trying to drown with the blasting music in my earbuds, their talk escalated to fucking. I can't blame them, though. Chloe spent every second since we left my apartment holed up with me in one of the many bedrooms of the royal penthouse suite.

"Harder, Knox. Please!" Chloe's desperate whimper travels through the thin wall.

"So greedy today, kitten," Knox rasps.

After a few minutes, Chloe's voice booms again, "Yes. Yes! Oh, aaah, I-I'm gonna come."

Aaand I'm going to throw myself off the balcony if I have to hear them fucking one more time. But sure enough, after a few minutes, they start again. You would think Knox wouldn't spend so much energy before a show since he usually plays the drums like he's possessed. This is, for sure, one of those moments I wish my hearing wasn't supernatural. I really didn't want to find out how my best friend sounds during an orgasm. I can't unhear it now. Don't get me wrong, I'm happy she's getting some. I just don't want to witness it on such a personal level.

With a light dusting of powder on my nose, I finish my makeup, take off my robe, and get out into the bedroom to look through the clothes Chloe packed for me and see if I can find something decent to wear. Knowing her, she probably packed a few outfits in the eventuality that I would decide to go to the concert after all.

When I step over the threshold, I slam into a wall of cinnamon and something spicy. I whip my head toward the luxurious teal armchair in the corner near the door to lock, involuntarily, with hazel eyes.

Mierda.

I was so distracted by trying to drown my best friend's sex noises with music that I didn't notice Jude coming into my room. I take out my earbuds. "What are you doing here?" I hiss, heat crawling up my neck and blazing in my cheeks with the realization that I'm only wearing a lacy thong and a push-up bra. At least I don't have on my period panties like that night Logan undressed me and put me to bed. It seems like all that happened a lifetime ago.

Jude gives me a lopsided grin, a mischievous glint shining in his eyes. "I wanted to see you, Ava." He's as breathtaking as ever, decked in all black, the tattoos on his corded forearms catching my eye as he leans forward in the armchair, resting his elbows on his knees. "And what a sight." Licking at his lower lip, his eyes travel over my body in a slow perusal from my toes all the way to my breasts and stay there.

I arch an eyebrow. "I'm surprised you remembered my name. I thought for a second there you were going to call me gorgeous," I say dryly, duck into the bathroom, and hastily put the bathrobe back on.

His footsteps reach my ears before he appears at the bathroom door. "Hardy har har." He leans on the door frame with a grin that's all teeth. "You do look gorgeous," he purrs, his voice as smooth as I remember, though this time, my body doesn't react in any way to it. There's no spark…*nada*.

I roll my eyes and push past him into the bedroom, plopping down on the pristine white bed with the silky eight-hundred-thread sheets. "What are you doing here, Jude?" I ask him again, my tone calmer now that the shock of him being in the same room with me has worn off. I knew I would have to face him eventually, it's his band's penthouse and concert after all. I just hoped I would manage to keep avoiding him.

He sits next to me and tilts his head. "I never got the chance to tell you how sorry I am for that night on the bus," Jude says, lifting a shoulder, his kaleidoscope gaze turning serious.

"I got the flowers and the card you sent, so I got the message."

He sighs and looks down for a moment. "I should have never pushed you. You almost died because of me—"

I cut him off. "It's not your fault, Jude. You don't need to apologize for that. I was dying anyway. Plus, I'm an adult, and I made my own decisions. I knew it would be a bad idea to do drugs with my heart condition, but I did it anyway, and on top of drinking a lot of alcohol." I shrug. "I was reckless…so desperate to cram all these life experiences in the short time I had left, and I let that cloud my judgment. But in the end, I don't regret any of it."

His eyebrows furrow in confusion. "So you don't blame me?"

"No, of course not."

"Then why did you block me on everything when I tried to contact you?"

"It just felt weird talking to you, you know? I guess I didn't want a reminder of that night. Plus, I didn't think you would care all that much anyway."

"Okay, I totally understand that, but I wanted to see you again… talk to you."

I snort laugh. "Why? C'mon, Jude…be real, I was nothing more than a groupie to you. You couldn't even remember my name. I was just a mindless fuck to add to your list, and that was fine by me because we were only going to use each other."

His cheeks turn red at my words, so contradictory to his bad-boy looks. "True. But then I couldn't forget your name or face after that night. You know, you're the reason I got clean." He swallows. "When I saw you collapse, I saw an image of me a few years from then in your exact position. I was going down a slippery slope…"

"I'm happy you got clean," I say, a small smile curving my lips.

A tense silence stretches between us before Jude speaks again. "I'm sorry about your friend. Chloe told me you lost someone."

"Yeah…thanks," I mumble.

His eyebrows furrow. "So, I heard you're with a guy. Is it serious?"

Shaking my head, I huff in fake annoyance. "Oh God, I need to have a talk with my best friend if she's sharing every detail of my personal life with everyone." Then, shrugging, I say, "It's pretty new, but yeah…I think it is."

"Knox told me about it. I think he's tired of my obsession with you. He told me in hopes I'll finally move on," he says and lifts his hand to wrap it around my jaw. "You know, I wish you would have given me a chance," he whispers as he drags his thumb over my bottom lip. "I think we would have been amazing together."

My wolf growls inside my head. She is not pleased that a man other than my mate is flirting with me in a hotel room where anything can happen. I pull back from Jude's hand and stand up. "Okay, mister, time to go. I need to get dressed," I say.

He stands with his hands lifted in mock surrender and strides to the door, opening it. "I'll see you later," he says over his shoulder.

One hour later, a hunky bodyguard that's all muscles and wavy auburn hair escorts Chloe and me separately from the band toward the two blacked-out SUVs waiting for us at the back entrance of the hotel. He is wearing dark sunglasses even inside, which I find pretty weird, and when he touches the back of my arm to guide me through the door, an ominous shiver skates down my spine. I shake it off and chalk it up to nerves.

Everything that's happening seems too freakin' surreal to me, especially that my best friend is now living like a celebrity. She's already used to all of this, but I feel trapped in some kind of alternate universe. Like, how is this real life?

The bodyguard opens the door, and I get in after Chloe. The only seat available is the one in the back next to Jude since Chloe and Knox took the middle seats, the car being one of those fancy SUVs that looks more like a limousine.

Jude gives me a rueful smile and pats the seat next to him. "C'mon, Ava. I saved you the best seat," he drawls with a devilish wink.

Rolling my eyes at his remark, I sit down as far as I can from him. The bodyguard closes the door with a loud thud and gets in the passenger seat. There's something about him that irks me; I just can't put my finger on it. The engine starts, and the car glides out of the alley into the evening traffic. Jude's eyes burn a hole through the side of my face as I try my best to feign ignorance and scroll on my phone, though I won't be able to do that for long. The battery is at one percent since I listened to music in a failed attempt to drown out Chloe and Knox's sex noises, and I forgot to charge it.

I've barely spoken to Logan these past two days. Not by choice. Josh's funeral was today, and between organizing the service and new patrols at their community borders, we didn't get much time to talk, but I don't mind. He has a lot on his plate at the moment. He also wasn't happy when I told him I was going to the concert, but he saw the state I was in while grieving for Tony, and he agreed that I needed to do something to keep my mind off the horrible way he died, especially since the security will be tight at the concert.

When my phone dies, I watch the city pass by in a deep scarlet blur as the sun sinks in the horizon. It takes us about forty minutes to arrive at the venue. We all file out of the two SUVs, Chloe, Knox and the rest of the band getting into the building before Jude and I.

Just when I'm about to wrap my hand around the club's door handle, the heel of my right boot gets stuck in the uneven pavement. *Ugh, why does this keep happening to me?* I want to kick myself for borrowing Chloe's high-heeled spiky boots. It seemed like a good idea at the time since they go really well with my leather mini-skirt and see-through mesh turtleneck. I pull my leg back with too much force, and I almost topple over Jude, who was walking behind me.

"You okay?" he asks as his hand wraps around my elbow.

"Yeah. Thanks," I respond, turning my head over my shoulder to look at him.

His eyes lift over my head before snapping back to mine. Before I realize what's happening, he steps into my space and kisses the corner of my lips briefly. I'm too stunned to act at first.

Suddenly, someone yells, "Jude! Are you two together? Is she your girlfriend?" Loud camera clicks and bright flashes of light follow before one of the bodyguards drags the paparazzo away.

"What the fuck? Why'd you do that?" I ask him through gritted teeth and push him a few feet back from me.

His eyes widen, probably not expecting me to be so strong. Then he shrugs nonchalantly as he ambles toward me. "Relax. It wasn't even a real kiss."

"You had no right." My fists clench and unclench, and I have to take a few calming breaths before the need to shift and tear Jude to pieces subsides. "I told you I'm with someone, Jude," I clip out with narrowed eyes and fling the door before he can reach me, stalking forward and almost barreling into Chloe.

Her eyebrows pinch with worry at seeing the fury clearly written on my face. "You okay? Did something happen?"

"Not here," I mutter as all the band members turn their heads in my direction, probably alerted by the high pitch in Chloe's voice.

"Follow me," Chloe says, grabs my trembling hand, and drags me backstage. "What happened?" She sits down gracefully on the brown leather couch in the backstage area, lifting a water bottle from the table in front of us and taking a few gulps.

I plop down next to her. "Jude kissed me, and a paparazzo caught it on camera. Well, it wasn't a full-on kiss. He only touched the corner of my mouth, but from the angle that paparazzo took the photos…it must have looked like a real one. I think he did it on purpose." I pinch the bridge of my nose. "Do you have a charger with you? My battery is dead, and I need to tell Logan what happened."

She puts the bottle back on the table. "No, sorry. You can use my phone if you want."

"I don't know his number by heart."

"I'm sure it's fine. You can tell him tonight after the concert."

Worrying my lower lip between my teeth, I say, "But what if that paparazzo sells the photos, and then Logan sees them and—"

Chloe's hand wraps around mine as she interrupts me. "Calm down, you spaz. It usually takes some time before that happens. If there is going to be an article, it's going to appear tomorrow. Plus, Logan doesn't seem like the type to read trashy tabloid stories, and you can call him at the hotel tonight and tell him everything, all right?"

"Fine," I relent with a deep sigh. Chloe is right. I can do damage control after the concert. "Ugh, I want to fucking strangle Jude."

"Maybe you shouldn't be so harsh on him, Ave. He's still hung up on you," she tells me after a few beats of silence.

"Well, he knew I was in a relationship and did it anyway. He came into my room earlier while you were busy talking to Knox." I waggle my eyebrows and exaggerate the word *talking*.

A laugh bubbles out of Chloe, and she shrugs unapologetically. "Knox likes to fuck before he plays. Says it brings him good luck. So, what did he want?"

"He wanted to talk about that night in the tour bus when my heart stopped."

"And?"

I pop a shoulder and start unzipping my boots. "I told him he has nothing to feel guilty about." Dropping the boots to the floor, I roll my ankles a few times and tuck my legs under me, sinking into the cushion at my back.

"You know, he truly has changed. I told you, the other guys have brought girls to their hotel rooms every night, and Jude hasn't. He also hasn't touched drugs or alcohol since the tour restarted. Maybe you should give him a shot, and then we can all travel together."

I huff. "Like a big happy family?"

"Exactly, can you imagine? We'd be having so much fun, and we would travel the world like you always wanted." Excitement dances in Chloe's eyes, and I can see on her face how her mind is spinning with the possibilities.

"That's a nice little fantasy, Chlo. Unfortunately, I don't feel anything for Jude. I'm with Logan, and he makes me happy, even if we haven't been together for long. I think he's it for me."

"Aw, my bestie is in looove," she says in a sing-song.

30

Logan

Standing in between Emily and my mother, heart heavy and shoulders weighing a thousand pounds, I watch Josh's coffin be lowered into the ground carefully by two of our men. We're all gathered in the cemetery at the edge of our community, surrounded by ancient trees that stand tall like sentinels, witnessing the grief and pain seeping out of us. Thick, gray clouds cover the sky, and an icy gust of wind bites into my cheeks and ruffles Emily's curls, blowing them into her face. She pushes them away and looks at me with glistening eyes.

Josh's body was left torn to pieces on the blood-soaked ground, freshly shifted from his wolf form with a gaping hole in his chest and his heart missing, a note nailed to his forehead that said, 'I'm coming for you, Alpha. I'm going to take everything you hold dear as you took everything from me.'

A keening wail rips from Layla's chest when the wood meets the ground at the bottom of the hole with a loud thud, the powerful cry folding her in two as she throws herself toward the hole. Her brother pulls her back just in time. Needles stab the back of my eyes as my gaze flits to Ryan, Josh and Layla's son. He seems so small and lost, crushed.

No child should bury their parent at his age. I can't even imagine what he's feeling right now. I swallow hard and grit my teeth to stop the tears from making an appearance. All the members of our pack surround us, and everyone needs me to be calm and calculated. I can't show weakness, even in a moment like this.

As if sensing the despair raging inside of me, Emily takes my hand in hers, squeezing it in a silent show of support, letting me know she's here for me, always by my side. I squeeze back and let go of her hand as I stride forward to the edge of the hole, bend down to pick some dirt, and throw it on top of the coffin. It's customary for the pack's Alpha to do so at burials.

Turning around and looking at every single person in attendance, taking in their tear-streaked faces and somber expressions, I clear my throat loudly. It takes a few moments before I can speak through the heavy knot lodged in my throat.

"Josh was a close friend of mine and loved by many in our community. I always considered him an example of what a father and loving husband should be. The love he held for his family and the devotion he showed to our pack will never be forgotten. He died protecting our community, and he will always be remembered as a hero. Rest in peace, Josh. We will never forget you."

Gaze lowered, I leave the cemetery with the pack at my back, giving Josh's family privacy to say their last goodbye.

The sky glows crimson through the windows of my living room, the same color as the blood-soaked ground beneath Josh's body when he was found. I shake my head to rid my mind of the image of him lying dead with his chest cleaved open as I finish pouring the whiskey into the three glasses I laid out on the wet bar in the corner, behind the navy couch.

"Is Ava still at the hotel?" Malik asks when I turn around to hand him his glass. He came by earlier with Kaiden and Dominic to pay their respects since I held the reception after the funeral at my house. Everyone from my pack except him and my sister left an hour ago. Kaiden and Dominic had to leave as well.

"No, she went to the concert with her friend," I answer, rounding the couch and extending my left hand with my sister's drink toward her.

She accepts it with a quiet "Thanks," and I plop down next to her, taking a hearty sip from my tumbler and welcoming the burn. With all the shit that's been happening, I have acquired a taste for stronger beverages.

"Do you think that's a good idea?" Malik asks.

My nostrils flare. "No, but I can't lock her up in my room and never let her out until we find the rogue, even if that's what I want. Besides, she took Tony's death badly, and she needs a distraction."

Nervous energy thrums through my veins, and my wolf is getting more and more impatient with our fated mate so far. I don't know how much longer I'll be able to hold back and not go to her. When she ran off, I felt the rift between us like a gaping wound in my chest, and even if we're good now, I still need her like I need my next breath.

My phone vibrating with a news alert pulls me out of my thoughts. I programmed it to alert me of every new article about Ashville that pops up online in case the rogue takes another victim we couldn't save. Emily and Malik are talking between themselves, their murmured conversation fading into the background when I see the title of the article.

"Is the lead singer of the band Deadly Sins in love?"

Under it is a photograph with a tattooed dickbag kissing someone that looks exactly like *my* Ava.

WHAT. THE. FUCK.

My stomach takes a dive all the way to my feet as the glass I'm holding explodes into tiny shards. Emily's surprised yelp barely penetrates through the war drum in my ears. The burning spirit carving a path through the fresh cuts in my palm doesn't even phase me because the heat of a thousand suns blisters my skin while I shoot up from the couch like an arrow. I start pacing the room, wearing down the carpet.

I vaguely hear Malik and Emily asking me questions. Still, I can't speak because rage, like no other, ravages me like wildfire. I suck in a jagged breath and stab at the screen. It cracks down the middle, but I still manage to dial Ava's number. It rings as if her phone is turned off. Ice sloshes through my veins with every second that passes.

"Motherfucking fuck!" I bellow and send the phone flying into the wall in front of me. It smacks the middle of the flat-screen TV with a loud thud and leaves a gaping hole behind.

"What the hell, Lo? What happened?" Emily asks from behind me, her eyebrows pinched with worry.

For a second, I lose control of my shift. My fingers extend into claws, and I snap my eyes shut and suck in a deep breath to prevent any more change. I haven't lost control of my body to my wolf like this since I was a kid. Soon, the shift recedes, and my fingers are back to normal. I realize it's because Malik has grabbed my shoulder and started chanting something under his breath. Anger still burns through me, but I no longer feel like I'm out of control.

"Give me your phone," I demand of my sister through gritted teeth.

She takes her phone out of her purse on the couch, unlocks the screen, and extends it to me. I dial Ava's number, but it still rings as if her phone is turned off. I try again and again and again. *Fuck*. I wish I had gotten Chloe's number.

When I give up on calling Ava, my sister picks up my phone from the floor in front of the TV. Surprisingly, even though the screen is cracked in multiple places, the phone is still working, and the moment I catch a glimpse of the distorted picture of Ava with that douchebag, rage threatens to swallow me whole again.

"Shit," Emily says, folding her lower lip between her teeth. "If I'm not mistaken, that's Jude, the lead singer of the band Chloe's boyfriend is in. Ava mentioned one time when we were working that they were going to hook up in their tour bus the night she had her second heart attack." She keeps looking at the screen. "Sheesh, I can't believe she's kissing Jude. He's super hot," she murmurs mostly to herself, but I hear her loud and clear.

My nostrils flare as I whip my head toward her.

"I would shut up if I were you, Em. Unless you want your brother to wring your neck," Malik pipes up as he stalks toward the wet bar and pours whiskey in a tumbler to the brim then shoves it in my chest. "Here, drink this. You need it."

Emily grimaces and shrugs. "Sorry, Lo, but you've got some tough competition; he's hot and a rock star on top of everything."

I down the whiskey in one go and make a beeline for the door.

"Where are you going?" Emily asks, hot on my heels.

"To get Ava, obviously. And to kill a fucking rock star for touching what's mine," I mutter the last part under my breath.

"You need to change; no one is going to let you enter the club like this. You're shirt got splattered with blood when you smashed the tumbler, and your pants are soaked in whiskey," Malik chimes in as he leans on the door frame.

Looking down, I realize he's right, and I charge in the direction of the stairs to get changed and get my mate. I'm going to fuck her so thoroughly I will erase every trace of that fucker from her skin. She's mine, and she's going to remember that.

31

Ava

We spend the first half of the concert dancing, sweating, and having lots of fun, even if the crowd is crazy tonight and is pushing us toward the stage from all directions. They're all screaming the lyrics so loudly my ears are ringing. Even with the earplugs I brought from the hotel, I still feel like my eardrums are bleeding, and my brain is being scraped with sandpaper.

When I can't take it anymore, I tell Chloe I'm not feeling that good, and we weave our way out through the throng of sweaty bodies accompanied by one of the bodyguards. A multitude of people mingle in the small room that serves as the backstage area. They nurse drinks and shoot the shit as they wait for the guys to finish their set. Chloe introduced me to so many people earlier, from the band's publicist to their stylist, and I quickly forgot all of their names.

One of the bodyguards brings in a group of long-legged beautiful girls, their eyes ravenous, glinting with excitement as they shuffle nervously on their feet. I wonder if Chloe and I looked as desperate as them when we were brought to the band's tour bus a few months ago. Who am I kidding? Of course, we did.

The guys finish their set with an encore of their most popular song, and a deafening chorus of screams and applauses erupts from the crowd, making me grind my teeth together and push my fingers into my temples, trying to stop the imminent headache from taking over completely. I don't think I'll attend a concert too soon or ever again if this is what it's going to be like. They're all sweaty and high on the crowd's excitement as they file in from the stage, their bodies brimming with pent-up energy. Chloe squeals as Knox stalks forward, lifts her, and circles her legs around his waist. He pushes his tongue into her mouth and kisses her like she's the last drop of water in the desert and he's dying of thirst.

A small smile lifts the corners of my lips at their enthusiastic display of affection. And I'm not sure why, but the sight gives me a weird tug in my chest as if the mating bond is telling me Logan is close. I ignore it, dismissing it as wishful thinking. I've been missing Logan like crazy, even if I just saw him two days ago. It's disgusting how clingy I'm becoming, but I can't help it.

I turn around, but as soon as I take a step away from the band members, a hand wraps around my wrist, whirls me around, and pulls me into a sweaty, naked chest before soft lips seal over mine.

Cinnamon mixed with fresh sweat. Jude takes advantage of my shocked gasp and pushes his tongue through the seam of my lips, groaning in my mouth. My wolf claws at my mind desperately as the sense of wrongness washes over me, and before I can push Jude away, he's ripped from me and tackled into a wall by a big, muscular body.

Chaos erupts in the next second, and my heart trips over itself at the sight of Logan pinning Jude to the wall with a hand around his throat.

My eyes drink him in ravenously. He looks amazing, with his black jeans and simple dark green Henley hugging his muscular body. And yes, I am aware of the incredulity in the way I'm ogling him while he chokes the life out of the Deadly Sin's lead singer.

The band members and two bodyguards try prying Logan off Jude but are unsuccessful. They don't know they're dealing with a dark creature, not a human. Jude manages to sneak an uppercut, but Logan seems unfazed as he growls menacingly, "She's mine!" at him and starts a round of body shots that would send any man into a coma.

My wolf is pleased with how Logan is claiming me, but I can only imagine how this is going to end if Logan doesn't stop—with a dead singer. I finally snap out of it and take long, purposeful strides toward them, grabbing Logan's shoulder while dodging his vicious elbow that almost breaks my nose as he cocks his fist. I use all my strength to pull him away and scream loudly, *"Stop!"* into his mind. He lets go of Jude, who leans on the wall, sputtering and gasping for air.

Logan's chest is heaving, anger rolling off him in noxious waves as he turns toward me with a crazy, animalistic glint in his eyes. He's more wolf than man as he crushes me to his chest, and his whole body shakes while he bands his arms around me. Immediately, I melt into his punishing hold. The air between us crackles with the singing energy of the mating bond.

"Let her go!" Jude booms as he spits out blood and takes a step toward us, holding his ribs protectively. Nasty bruises are already forming on the side of his face, blood seeping from his split lip.

"Come any closer, and I'll rip your spine out and strangle you with it," Logan growls at him, his tone dripping with menace and iciness. His nostrils flare, and I can sense how close he is to losing control of his shift.

Three more bodyguards come running into the room, joining the other two, and form a protective barrier in front of Jude.

"Are you okay, Ave?" Chloe asks. She pops her head over the side of Logan's shoulder, concern evident in the lines etched around her eyes and in her high-pitched voice.

"Yeah," I answer.

"I'm so sorry, Logan. I didn't know he was going to do that. I didn't kiss him back, I swear."

"Fucking hell, Ava. If you would have shot me with a bullet dipped in aconite, it would have hurt less than seeing you with another man."

His words land like a punch to my solar plexus. Fuck. *"Let's get out of here, and we can talk."*

"I can't move. My wolf will end up shifting and killing him." He dips his head and buries his nose in my hair, inhaling deeply, sending a shiver down my spine and my pulse in overdrive. *"Fuck, baby, how I missed your scent. How I missed you. You're mine, Ava. Fucking mine!"*

"I know, baby. I know," I tell him. *"I'm yours and only yours."*

"Let's get some fresh air, Lo," a voice I vaguely recognize says, and then Malik approaches us and grabs Logan's shoulder. "Hey, Ava. Long time no see." He winks and gives me a roguish grin. "You look beautiful." He looks like sex on legs with his leather duster and silver mane glinting in the overhead lights, his cat-like eyes fixating on me.

Logan glares at him.

My cheeks flush red. "Hey, Malik. Thanks."

"If you don't leave in the next five minutes, we'll call the police, and I'll press charges for assault," Jude bites out, crossing his arms in front of his chest.

"We'll go, right, Logan?" Malik's fingers flex around his shoulder, and Logan finally disentangles himself from me. The dangerous edge in his eyes softens, and his muscles relax as if Malik sedated him through his touch. Then I remember he is a warlock and probably used magic to calm him down.

I step back from Logan's hold. "Wait for me outside. I'll be right back."

"I'm not leaving without you," Logan snaps, his nostrils flaring.

"I'll be right with you, okay?"

Logan's eyes search mine, and then he nods and stalks toward the exit, spine rod straight and fingers clenching and unclenching at his sides as Malik follows closely behind him.

"What the fuck are you waiting for? Aren't you going to escort them out?" Jude snaps at the bodyguards. "And how the motherfucking fuck did they get in? You're useless. All of you."

Two bodyguards stride forward, catching up with Logan and Malik, and when one of them tries to grab Logan's arm, Malik says, "I wouldn't do that if I were you…unless you want to lose that hand. If that's your intention, then by all means." He chuckles darkly, and then they disappear through the door.

"Hey, you okay?" Chloe asks, taking my hand in hers, squeezing lightly with Knox glued to her side.

Swallowing through the heavy knot lodged in my throat, I murmur, "Yeah," and pick a piece of imaginary lint out from the sleeve of my turtleneck. All the groupies are huddled in groups, whispering and pointing at me, and it makes my skin crawl.

"Ava, can we talk?" Jude approaches us with a grimace.

I gasp with a hand over my mouth at the state he's in. He looks like he was run down by a speeding car. His torso is already marred with nasty bruises and caked blood. "Holy shit, Jude. You need to go to a hospital."

"I'm fine," he says, and waves a hand in front of him like it's nothing, but I don't miss the way he winces with the small movement.

Knox glares at him and pulls out his phone to make a call. "You're clearly not, you idiot. I'm calling you an ambulance."

Jude looks at Chloe and Knox. "Can you give us some privacy?"

They both nod and step away, but Chloe's eyes are still fixated on me as she nibbles on her lower lip.

"You shouldn't have kissed me. Especially after what happened outside," I tell Jude. "Wasn't my earlier reaction a clear indication that I didn't want you to kiss me?" My gaze flits over his battered body and then locks with his, now greener against the splash of red and purple.

He shrugs. "It was worth it, but you're right, I shouldn't have...I'm sorry," he says sheepishly and runs a hand over the back of his neck. "But you look so fucking beautiful tonight, and I thought that if I showed you how good we can be together, then you'll leave that guy for me."

"Yeah...you took what you wanted without thinking of the consequences." I sigh and tilt my head slightly. "Are you going to press charges?"

He looks down, ponders my question, and after a while, he says, "I don't know."

"Well, consider this, Jude. If you do press charges against Logan, I'll press charges for sexual assault. I don't know what got into you tonight, but I hope you learned your lesson. Women throw themselves at your feet all the time; just pick one who is willing."

His jaw locks with anger. "But I want *you*."

"Only because you see me as a challenge, and you're used to getting everything you want. Being famous doesn't grant you the privilege to act like that, Jude. Now go sit; I don't think you're supposed to stand right now." I turn on my heel, but he grabs my wrist, making me look over my shoulder.

"I'm coming with you. That guy is dangerous."

I shake his hand off, annoyed. "Do you have a death wish? Logan is going to kill you if he sees you again. Plus, I don't want you near me, and he would never lay a hand on me. Please, just go sit and wait for the doctors to come take a look at you."

"Then, at least take a bodyguard with you."

"Fine," I huff, relenting, knowing he won't let this go until I accept.

"One of you, go with her," Jude commands behind my back.

I don't wait around for any of them, though, and stride directly toward the bathroom on the club floor instead of the door at the back that leads outside, where Logan is waiting for me. I need a moment to compose myself before facing him, and I don't want to stumble upon any of the spectators to the earlier shit show that has become my life by going to the bathroom closest to the backstage room.

People are waiting in line to get out of the club, talking excitedly, some of them slurring their words and barely keeping their balance. I walk past them and descend the stairs to the dark bathroom corridor while the steady beat of the bodyguard's footsteps echoes behind me.

I push the bathroom door open and sigh with relief when I see I'm alone. Ambling to the sink, I splash some ice-cold water onto my face, my mind reeling with tonight's events. Jude acted like a proper *pendejo*. I can't believe he kissed me…again. I have the urge to use bleach as mouthwash to somehow erase him from my skin. Even if Logan pummeled him into the wall and almost killed him, my wolf doesn't deem his actions as enough.

She's been clawing at me to get out since Jude's lips crashed to mine, but I repressed the urge. Getting Logan settled and out of there as soon as possible was my top priority. But now, she demands I deliver my revenge on a platter of snapping teeth and sharp claws. My whole body trembles as I drop my head between my shoulders, white-knuckling the sink.

My wolf's bloodthirsty thoughts are interrupted by the door to the bathroom swinging open, and I lift my head to see the bodyguard with auburn wavy hair cross the threshold, only he is not wearing sunglasses anymore. His pale blue eyes collide with mine.

Why the hell does he seem so familiar?

His eyes, I have seen his eyes before.

But where?

"Um, this is the women's bathroom. What are you doing here? Did something happen?" My eyebrows pull together in concentration as I'm racking my brain, trying to remember where I have seen him before.

He smirks, and a wolfish grin curves his lips. His eyes are like two icicles as his gaze rakes over my body lazily. "I'm here for you, little wolf," he mocks, using the pet name Logan likes to call me.

My heart slams violently to a stop.

Those eyes. He's the rogue.

Adrenaline gives my eyes a fuzzy edge while I frantically scan the room for an escape route, but there isn't one. If I want to get out, I have to pass by him.

He stalks forward and backs me into the tiled wall. I widen my stance, my fists at the ready. I don't exactly know how to fight aside from the brief self-defense lessons I received from Ben, my mother's boyfriend, but I can be a scrappy bitch if needed. He shoots out his hand and grabs my upper arm, his fingers digging viciously into my skin.

"Let me go!" I snap, cock my fist, and send it flying at his face.

He easily dodges and barks out an amused laugh as if I'm no more than an annoying fly. He grabs my wrist and twists it painfully. "Now, where would the fun be in that?"

I let out a strangled cry of pain, and then I dip. My teeth elongate in my mouth, and I sink them as hard as I can into the meaty part of the hand gripping my wrist. I feel his skin breaking and the taste of copper floods my mouth. The rogue lets out a sharp curse and lets me go for a flitting second. That's all I need to drive my knee into his crotch.

"You stupid bitch!" he spews, his features twisted in a grimace as he grabs his junk protectively.

My victory cry is short-lived because the moment I try to push past him, he grabs me by the throat and slams the back of my head into the wall so hard I feel the tiles shatter and something wet and sticky coat the hair at the nape of my neck. My world tilts upside down.

I try to contact Logan through our mental link. *"Logan, the rogue, he's – "*

Before I can finish my sentence, blankness washes over me.

32

Logan

"Would you stop pacing already? You're giving me a fucking headache," Malik says with a bored expression, leaning on the side of my truck.

I scowl at him and check my new phone's screen for the umpteenth time. Fifteen minutes have passed since we were escorted outside the club, and Ava still hasn't come out. "What the hell is taking her so long?" My breath plumes in front of my face with how cold it is, but I don't feel it. The anger burning through me is red hot and all-consuming.

He shrugs. "I don't know. She might smooth things over with that dickbag. He could press charges against you."

My jaw ticks at Malik's words. "Fuck it, I'm going after her," I grit out and stalk toward the back entrance of the club.

"I can't let you go in," one of the asshole bodyguards who escorted us earlier says, blocking the entrance. He crosses his arms in front of his chest and squares his shoulders. He does it like it's rehearsed, like it's worked on many people before. Sure, he's big and muscly, but he has nothing on my frame and still has to look up when he addresses me. Even though he tries to play it off as if he isn't afraid, I don't miss the way his Adam's apple bobs in his throat when I throw him a scathing glare.

"Just give her five more minutes," Malik tells me from my back, tone coaxing. "If she doesn't show up, we'll go back inside."

I snap my eyes shut, willing patience to come to me, but it's futile. I've been running on fumes since the moment I saw that goddamn photo. And then the universe had to take a step further and make me witness that piece of shit kissing her right in front of my eyes. It filled me with such rage, such contempt that I was ready to kill every single person in that room, consequences be damned. My wolf had gone off the deep end, and if I didn't have Ava in my arms, tethering me to reality, I would have shifted right then and there and left a blood bath in my wake.

Even after everything, my chest is still an open wound, the sting of jealousy burning brighter and cutting deeper than anything I have ever felt before. I clench and unclench my fingers to pass the brutal time, my bloody knuckles screaming in protest.

All of a sudden, dread fills my veins. It coils beneath my ribcage and wraps around my lungs until I can no longer breathe. It's pure, unadulterated fear, and it takes a few seconds for my mind to catch up and realize that it's not mine; it's Ava's. I can feel it through the mating bond as if it were mine.

Then I hear her voice in my head: *"Logan, the rogue, he's —"* She doesn't finish the sentence. Terror grips me by the throat with sharp claws.

"Ava, baby, what happened?" I send back to her.

She doesn't answer. "Ava?"

Nothing.

Fuck. Fuck. Fuck. Fuck.

"I'm coming for you, baby," I tell her.

Still nothing.

Immediately, I push the bodyguard out of my way. He lets out a sound of protest and grabs my shoulder to stop me. As Malik warned him before, it is a horrible decision on his part. Blinded by the fear of not getting to Ava in time, I send my fist flying in an uppercut. His eyes bulge out of his head in surprise, and before he can make a sound, his body is sent backward into the air, slams into the side of a parked SUV, and his head smashes the passenger window. He instantly blacks out, falling in a heap on the asphalt, blood pooling beneath him. Malik swears loudly, jogs to get to the bodyguard, and crouches next to his unconscious body to check for a pulse. I don't stay around to find out if I killed him or not. I need to find Ava.

Ripping open the door, I start running, turning right toward the stairs leading to the backstage room. In my desperation, I almost miss her vanilla and caramel scent. With how strong it is, I can tell she's been here only minutes before. I turn on my heel and follow it back into the club, pass the back door I entered through, and make a beeline to the bathrooms on the underground floor.

A horrible feeling churns in my gut as I barrel into the women's bathroom and take in the blood smeared on the dented tiles in front of me. I don't have to get close to know it's Ava's. I can smell it from here. What I assume is her phone is smashed to pieces on the floor, and I catch something in the corner of my eye. It's a message scribbled in Ava's blood on the mirror.

'Eye for an eye. Heart for a heart. How does it feel to know I have her?'

My knees buckle under me, and the blistering fear that I will find Ava in the same state as Josh seeps into every crack and crevice of my chest until I choke on it.

33

Ava

Temples throbbing fiercely, I try to pry my eyes open, but the only movement I manage is that of fluttering eyelids. The sensation throws me back to the day I woke up in Logan's basement. There's something different now, though. I still smell wood and pine sap, but it's overpowered by a repulsing odor carving a path down my throat. As if someone decided to make a soup of burned hair, coagulated blood, and melted plastic with a healthy dose of soured meat on top. It's so foul, I have to swallow down the urge to projectile vomit.

C'mon, Ava, open your damn eyes! When I finally do, I realize I am tied up in another cabin. And this time, instead of hanging from the ceiling, heavy, fiery chains pin me to a wooden chair as the skin on my wrists and ankles sizzles under them.

It's me…the sickening smell is coming from me.

I struggle against the restraints, and my own strangled scream obliterates every coherent thought. The pain is so intense I feel like I might black out again. Taking a few deep breaths in and out, I let my eyes wander over the room I'm in, trying to distract myself from the blinding pain. The windows are all boarded shut, and a thick layer of grime covers the floor and wooden walls. The only pieces of furniture are the chair I'm tied to and a big old dusty bookshelf on my left, pushed against the wall and lined with huge jars and lit candles. The jars all look the same, filled with some sort of liquid, and something is floating inside them.

¡Mierda! Is that? Are those…are those organs? No, not just organs… they're all hearts.

Jesus fucking Christ.

Tearing my eyes from the gruesome picture before me, I look down. There's a weird drawing under my chair on the floorboards, a red circle filled with intricate symbols, and I'm sitting right in the middle of it.

The sound of shoes slapping against the creaking floor reaches my ears before a woman enters. She's wearing a long, dark blue dress under a black cloak—the same cloak I saw in the woods when Tony was torn to pieces. She must be the witch.

"Ah, you're finally awake," she says. The first thing I notice about her are the inky black tendrils covering every available surface of skin as though her veins are filled with tar-like blood. Even her face is full of them. The strange veins seem to be shifting and moving under her skin with a mind of their own. She's holding an ancient copper bowl with symbols etched on it, and she saunters toward me, her white as-snow hair flowing at her back.

"What do you want from me?" I manage to grit out in a scratchy voice.

She pins me with a sinister smile. It's unsettling how wrong it looks on her face. And you know that saying, "Eyes are the mirror of the soul"? Well, hers are…empty. Said soulless eyes lock with mine. "Just your blood…for now. Then your heart, of course." She lifts the sleeve of my mesh turtleneck roughly and takes out a knife from the holster hanging from the belt at her waist. The sharp blade slashes through the skin of my forearm, right over a fresh cut that's oozing blood.

Muttering a sharp curse, I struggle against the chains holding me to the chair, but the intense pain explodes through my nerve endings again as the metal burns through another layer of my skin. I still immediately, taking jagged breaths through a clenched jaw. A bead of sweat gets stuck in my eyelashes, and I blink it away.

"I wouldn't do that if I were you. The chains are made out of pure silver." Shadows obscure half of her face, and the other is illuminated by the flickering candles. She places the bowl under my arm to catch the blood flowing from the deep gash in rivulets, painting the inside of the bowl red.

My nostrils flare. "Why are you doing this? Why kill so many innocent people?"

She shrugs nonchalantly with a bored expression. "It's nothing personal. I just needed their hearts for a spell."

My eyes widen in shock. "All that for a spell?"

She smiles like a cat. "No, not just any spell. A demon summoning one."

"Why would you want to summon a demon?" I sputter.

No, seriously, why would anyone want that?

She looks at the blood that's still dripping in the bowl, eyes fixated on every drop as she speaks. "Well, you see. I was in love once. Hundreds of years ago." She pauses. Sighs as if reminiscing her long-lost life, and then her dead gray eyes lock with mine. "Me and Beelzebub were happy for many years until those foul archangels came and took him back to Hell. They imprisoned him in blessed chains so he could never escape. I have waited five hundred years to come back and break him out." She turns her head and bellows toward the door she came through, "She's awake, Clayton. Bring your phone."

When the bowl is half full, she takes a few steps to my right and crouches, dips her fingers into my blood, and starts to draw another circle on the floor the same size as the one beneath my chair. The sound of a door opening and closing echoes through the cabin, and then heavy footsteps follow before the rogue wolf prowls into the room like a predator cornering its next meal.

"Look who decided to join the party. How's that pretty little head of yours?" Clayton taunts, wrapping my jaw in a punishing grip.

"Fuck you!" I shake his hold before I spit at him. My saliva hits his cheek and runs down his face.

"You fucking, bitch," the rogue sneers. He wipes at my saliva with his fingers. In the next second, the back of his hand collides with the side of my face, sending my head flying to the side.

Despite the exploding pain, I straighten my head and give him a bloody smile. "That's all you got?"

His fingers clench at his sides, and he bends his knees to be at eye level with me. "You're going to regret disrespecting me like that, you stupid cunt," he spews, and his big hand wraps around my throat, cutting my air supply and crushing my windpipe, making my eyes bulge in my head.

"Stop playing with the sacrifice and call her mate already. She can't talk if you crush her larynx, you idiot," the witch admonishes him from my right, still painting with my blood on the floor.

The rogue finally lets me go with a sly smile and an icy glare. "This is how this is going to go. I'm going to call your mate, and you're going to convince him to come get you."

Panic trashes beneath my skin with the force of a hurricane. I can't let them lure Logan here. They're going to kill him. "No, just leave Logan alone. You have me. You don't need him." I swallow hard. "Please."

"Actually, for the spell to be completed, I need the hearts of two fated mates," the witch tells me as she lifts from her crouch and judges her bloody circle. "Perfect," she mumbles to herself.

Clayton taps on the screen and then puts it on speaker as it rings.

Logan answers on the first ring. "Who is this?" he asks.

The rogue brings the phone to my lips and mouths at me, "Talk to him."

I press my lips in a thin line and give him a defiant glare. Silence stretches between us, and then Logan's voice breaks through. "Ava?" He pauses before inhaling sharply. "Ava, is this you? Where are you, baby? Please talk to me." His voice is coated in desperation, and I can almost see the anguish etched on his face as if he's in front of me.

"She's right here," the rogue answers after a few moments and pushes his thumb into the deep gash in my forearm.

My eyes roll to the back of my head, and I bite my tongue so hard I draw blood, but I refuse to scream and do his bidding.

"Oh, you wanna play, little bird? Let's hear you sing." A sadistic smirk lifts the corner of his lips, and something flashes in his eyes before he takes out a knife and stabs it into the middle of my right thigh.

This time, I can't stop the bellowing scream that rips from my lungs as he twists the blade. The metal slices through skin and bone and burns my flesh from the inside out. The acrid smell of charred meat—my own charred meat—coats my lungs, and the fiery pain is so intense I throw up in my mouth.

"AVA! What the fuck did you do to her?" Logan snaps into the phone.

"I just stabbed her with a pure silver blade, and I'll do worse if you don't listen carefully to my demands."

"What do you want?" Logan seethes.

"I'm going to send you a location, and you'll come here alone. If I sense you're not, she'll be dead before you can lay eyes on her. And make it fast. I don't like to wait. For every ten minutes that pass, I will carve a new mark into her skin and make her sing like the pretty little bird she is."

Logan's voice softens, and I can hear his ragged breaths through the phone speaker. "Ava? Hang tight, baby. I'm coming to get you, all right?"

"No, Logan! Don't! They're going to k—" I try to warn him, but Clayton ends the call abruptly and twists the knife again, eliciting another agony-filled scream from me.

He curls his upper lip in a sneer. "You. Only. Speak. When. I. Allow. You. To."

34

Ava

There are eighty-six scratches and dents in the wooden wall in front of me. I would know. I've counted them all. Over and over again. True to his word, Clayton started carving me up like a Halloween pumpkin the moment he ended the call with Logan. Only he grew bored waiting ten full minutes between cuts, so every three minutes, he sinks his blade into me, taking a fresh piece of flesh. The pain scorches me from the inside out. Yet, I don't make a sound.

Seventy-nine.

Eighty.

Eighty-one.

Eighty-t-two —

Clayton carves into my right cheek with meticulous, slow movements. I can tell this is definitely not the first time he's inflicting this type of torture on someone. He's such an expert on the matter he could write a book. I would be impressed if it wasn't my skin and muscle that his blade splits like a hot knife going through butter. The fiery imprint it leaves behind locks my jaw as my vision blurs slightly.

I breathe in and out shallowly as I stare blankly at the wall. I screamed the first five times he marked me, but now I have come to welcome the pain in some capacity. At least, it means that I'm still alive. Moreover, it distracts me from the silver chains burning through the skin on my wrists and ankles. I also don't want to give this bastard the satisfaction of coaxing a reaction out of me. I can tell he gets off on it. The only problem is that when I don't make a sound, he takes it as a challenge, and every time, the blade sinks deeper and deeper.

Eighty-three.

Eighty-f-four.

I think he just hit the bone. This time, I can't stop the strangled whimper that tumbles free. His lip twitches in the corner of my eye, so I know he heard it.

Eighty-five.

Eighty-six.

One.

I let out a trembling sigh of relief through my nose when the blade stops its torturous glide through my flesh.

"Would you look at that. An hour has already passed," Clayton says. "Time flies when you're having fun, huh, little bird?"

It's only us in the room. The witch left after she drew some more symbols on the walls with my blood and brought in another chair, which she placed in the middle of the bloody circle to my right.

"I have to give it to you, little bird. You're tougher than you look." He bends slightly and traces the mark he just carved from my ear lobe to the corner of my lips with his calloused finger. His touch is rough, and I have to bite my tongue to keep from screaming in pain. "Such a shame Marion needs your heart. Otherwise, I would keep you as my pet. Carve your pretty skin and fuck you whenever I want."

I pull away from his touch, swallowing the bile that rises in my throat at his repulsive words. My wolf growls in my head loudly. She wants to shred him to pieces for what he's done to us. "What's in it for you?" I grit out, not being able to stop my curiosity, and wince at the way the skin on my cheek stretches as I move my lips. "I understand her motive. She wants to be reunited with her love, but why would *you* help her?"

His hands fist at his sides. "Your mate killed my sire, and ever since, I've been biding my time to get my revenge. After I kill him, I will take my rightful place as an Alpha of his pack. I'll take everything from him just like he took everything from me."

So he was sired by another wolf shifter's bite. No wonder he is crazy. Or maybe he was already a psychopath before he was bitten—one of those who like to kill animals before escalating to human beings.

I feel the tug of the mating bond. *Fuck.* Logan is here. I prayed he wouldn't come after all…that he didn't care enough about me so he wouldn't be in danger. Clayton straightens, lifts his nose in the air, and sniffs it. In the next second, a wolfish grin takes over his features, and he leaves the room with hurried steps. There's a struggle outside before the cabin's front door opens and closes with a loud thud, two sets of heavy footsteps coming my way.

Logan enters the room with Clayton at his back, who's keeping him at gunpoint. My heart flutters at seeing Logan before me. He's naked, so he must have shifted to get here, and even in the state I'm in, the mating bond purrs in my chest like a cat. My eyes flit to Clayton; he has a split lip, and blood trickles from the side of his head. I wish Logan would have done more damage.

"Ava," Logan's voice is barely above a whisper, and a ripple of shock passes through his features the moment our gazes collide, and he sees the state I'm in.

He hurries his steps to get to me, but Clayton stops him when he says, "One more step, and I'll put a silver bullet into your brain. And I'm going to let you in on a little secret: all the bullets are dipped in aconite."

Logan's eyes blaze with fury, transforming to burnished gold. A muscle thrums in his jaw as he lets his eyes roam over every inch of my body. When they snap back to mine, they flash with a promise, as if he filed every single injury and will deliver a hundredfold in return. "What did you do to her, you sick fuck?" he growls, his fists clenching and unclenching at his sides. In the next moment, he spins on his heels and sends one said fist flying in an uppercut that catches Clayton by surprise. Spit and blood dart from his mouth as his head snaps backward, and he loses his balance.

"Enough!" Marion, the witch, screams loudly as she appears in the doorway and extends her hand in front of her. A blast of her power sends Logan flying through the air. His big frame hits the wall behind me with a loud thump and cracks the wood. "I don't have time for your nonsense." She takes the gun from Clayton, pointing it at me. "Do as I say, or I'll shoot your mate. Do you understand?"

Logan pushes up from the floor, rubs the back of his head, and nods, his nostrils flaring.

"Good, now go sit down." She lifts her chin and points it to the vacant chair at my right.

Logan cuts through the room and plops down on the chair, his eyes never leaving mine. "I'm going to get you out of here," he tells me.

Marion huffs. "Don't make her promises you can't keep."

She passes the gun to Clayton, who keeps it pointed at my head. She then takes four thick silver chains from the dusty bookshelf and strides toward Logan, securing his wrists and ankles. His skin sizzles the moment the metal makes contact with it. Logan doesn't even flinch, though. The only indication that he feels some sort of pain is that of a vein bulging on the side of his forehead and the way his jaw ticks.

"Oh, I'm fully intending to keep my promise," he tells the witch, his tone low, menacing. "And I can make you one right now, too. You're both going to pay for this."

Marion cackles as she straightens, lifting a mocking eyebrow at him. "I'd like to see you try, mutt." She walks to the dusty bookshelf, picks up the copper bowl, and glares at Clayton, who's leaning on the wall in front of us with a smug look on his face. "Bring my grimoire."

He simply nods and strides out of the room. Marion goes back to where Logan is seated and takes out the knife she used to cut me earlier. The moment the blade slashes through Logan's forearm, fury blisters my insides like napalm, and my wolf goes off the deep end as I struggle against the silver restraints, not even caring about the intense pain and the metal singeing me. A menacing growl rumbles out of me with the promise of bloodshed.

Logan swears under his breath. *"Ava, I'm okay, baby. Stop struggling; you're only hurting yourself."*

His words are able to cut through my wolf's haze of rage, and I immediately stop moving as our gazes lock. I let out a shuddering breath. In the momentary silence without screaming or melting flesh, I feel beads of sweat go down my face and between my shoulder blades like tears.

Marion collects the blood she needs from Logan into the copper bowl and drops to her haunches in between the bloody circles. She starts painting another intricate symbol on the floorboards between our chairs, interconnecting the circles like a three-way Ven diagram as Clayton returns to the room, holding a leather-bound, ancient-looking book.

She stands, wipes her bloody fingers on her dress, and takes the book from Clayton's outstretched hand. "Bring the hearts. Take them out and place them over the symbol in the middle. Carefully, don't smudge the blood."

Like a good little soldier, Clayton does as she instructed, and with each heart that he pulls out of a jar, my stomach constricts painfully. I wonder which one of those is Tony's.

While Clayton is busy with the hearts, Marion arranges some unlit candles around the circles. As soon as he finishes placing all of the hearts in between our chairs, he steps back, and Marion flits through the pages of the book until she settles on one. "I can't wait to see you, my love," she murmurs and then starts chanting loudly in a foreign language that sounds like a combination of Latin and Hebrew, the black veins under her skin pulsing with power and shifting relentlessly.

As her verses reach a crescendo, giant flames flicker to life from the candles, and the floor starts shaking as if we're in the middle of an earthquake. Deep crevices form in the floorboards and walls. They bypass the symbols completely as wood splinters fly everywhere and the air thickens with a suffocating, black fog.

The witch turns to Clayton and says, "Now." Then she continues chanting.

He prowls toward me with a predatory gait, and when he reaches my chair, he takes the silver knife out of its sheath strapped to his belt. His demented gaze flits to Logan. "You're going to watch as I carve her heart out of her chest just as I watched you kill my sire in cold blood. You're going to feel what it's like to lose everything."

I'm already lightheaded with how much blood I've lost, and my heart thunders in my ears with the realization that this is it. This is how I die. At least I had a few more months to live on my terms. At least I found my fated mate.

"Ava, look at me, baby! Give me those beautiful greens."

Clayton plunges the blade into the center of my chest.

As blood floods my mouth, I look one last time at Logan, memorizing his striking features. The slope of his eyebrows over his honey eyes that are now filled with anguish and swimming with regret. The fullness of his wicked lips and the hard set of his jaw. "I wish we had more time," I whisper as a tear crests over my eyelashes and rolls down my cheek.

"No, no, no, Ava! Stay with me, baby! PLEASE! Don't you dare close your eyes!" Logan pleads, his voice raw, desperate. "AVA!" He struggles against the restraints, his skin sizzling. "AVA!"

I try to keep my eyes open, I do, but my eyelids are so damn heavy. "I'm sorry," I murmur brokenly.

I don't want to die…

I think I'm in love with you.

The last thing I hear is Logan letting out a sound so visceral, so full of agony it hurts more than the blade cutting into me.

35

Logan

I have never been more helpless. Never more than in the moment I watch the blade go through Ava's chest.

The image of her eyelids fluttering closed is forever seared into my brain. I cling with desperation to every shallow breath she takes into her lungs as I struggle against my restraints, the silver not letting me shift. I grit my teeth and push through the white-hot pain, ignoring how the chains burn through muscle and bone. I finally manage to break my right hand and slide it out of the thick silver chain.

Fuck. She's losing so much blood.

Too little too late, Kaiden pops out of thin air behind the witch. She stops chanting and turns around. Her hands lift into the air and blasts Kaiden with power from both palms. He blocks them easily, his eyes churning with his own power—flecks of gold swirling with red.

"W-what are y-you?" she stutters, and her eyes widen in fear.

Kaiden disappears again and appears right in front of her. He easily twists her neck, breaking it with a sickening crack, and her body thuds lifelessly on the floor. The rogue whips his head around, and the moment he senses the unadulterated power coming from Kaiden, he lets go of the knife still embedded into Ava's chest, shifts, and takes off through the door on four legs. The glass from a window shatters as he jumps through it, making his escape.

"What the fuck took you so long?" I bellow while I manage to free my other hand.

Kaiden crouches and helps me with the chains around my ankles. "The witch used strong blood magic for the wards. It took longer than we anticipated for Malik to break through them."

I immediately slice through the small space separating me from Ava and take off her restraints, not caring about the silver chains scorching my palms and fingers. I pull her from the chair into my arms and tap her cheek softly. "Ava, baby. Wake up! C'mon, I need to see those beautiful greens."

Fuck. Fuck. Fuck.

She doesn't even stir, her breaths becoming shallower and her heartbeats fading with every second that passes. Like an anchor, my heart sinks to the bottom of my feet, and I swallow through the heavy knot in my throat. "Where the fuck is Malik? Ava is dying."

"I'm here," he says as he barrels into the room. He swears sharply under his breath when his eyes find Ava. "Put her down on the floor. Kaiden, I'll need to pull power from you to heal her."

Kaiden nods as I gently lay Ava on the floor. We all kneel beside her, and Malik's eyes find mine. "You'll have to take the knife out; I can't heal her with it still embedded into her chest. On three, two, one."

The second I pull the knife out, blood shoots from the wound, and Malik covers it with pressure from his right hand to staunch the blood while he grabs Kaiden's forearm and begins chanting. The black magic swirls into his veins and thickens the air.

But Ava's heart stops beating. The silence screams a panic like I have never known. I can't think. I can't breathe. If she dies, I'll die with her because I can't accept living in a world where Ava is no more. I close my eyes and pray to a God I don't even believe in to give her back to me.

Then, her chest rises with the softest inhale. I hang to that tiny flutter that ensues like to a lifeline. Her heart starts beating rhythmically again. Stronger. Surer. The gaping wound in her chest pieces itself together right under my eyes. I feel like I'm taking my first breath of air as Ava's cuts and bruises disappear before my eyes. The tears clouding my vision are now spilling over my cheeks. I haven't cried since the day I found out my father died. I don't even care that Malik and Kaiden are here to witness my breakdown.

When Malik finishes healing her, I pull Ava against my chest, my trembling fingers hanging on to her like she's my salvation. Someone is speaking to me, but I can't hear them as the terror filters through my veins and pulls me down, down, down. It's never-ending, like falling into an abyss. I sink into it and let my wolf take over. He's the only one who can fully protect Ava. No one is going to lay another finger on her. No one is ever going to take our mate from us.

Everything fades.

There's only black.

The distant echoes of footsteps chip at the haze of madness I drowned in bit by bit. I don't know how much time has passed. It could be an hour or days, but with each choppy inhale that fills my lungs, the blackness dissipates like smoke in the wind, and the cabin slowly comes back into focus.

"C'mon, Lo. We need to get Ava to a bed. She'll be more comfortable," Emily's soft voice snaps me out of the deep end.

I look at her, confused. "Em, what are you doing here?"

"Kaiden called me. Your wolf wouldn't let her go. You almost killed

Malik when he tried to take her from your arms so he could heal you."

My eyebrows crinkle. "What? I don't remember any of it."

She crouches next to me. "C'mon," she repeats. "I brought you some clothes. I can take Ava while you get dressed, and we'll bring her home so she can heal properly and rest." Her tone is soft, and worry is etched into the lines around her eyes.

"Don't touch her," I growl when Emily outstretches her hand toward Ava.

Emily puts her palms up in a show of surrender. "Okay," she says soothingly as if talking to a rabid animal. I guess, to some extent, she is. "Just come to the car, and I'll drive you both home."

"The rogue escaped," I tell her as I push up from the floor and carry Ava to the front door of the rickety cabin. My eyes skitter over the place, and I notice that the witch's body is no longer lying lifelessly on the floor. "We need to have everyone from the pack on alert."

"Dominic immobilized him as soon as he jumped out of the window, and Malik put a binding spell on him. Dominic is on his way to put him in one of the cages in the basement you use for the Conclave. He said you would want to be the one to kill the rogue."

An icy gust of wind ruffles my hair when I step out of the cabin, and I pull Ava closer, concerned that she might feel the cold. The sky is a deep crimson as dawn breaks, casting a warm glow on the thick canopy of trees. The rundown cabin the rogue and the witch used to hide is only at a half an hour drive from our community, and it's embarrassing no one fucking noticed or found them until now. Though, with the wards hiding it in plain sight, we couldn't have sensed they were inside.

Malik and Kaiden are waiting for us near my truck and Kaiden's Escalade. Malik's throat is all bruised, the imprint of my hand standing out on his taupe-hued skin. My shoulders slump, and shame slams into me. I swallow the heavy knot in my throat as our gazes lock. "I'm so sorry, man."

"S'ok, I should have known better than to approach you when you got all feral and growled at us like a cornered animal."

Emily gets a blanket out of the back of my truck and approaches me with long strides, carefully draping it over Ava and me. It takes everything in me not to snarl at her despite the fact she is my sister and my Beta.

"Thank you to all of you," I tell them and get in the back of the car, careful not to jolt Ava too much. She seems so small. So fragile. I close my eyes and listen to her every inhale and heartbeat as my sister opens the door, settles into the driver seat, and starts the car.

36

Ava

If this is what being dead feels like, I'm not mad at it. An earthy, woodsy smell envelops me, and I no longer feel that gaping pit of sadness in the center of my chest. I feel whole. Complete. At utter peace with myself and the world.

Huh, would you look at that? I think I'm in Heaven. At least it feels like it.

My eyes pop open, and I blink a few times, the bright light slanting through the windows, blinding me momentarily. The wall in front of me is made of glass and offers a breathtaking view of the sprawling pine forest and the snowed mountain peaks in the distance.

It takes a few seconds before I can make out the room I'm in. I lift my head and realize I'm lying on a king-sized bed in a large bedroom, but I can't move. I'm tangled in between Logan's arms and legs. He's holding me like he's afraid I might disappear into thin air, his full lips parted slightly in relaxed slumber.

Swallowing hard, I bring my hand to the center of my chest and run it over the spot where Clayton stabbed me with the silver knife. The memory of the excruciating pain folds my lungs in two. But I can't feel anything aside from the skin being slightly raised. My eyebrows pull together, and I bring my fingers to my right cheek where I should have a nasty cut, but again…there's nothing aside from a line of slightly puckered skin.

How is this even possible? Well, I guess if I'm dead, then I shouldn't have any wounds, right? But what is Logan doing here if I'm dead? Does that mean he is, too?

No, no, no, no, no, no, no.

A sinking feeling of desperation and then a sob, tears rolling down my cheeks.

Logan's eyes fly open. "Ava, what's wrong, baby? What happened?" His voice is gravelly and rough from sleep. He disentangles himself from me, pushes up on his elbows, and frantically searches the room.

"Y-you're dead. You're not s-supposed t-to b-be d-dead. I know I died, but I hoped that you would save yourself somehow."

He pulls me into his arms with a deep sigh of relief and kisses my forehead. "None of us are dead."

Sniffling, I saw my lower lip between my teeth. "We're not?"

"No, baby." He chases my tears with the pad of his thumb, wiping at my cheeks gently.

"Oh," I whisper. I take a deep breath and let it out through my nose. "But, how? I don't understand. He carved me up, and I don't feel any pain."

"After you blacked out, Kaiden arrived and killed the witch. Then Malik healed you. It took a long time for them to break through the wards the witch put around the cabin. Longer than we expected."

"Malik healed me?"

"Yeah, I told you about his healing abilities."

"Oh….so, is it over?"

"It is. The witch is dead, and we imprisoned the rogue."

"Okay…that's good," I mumble. The sense of relief filling my veins gives me whiplash, though. I need a little more time to come to the terms that it's finally over. We're safe. Both of us. Thank God, baby Jesus, and every other deity out there. The tension in my muscles leaves bit by bit as I inhale a lungful of calming air, but then I remember the concert, and I jackknife into a sitting position, startling Logan. "Fuck! Chloe! I need to let her know I'm okay. She's probably freaked out of her mind."

Logan pulls me back into his embrace. "She doesn't know the rogue took you. I asked our hacker to message Chloe pretending to be you. He told her you spent the night with me."

My brain is too scrambled to think of the implications of that. At least she knows I'm safe. Still, I probably have at least a hundred messages from her. "Where are we?"

"At my house. We're in my bedroom."

Looking again toward the floor-to-ceiling windows, I say, "The view is stunning. I love it."

"I know. Me too," he says, but his burning gaze fixates on my face. Cheesy, lovely man. "God, Ava. I have never been more scared in my entire life. I thought I lost you." His voice breaks while tremors wrack his body. My wolf and the mating bond are purring beneath my ribs at our close proximity. The desire I feel for him gets a new meaning when the euphoria that I'm alive in Logan's arms registers. It makes my clit throb, hard. It also doesn't help that Logan is only wearing a pair of boxers, his glorious, taut muscles on display, rendering me stupid.

For a moment, I consider jumping his bones, but then I remember how we left things before Clayton kidnapped me, so I say instead, "Listen, Logan…about the whole Jude situation—" I don't get to finish the sentence because Logan traps me under his massive frame, with my wrists pinned above my head as he settles in between my legs. He thrusts his hard-as-steel erection over my aching clit. Instantly, I'm made aware of the fact that I'm not wearing anything underneath his T-shirt.

"W-what are y-you doing?" I stutter out. "We should talk."

His half-lidded gaze is molten gold as his right hand lowers, fists my T-shirt, and yanks it off me, discarding it on the floor in tatters, while his other hand keeps me bound against the bed.

"Reminding you who you belong to," Logan growls before he dips and licks at the seam of my lips. He pushes down his boxers. The moment his velvety skin meets my soaked slit, my eyes roll in the back of my head. The mind-numbing friction he creates as he slides his cock up and down over my clit is almost too much to bear. I can't stop the loud moans that escape my mouth.

He lowers his face to mine. We are practically sharing the same breath as he nips my lower lip until he draws blood. A guttural sound of pleasure leaves his chest when he pushes his tongue into my mouth, gliding it against mine expertly. *"Your pussy is dripping all over my cock, baby,"* he rasps into my mind.

My pulse skyrockets with every thrust of Logan's hips, the friction between our bodies, and the way he feasts on my mouth, bringing me to the brink of orgasm.

"Were you this wet when he kissed you? Did your pussy beg for his cock like it begs for mine?" Alarm bells go off in my head at Logan's clipped tone. I know I should say something…anything, but I'm about to break at the seams, and all words are lost to me. All of a sudden, Logan stops thrusting, his lips no longer touching mine.

I let out a frustrated whimper. "No, Logan! I was about to come."

Before I can answer his question, I'm flipped on my belly with a heavy hand between my shoulder blades, pinning me to the bed.

"Jesus, Ava…when I saw him kissing you, I wanted to kill him, to shift and tear him to pieces and then bathe in his blood. You don't know how much that hurt me…seeing you with someone else. It fucking destroyed me."

"I'm sorry, Logan," I cry out. His raging emotions travel through our mating bond, and I feel his turmoil as if it were my own.

"Do you feel anything for him?"

"No, I—"

"Did your pussy get wet when he kissed you?"

"No, Logan. I don't feel anything for him. He kissed me. I didn't kiss him back—"

"Were you going to fuck him that night your heart stopped?"

"Y-yes."

"Why didn't you tell me about it before going to the hotel?" he roars.

Tears stream down my face, wetting the pillow under my smooshed face. "I-I didn't think it was important…I never felt anything for Jude."

"Did you fuck him?"

"No, I swear…We only kissed once, that's all, and it was months ago."

Logan lets out a shuddering breath at my words. Then he plunges two thick fingers inside my drenched pussy, massaging them expertly against my G-spot, making my eyes roll in the back of my head. "Who do you belong to, Ava?"

"Y-you, Logan."

"Who owns this pussy?"

"You! Only you!"

"Mmm. That's my good girl," he breathes gravelly in my ear, his voice drenched in sex, his breath fanning over the side of my neck, eliciting tingles all the way down to my toes. A guttural moan leaves Logan as he sucks his fingers clean before his mouth crashes to mine. He pushes the fat head of his cock at my entrance and slams to the hilt, his balls slapping against my pussy. I only get a few seconds to adjust to his impressive length before he starts fucking me hard.

Pleasure entwines with pain, and Logan doesn't let up. He hammers into me like he's possessed, swallowing with his lips and tongue the loud moans coming out of my mouth, the front of his body fused with my back. Just as I'm about to crest and fall over the edge, Logan stops, denying me another orgasm. I cry out his name in frustration as tears blur my vision and roll down my cheeks. Clearly, he isn't done punishing me, but I don't know how much more of this I can take.

I feel empty as he pulls out of me. With equal parts of irritation and curiosity, I crane my neck a little more to the side to gauge his next move. Honestly, with the raw pain that filtered through our bond, I expect him to walk away. What I'm not prepared for is the moment he palms his cock before he starts pumping his hand furiously over his shaft. I lick my lips at the bead of precum dripping down my ass, hungry for him, the eroticism of this moment sucking all the air from my lungs.

He looks like a sex god, jaw slack, taut muscles, and bulging veins while he bites into his lower lip, his eyes at half-mast, watching me. His expression smolders as he comes with my name on his lips. Thick ropes of cum jut out and paint my lower back and ass cheeks as his heated gaze travels the length of my body in a slow, sensual perusal, setting my blood on fire.

"Fuck, baby, you look so hot covered in my cum," he growls, wipes up his cum with his hand, and pushes it into my pussy with two of his fingers. He continues to move them inside me, slow and maddening, keeping me just out of reach of the high I'm so desperate for.

I push back on his hand, seeking more friction, and he purrs, "Is there something you need?"

"Fuck me! Please, Logan, please, I need you!" I snap my eyes shut, unable to take the assault on my senses anymore. I need to come like I need my next breath.

Suddenly, Logan flips me onto my back. "Open your eyes, baby.

Give me those beautiful greens." His tone is soft now.

With a loud sniff, I open them. Our gazes hook and snare. My breath catches in my throat at the mix of adulation, lust, and tenderness brimming in his. He has me caged against the mattress, his lips a hair's-breadth away from mine.

Logan's cock twitches against my slit, making me whimper loudly. This time, he enters me slowly as if trying to savor every single point of new, delicious contact. An inferno blazes through me at the way his thumb circles my engorged clit, with the perfect amount of pressure. His eyes never leave mine, and our connection runs deeper than ever before; our pleasure intensified tenfold by the way we feel everything the other does through our mating bond. Our chests move in unison, heart to heart, beating at the same maddening rhythm.

"You own me, Ava. Every piece of me. Every piece of my heart. I love you, and I can't live without you."

His words bounce between us and sear into my soul while breathing life into my lungs at the same time. "I love you too, Logan. So much it hurts," I say earnestly, and we lose ourselves in each other's rapture, my admission pushing us both over the edge into an abyss of ecstasy.

37

Ava

Heart raw and cheeks streaked with old and fresh tears, I look through the window, watching the city pass by in a blur from the passenger seat of Logan's truck. We just left Tony's funeral service, but I couldn't bear to see him being lowered into the ground, so we skipped the burial at the cemetery. Emily went for both of us.

So many people showed up at the service. I'm not surprised Tony was popular with his kind nature and effervescent personality. I cried and laughed as I listened to the speeches. Almost all of them were filled with funny stories, my favorite being those his mother reminisced. Even if I'll never be able to forget the way I found Tony on the cold, blood-soaked ground on the night of the Halloween party, I refuse to remember him like that. He will always be my sweet Tony, who knew the exact thing to say to lift my spirit, a sparkling light in the darkness and a force of nature.

Logan's hand squeezes my thigh and pulls me out of my thoughts.

"You okay?" he asks, his voice thick with concern. His amber gaze captures mine briefly before fixating again on the traffic. He's been nothing but perfect since I woke up at his house three days ago, which we didn't leave until today. We spent the whole time in bed, consumed by pleasure and only getting up to shower and eat.

"I just miss him," I sigh and wipe at my cheeks, not used to the feel of the scar under the pad of my finger. Even though Malik managed to heal me, silver is poisonous to wolf shifters, and my face and body will forever be riddled with the scars left behind by Clayton's blade. The ones in the center of my chest, on my thigh, and my right cheek the worst.

I cried when I first saw them, but then Logan wiped my tears with gentle fingers and fucked me in front of a mirror, telling me how beautiful I am to him, more now than ever. How these scars mean that, above all else, I'm a survivor. And how they serve as a reminder that I'm a badass for enduring torture that anyone else in my position would crumble under.

Deep down, I know Logan is right. There will probably be a time in the near future when I won't flinch when catching my reflection in a mirror, but they're still fresh. And as much as I hate being vain, I can't help but wish I didn't have them at all because every time I feel the puckered skin with my fingers, I get a flashback of the blade slicing through my flesh.

Logan nods in understanding. He is battling his own grief. "I have a surprise for you," he says after a few beats of silence.

"Oh, do tell."

He chuckles. "Well, it won't be a surprise anymore if I tell you what it is, now would it? But I think it will be cathartic."

Half an hour later, Logan leads me by the hand through the glass doors of the building Kaiden owns in the most exclusivist neighborhood in Ashville. I've never been to this part of the city before, but apparently, it was a dump when he bought this building, and now it's filled with skyscrapers, coffee shops, fancy restaurants, and high-end stores. The type that I couldn't even afford to make it through the threshold.

"Wow, this place is swanky," I say, marveling at the luxury, finally grasping how influential and rich Kaiden must be. I don't even know what to take in first: the opulent chandelier in the lobby or the marble gracing every surface. "Kaiden must be loaded."

Logan guides me to the elevator, and his warmth seeps into my skin as he places his hand at the small of my back. "He actually owns the whole neighborhood."

I gape at him. "You're kidding me."

"Nope. You should see his car collection, though he prefers riding his fancy-ass bike."

"Sheesh. And I guess when you say bike, you're not talking about the type you would use to ride in a park." The look Logan gives me is answer enough. The elevator doors close after he jabs the minus four button. "So, are you going to tell me why we're here?"

"You'll see in a few minutes."

After we exit the elevator, Logan guides me through some winding hallways until we reach a big steel door. He punches a code into the keypad on the side, and then he approaches what I assume is one of those biometric scanners you only see in spy movies. It scans his eye before the door opens with a soft click.

"Malik put powerful wards on this place, but you can never be too careful, so Kaiden made sure it also has top-notch security," Logan explains when he sees my quirked eyebrow.

A million questions sit on my tongue, but I refrain from bombarding Logan.

He turns to me and cups my jaw in his big hand. His gaze softens, and I inevitably melt under his touch. "As I told you before, the Obsidian

Conclave is responsible for protecting and ensuring the dark creatures follow the rules the Celestial Treaty imposes on us. But at the same time, Kaiden has the obligation to punish anyone who doesn't follow them. When I open the door, you'll see Clayton strapped to a chair, just like I found you. I was going to exert his punishment, but I think for what you endured at the hands of this piece of shit, you should be the one to do it." He pauses, his eyes searching mine before continuing, "If you're not up to it, that's okay. I just thought that today…after Tony's funeral, you would want to get your pound of flesh."

Logan's words imbue me with a sort of nervous energy, but I'm not sure if it's eagerness for revenge or simple panic at Clayton's proximity. Can I do this? Am I capable of taking someone else's life? No, not just someone, a monster. Taking a deep breath in, resolve settles deep into my bones. I want to do this. I want to get revenge for what that motherfucker did to me, Tony, and countless other innocent people.

There must be some spark that Logan sees in my eyes because his lips curve in a dangerous smile, and before I can say anything, he lets go of my face and opens the door. There, in the middle of the room, sits Clayton, secured with silver chains to a chair, gagged. His nostrils flare when our gazes lock.

"Remember, if anything makes you feel uncomfortable, or if you change your mind at any time, we'll go. I can deal with him later," Logan tells me through our mental link.

"I won't be changing my mind. I want to do this."

"You sure?"

I simply nod, and we stride together to the big table on top of which torture instruments are laid in a very orderly manner. Turning my head, I take in the room the Conclave uses to exert the punishment on the unruly dark creatures. It looks like a big underground warehouse, and it even has cages lining the walls with symbols drawn on the floor, all empty now.

Logan picks up something from the table and extends it toward me. I recognize it immediately. It's the knife Clayton used to carve me up. "You have to be careful so the blade doesn't touch you since it's made of pure silver. You can use everything you see on the table here, but I thought you might want to start with this one."

I gingerly take the knife by the hilt from Logan's hand, and with sure, measured steps, I approach Clayton and untie the gag around his mouth. I want to hear him suffer.

"Hello, little bird. I see you managed to survive." Clayton tilts his head, and his eyes fixate on the nasty scar he slashed across my right cheek. The one that runs all the way from the lobe of my ear to the corner of my mouth. It's the one I'm the most insecure about because I can't exactly hide it under clothes. "Remember how beautifully you sang for me?" the bastard croons and has the audacity to smirk at me.

Red-hot rage blinds me, and my knuckles turn white on the hilt before I thrust the blade into his thigh as deep as I can, eliciting a surprised, agony-filled scream from him. Dragging the blade all the way to his knee, I smile—all teeth and sharp edges. He thought I didn't have it in me.

Well, tough shit, hijo de puta, you're going to get exactly what you deserve.
"Who's the little bird now?" I taunt.

"You fucking, bitch!" he spews and struggles against the restraints, but he only manages to dig them further into his skin.

The smell of burned flesh crawls up my nose as I take the blade out and then lodge it right between his legs. He howls like an injured animal as blood flows from the wound in rivulets, and pure satisfaction blooms inside my veins. "What was that? I didn't quite hear you."

"*That's my girl,*" Logan says proudly in my head. "*You're so goddamn sexy right now. You look like a warrior goddess. Fuck, I'm hard as stone, baby.*"

I turn around, and the heated look in Logan's eyes turns my blood to liquid fire. The air between us sparks, and I want to go to him, but instead, I tell him, "Later," and wink before turning around to finish what I started.

"You know what they say about karma," I muse as I take the blade out of Clayton's dick with a wet pop. Lifting my hand, I drag the sharp tip on his cheek until I reach the ear lobe and start carving him the same way he carved me, with slow and meticulous movements, until I reach the corner of his mouth. But I don't stop there; I give him the full Joker smile.

He continues screaming as I glide the blade through skin and muscle. I should probably be worried about how thirsty I am for blood, but for some reason, I simply don't give a fuck. The old Ava would spill her guts all over the cement floor if she saw me right now. Still, I can't bring myself to conjure any feeling of guilt or remorse.

"This is for Tony, *malparido*," I seethe.

Slash.

"And this is for me."

Slash.

"For Josh and his family."

Slash.

"And for every other innocent person you robbed of their future."

Slash. Slash. Slash.

After I take everything I need to quench the thirst for revenge, I let Logan put a silver bullet dipped in aconite in Clayton's brain. When the light dims from his eyes, all I feel is a complete sense of peace. I wait for the crippling guilt to come, but it never does.

38

Logan

I say my goodbyes to Emily and my mother before closing the front door of my house and making my way to the stairs. We had a quiet dinner at my place to celebrate mine and Emily's birthday. Kaiden, Malik, and Dominic were here as well. They left earlier, and my mother and Emily stayed to help clean up. The big party will take place tomorrow, where the whole pack will be present.

Entering the bedroom, I almost trip on my own legs like an idiot. But my jaw still practically hits the floor when my eyes take in the image before me. The room is illuminated only by candles scattered all around, their flickering light bathing Ava in a soft glow. She's wearing the sexiest contraption I have ever seen, a fiery red lace bodysuit that leaves nothing to the imagination. All my blood travels straight to my dick, and I'm instantly rock hard.

"Happy birthday," Ava purrs and saunters toward me with feline purpose.

"Fuck me," I mutter under my breath shakily. "Are you trying to kill me, baby? Because I'm certain I'm having a heart attack."

Ava laughs huskily, but before I can grab her and devour her like I want, she sinks to her knees in front of me and unbuckles my belt. She lowers the zipper slowly as her teeth sink into her lower lip. I don't know what I did to deserve this, but I'm feeling like the luckiest bastard alive at this moment. She hooks her fingers into my boxers and lowers them alongside my jeans. My cock juts out, and she looks up, her eyes smoldering as our gazes lock. Topaz green fire singes my skin with flames of desire.

She licks her lips like she can't wait to taste me and wraps her right hand around my base, pumping once, twice before she takes me into her mouth to the back of her throat. Intense pleasure seizes my lungs as my blood drums in my ears, a staccato rhythm that incinerates me from the inside out. For a few seconds, I forget how to breathe entirely. God, this woman. She hollows her cheeks, and her eyes don't leave mine as she starts bobbing her head while her wicked tongue licks at the underside of my cock in a way that makes my vision blurry.

"Fuuuuck, baby. Your mouth feels so good," I growl and wrap her hair around my hand before grabbing the nape of her neck possessively.

She moans around me, the vibration increasing the pleasure tenfold. Her perfect, rosy nipples draw to hard tips and strain against the red lace. My mouth waters with the need to taste her. "I can smell your arousal, Ava. Is my dirty girl's pussy wet from sucking my cock?"

She whimpers in response. "Then play with that pretty pussy, little wolf," I command in a raspy voice. She lowers the hand that was massaging my balls, pushes the lacy material covering her pussy to the side, and drags her finger along her soaked slit before she starts to move it up and down over her clit.

Ava's muffled sounds of pleasure and the way she looks kneeling in front of me, like a wet dream come to life, are my undoing. I come with a roar, spurting thick ropes of cum down Ava's throat.

"That's my good girl," I growl when she swallows every last bit and licks me clean. Before she gets the chance to move, I hastily wrestle out of my clothes and bend to take Ava in my arms, circling her legs around my waist. "Best. Birthday. Ever," I rasp, and then close the space between us, devouring her plush lips in a soul-searing kiss.

I make a beeline for the bed, and lower Ava on top of it. Dragging my eyes slowly over her body, I take a moment to admire how perfect my mate is. She's all curves and creamy tan skin, her eyes alight with carnal need. "You're so beautiful, Ava. I can't believe you're mine," I say gravelly, my trembling voice betraying my emotions.

"*Te amo*," she murmurs in sentiment.

"Say that again," I demand, kneeling between her legs and spreading her thighs.

"*¡Te amo!* I. Love. You," she repeats.

Her words set me ablaze. "Fuck, I'll never get tired of hearing you say that to me. I love you too, baby. So fucking much!"

A gasp leaves her lips when I tear the bodysuit off her body and discard it on the floor in tatters. "Logan! I just bought it, and it was really fucking expensive," she whines and gives me a withering glare. "What's with you ripping everything off me?"

"I can't stand having something between us. I'll buy you a new one," I breathe against her skin, tracing tongue-filled kisses on her inner thighs. "Hell, I'll buy you ten, twenty if you want." I bypass her center altogether and continue my trail of kisses until I reach her gorgeous tits. Breath ghosting over her rosy buds, I take my time to lavish each of them with eager sucks.

My hand glides down her silky skin until I reach her pussy. I spread her arousal with the pads of my fingers and dip one finger into her, pumping it slowly. Then, I add another to the mix to crook them against that spot that turns her feral while I massage her walls. At the same time, my teeth sink into her nipple, followed by soothing, languid strokes of my tongue. A sound between a whimper and a moan pitches in her throat. I use it as my cue to add the third finger as the top of my palm creates friction on her clit.

I can't help but steal a kiss before continuing my way down, mapping her skin with my lips and tongue. When I reach her soaked center, I bury my face into her pussy and inhale her sweet scent of arousal. "Fuck, baby, you smell so good," I groan and blow softly on her clit.

"P-please," she whimpers. "Logan! Stop playing with me."

I chuckle and give my girl what she wants, flicking the tip of my tongue over her clit. Tremors wrack her body, and sounds of pleasure echo against the walls. They spur me on as I take a finger out to spread her arousal to her back hole. She tenses slightly at the sensation.

"Relax, baby," I tell her in her mind.

"It's just that…I, well, um…no one has ever done that before."

"Mmm, I'm going to enjoy fucking your virgin ass, baby, but not today. I'm just going to use my finger, okay? I need you to relax. Once you get used to the sensation, you're going to love it, I promise." I add the third finger back into her slick heat and use my pinky to probe at her puckered hole.

"Okay," she whispers and relaxes her muscles, allowing me access.

Continuing the assault on her clit and massaging her inner walls at the same time, I slip my pinky slowly into her back hole, and the moment I'm knuckle deep, Ava's back bows off the bed with a desperate whimper.

"Oh, God! I feel so full."

"Come for me, baby," I demand, setting a rapid pace with my fingers, sucking on her clit and then grazing my teeth over it.

"Holy fuuuck!" she screams as her orgasm rips through her. My cock twitches at the way her walls spasm around my fingers, and I continue fucking her through it while sucking lightly on her clit to erase the bite of pain from earlier.

When Ava comes down from her high, I slip my fingers out of her and lick them clean, not wasting a drop of her cum. Laying on the bed next to her, I turn Ava on her side and enter her from behind slowly, the contact making her moan loudly and me hiss and suck in a ragged breath as a ripple of electricity passes through my body. I bottom out, wrapping one of my hands around her throat and lowering the other to her clit. I press two fingers against the sensitive nub and circle them slowly. Rolling my hips, I fuck her hard and deep while tightening the hold on her throat.

"Take a deep breath, baby," I command, and after she obeys, I cut her air supply completely as I piston her pussy, my thighs slapping loudly against her ass. It doesn't take long before Ava breaks at the seams with sexy as fuck noises while calling out my name. The way Ava's pussy ripples around me sets me ablaze, and like a cord pulled too tight, I snap. The release whips through me with the force of a wildfire.

Hours later, we both lie in post-orgasmic bliss, Ava sprawled on my chest, making imaginary circles with her fingers on my abdomen and my hand splayed on her back possessively. I remember I also had a surprise for her, but the little minx managed to distract me in the best possible way, and it slipped my mind. "I have something for you," I say, turning slightly to grab the envelope I placed earlier on my nightstand.

Ava lifts her head and pushes to a sitting position on the bed before she takes the envelope. She looks positively sex rumpled and so goddamn beautiful my heart rattles against its cage, fighting to get to her while my dick stands up at attention like I haven't spent the last few hours inside her. With Ava, I'll never get enough. Enough smiles. Enough kisses. Enough of her silky heat wrapped around me. Enough of…everything.

Her eyebrows pinch and rise in surprise at the same time, a half-smile lifting her luscious lips. "What is it?"

"Open it, and you'll find out."

She opens the flap and fishes out the key I placed there. Her throat bobs, and her eyes flit to mine. "Is this what I think it is?"

I nod. My stomach is a nervous ball of energy as I fist my hands, trying to hide the way my fingers are trembling in anticipation. "Will you move in with me, baby?" Technically, Ava's been spending so much time at my house since she woke up here for the first time. It's like we're already living together, and I have never been happier.

"Oh my God, Logan, yes, there's nothing I want more." Her eyes glimmer, and a tear escapes, trailing a path down her cheek as she throws her arms around my neck, her naked chest fusing with mine. She kisses me. Deep. Sensual. Consuming. I almost sink into her again but manage to pull back before I lose all sense of control.

I clear my throat. "There's something more. Look again."

She takes out the two folded pieces of paper and looks at the first one. "Holy smokes! Tickets to Paris!? Logan, this is entirely too much. Today is your birthday, and you're giving me presents. You already got me that fancy thousand-dollar kitchen mixer for Christmas."

"Yeah, and you're going to need it. Look at the second page."

She gasps, her hand going to the center of her chest while her fingers grip the paper so hard it crinkles on the sides. It shakes in her hand. "Is this…" She lifts her eyes in disbelief. "No, Logan…I-I can't accept this—"

"You can and you will," I cut her off, lifting her chin with my finger, needing to look into her eyes.

She scrunches her nose like she often does when annoyed with me. "A forty-thousand-dollar tuition at the most prestigious pastry school in Paris? There is no way I can ever accept this; it's the equivalent of my rent for two freakin' years—"

I cut her off again, earning a huff in response. "I might not have

Kaiden's money, but I'm loaded. And you're the woman I love and want to spend the rest of my life with. Get used to it because I plan to spoil the fuck out of you for the rest of our lives. Plus, you've been talking about wanting to go to a baking school almost every day now, and that chocolate truffle cake you made for Em and me tonight was the most delicious thing I have ever eaten in my life aside from your pussy." I wink, and then my expression turns serious. "It's already been paid for, and it's nonrefundable."

She sucks in a sharp breath and brings the envelope to her ear, rattling it like she's expecting something else to be inside.

I lift a quizzical eyebrow. "What are you doing?"

"Trying to figure out if I'm supposed to also find a ring in there."

"There's no ring," I say, and she visibly deflates, like one of those helium balloons left for days in the sun. I roll on top of her and pin her to the mattress. "Make no mistake, Ava. I meant everything that I said. I plan on spending the rest of my life with you. I'm just not proposing tonight. And tonight is the keyword here."

"Now I'm going to be a nervous wreck, waiting at every turn for you to drop on one knee. That's just plain cruel."

I can't restrain myself from showing her just how cruel I can be; I dip and suck on her nipple. "You'll live," I breathe against her skin.

"Can't you at least drop some sort of a hint on when or how you're going to do it?"

"Of course not. It's a surprise."

"Fine." She takes a deep breath in, biting her lower lip to stifle a moan when my fingers find her soaked slit. "So, how is this going to work? I mean…if I attend the pastry school, and that's a big if, the program lasts for two months. What about the pack and our responsibilities here? I've just adjusted somewhat to being their Luna, and you're the Alpha. And then there's the Conclave."

"I rented an apartment in Paris near the school, and I'm going to spend half a week there with you, and the other half I'll fly back home. Then we'll both be flying back for the full moons. Emily will step up and be here full-time for these two months. She's taking a break from the bartender gig for a while since Marnie sold the bar anyway."

"Aren't you going to be tired spending so much time on a plane? You have so much on your plate…I just don't want you to resent me. And all those expensive plane tick—"

"Money is not an issue. Plus, I have never taken a vacation since I became Alpha. It is long overdue. With the children being cured and the pack back to its strength, we don't have anything to worry about. It's only two months. We'll manage it just fine."

"You thought of everything, didn't you?"

"Mmhm," I mumble against the column of her neck, licking at the spot that I know drives her crazy.

"I-I'll p-pay you back somehow," she stutters through sharp breaths.

"Sure you will. You'll pay me back in orgasms. Yours," I say, my voice thick with lust as I roll onto my back and position Ava on top of me. I thrust my hips and enter her in one swift motion as my fingers collar her throat. "Start moving, baby. I want to see you fall apart while riding my cock."

Eyes at half-mast, cheeks flushed, and lips parted, Ava sets a maddening pace, looking like a goddess on top of me. She loses herself in pleasure and me in her until the first rays of the sun break through the sky.

Epilogue
Ava

The happy trill of birdsong fills the air, and the sun radiates golden rays from a cloudless sky. It warms my face as I take in everyone in attendance. I couldn't have asked for a more perfect spring day. Since coming back from Paris, I've been stressed to the max, trying to get everything ready for the opening of my bakery, Silver Moon Sweets, while obsessing over every single detail and driving Logan up the wall with my craziness. He's been amazing through every single one of my mental breakdowns, and when I was too much to handle, he knew exactly how to calm me down.

Everyone from our pack is present. Chloe and Knox arrived a few days ago in Ashville, and surprisingly, my mother and her boyfriend Ben are here, too. Our relationship is not fully mended, but we have come to some sort of a truce, and she wants to be part of my life again.

A light breeze ruffles my hair, and goosebumps spread across my skin when I realize it carries a trace of Tony's cologne. Somehow, I feel his presence and know he is here with me, supporting my dream. It's the first time this has happened, but I know it's him because his spirit envelops me like a warm embrace. My throat burns while I send my thoughts to him. *I miss you so much.* I take a deep breath in, trying to keep the tears threatening to spill from my eyes at bay.

Nervous energy blooms in my stomach, but it's the good kind, even if my fingers tremble slightly on the scissors as my gaze flits to Logan, who's standing a few feet to my right. I wanted him to be next to me, but he said that this is my day and that I deserve to be in the spotlight all by myself. He winks, making my pulse scatter. He looks incredible in a button-down and cigarette pants that fit him like a glove. As I look back at the scissors, a ray of sunshine catches the oval moonstone in my engagement ring, making it sparkle. The day Logan proposed to me was brilliantly bright.

"C'mon, sleepyhead, wake up. We have a plane to catch."

I groan in frustration, placing the pillow over my head while mumbling profanities at Logan. The pastry final the day before, which was a theoretical exam, kicked my ass, and I've had so many sleepless nights trying to memorize everything that all I want today is to be a sloth.

He chuckles at my muffled protests, and before I realize what's happening, I'm thrown over his shoulder like a sack of potatoes. I yelp in surprise, and Logan smacks my ass lightly before he deposits me in the walk-in shower of our one-bedroom Parisian apartment that sits in a historical building in Montmartre.

We only have a few days left in Paris, and after I graduate and receive my diploma, we'll go back home. We've made so many beautiful memories here, and though I'll be sad to leave Europe, I miss the runs with our pack. I've only been back for the full moons, and my wolf hasn't been too happy about that. I never thought I'd feel this way toward them, but the pack is like family to me now, and I'm proud to be their Luna.

"Where are we going?" I ask as I massage the shampoo into my hair and

then start rinsing it.

Logan crosses his arms in front of his chest. His muscles bulge underneath the skin-tight T-shirt he is wearing, and an ember of heat kindles in my core at his masculine beauty. "It's a surprise." He props his hip in the door frame, his eyes running down my body slowly in a languid perusal, and I know we must be on a schedule because Logan would never pass an opportunity to ravage me, especially after our gazes lock. He can read the lust in mine and feel it through our bond.

With every day that passes, our bond strengthens. It's as if we're an extension of each other. It makes for the most intense sexual experiences, but at the same time, it's a bitch when we fight because we involuntarily heighten each other's emotions to the point where one of us either has to leave or we end up angry fucking.

As soon as I finish blow drying my hair, I do a light makeup look and step out of the bathroom. Logan hands me a bag with a chocolate croissant and a cappuccino in a to-go cup from the boulangerie across the street. I give him a peck and say a soft thank you before biting into the croissant. It's still warm, and my taste buds do a little happy dance at the explosion of buttery flavor.

Logan rolls my carry-on alongside his to the door, then waits for me to grab my jacket before we descend the stairs and climb into the cab idling at the curb. Instead of taking the normal route to the airport, we arrive at a hangar where Kaiden's jet is waiting for us. He was kind enough to lend us the jet throughout these months for trips between Ashville and here. Still, I wasn't expecting to use it today since we flew commercial every time we've had the opportunity to escape to a new European country, usually on the weekends when Logan is here.

Two hours later, we land in Rome and check into our hotel near Fontana di Trevi. A stunning sundress waits for me on the bed alongside a pair of flat sandals. It has a camellia yellow flower print with a fitted bodice and a flowy maxi skirt with three layers of ruffles at the bottom. We both change our clothes, Logan opting for a pair of dark blue chinos and a linen shirt. My pulse spikes at the way the clothes cling to his chiseled body, and when he sees me lick my lips and ogle him, he winks at me with smoldering eyes, and tells me, "Later."

It's an abnormally hot day, even for the first week of March, and I'm happy Logan decided to surprise me with the clothes. After a delicious lunch on the hotel's terrace overlooking the city, we take a private tour of the Colosseum and Palatine Hill.

The sun makes its lazy descent, casting a warm glow over the Roman Forum as we reach the top of the Palatine Hill. I have a sneaky suspicion something is going to happen since there are no other tourists when it should have been packed. I don't dwell on it, though, and enjoy our private tour, soaking as much of the history as I can.

The moment we reach the balcony on the terrace at the top of the Palatine Hill, a string quartet suddenly appears around us and starts playing "Can't Help Falling in Love" by Elvis Presley. With the Eternal City draped in fiery orange at his back, Logan drops on one knee in front of me, his eyes molten gold as he pulls out the most beautiful ring I have ever seen — an oval moonstone with delicate diamond accents on its sides, flanked by two crescent moons, set on a simple gold band.

His voice is gravelly, and his eyes glimmer with exhilaration. "Ava, I've never expected you to barge into my life and become the center of my universe, yet fate brought you to me, and even if I tried my hardest, I still couldn't resist you. You're everything to me, the other half of my soul. You complete me, and I have never known such happiness and peace as I feel when I'm with you. Will you do me the honor of being my wife?"

A sob escapes my throat. I kneel in front of Logan, not caring about the beautiful dress anymore. In my rush, I almost tackle him to the ground. Tears stream down my face as I say, "Yes! A thousand times, yes!" I tell him through our bond and then aloud when I can finally speak again.

I shake my head slightly as I drag my mind back into the present. With a smile that makes my cheeks hurt, I cut the ribbon and inaugurate the Silver Moon Sweets bakery. A cork of champagne pops, and applause from everyone in attendance ensue as my fiancé pulls me into his arms.

"I'm so proud of you." He plants a warm kiss atop my head.

It's in this moment I know that with Logan at my side, I'm capable of anything I set my mind to do, not because I need him to accomplish something, but because he supports me and my dreams and would do anything to make me happy. For the first time in my life, I feel like I have found my way. I no longer feel lost, adrift. I'm living life on my terms.

Logan

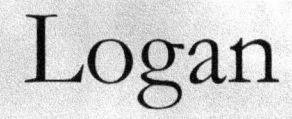

I'm buttoning my suit jacket when a knock comes through my bedroom door.

"Come in," I say and round the corner of my dressing room. Kaiden walks in and closes the door at his back.

He slides his hands into the pockets of his pants. "I know it's not the best time to tell you this since you're getting married today, but I also know you wouldn't have wanted to wait to receive the news. I finally managed to trace the shell company that owns the hospital Ava received the heart transplant at. I just got the confirmation that it's owned by the Kabal. The doctors, the staff, and everyone on the premises were working for them; that's how Ava got an infected heart, and that's why they disappeared and closed it down when we started to look into it."

Fuck. Fuck. Fuck.

It's not like we weren't expecting the Kabal to be behind the mysterious heart transplant and Hope's kidnapping and death. But this is the first time we've found some form of tangible proof.

Panic punches a hole through my chest, and my wolf claws at my insides, demanding to get to her right this moment, unsettled by the possibility that someone might try and take our fated mate from us. I suck in a choppy breath and say, "Do you think they'll come for her?"

"Well, they've had plenty of opportunities. Especially when she was vulnerable and in their care after the surgery. My best guess is that they wanted to see first if the heart transplant was a success and if she would actually shift. They must have noticed you two are together if they watched her progress closely. But our friendship is public knowledge within the dark creatures community, and I don't think they would dare come close to me or us after what happened in the Vatican. Although, we already know how unhinged and thirsty the Kabal is for power."

Kaiden's words settle like battery acid in my stomach. They burn through all of my organs and still ring in my ears on a loop after he leaves the room. I tried my best not to worry Ava, but the Kabal's implication has made me lose more sleep than I would like to admit in these past few months. When she was in Paris alone because I had to return to Ashville on pack matters, she had a security detail permanently on her without her knowledge. I didn't want her to worry. Even if no one made a move to harm Ava in any way, I still needed to take all the safety precautions so that nothing would happen to my mate.

My legs are filled with lead as I pace the length of my bedroom floor, my wolf waging war on my emotions. I snap off my bowtie, but my shirt collar still constricts my every breath, and I barely harness the restraint not to rip it to pieces. With trembling fingers, I take my phone out of my pants and call Emily. She picks up, and I hear Ava saying something to Chloe in the background, causing my heart to rattle hard against its cage.

"I need to see Ava," I choke out.

A door slams shut, and the hurried clicking sound made by heels against the hardwood floor travels through the phone. "What?" my sister asks in a hushed voice, probably trying to stay off the radar of Ava's hearing. "Did something happen?"

I swallow the lump in my throat. "I need to see her. Now!" I demand again, the hard edge in my voice not leaving room for argument.

"You know I don't care about bullshit wedding superstitions, but Ava does," she hisses at me.

"I don't give a flying fuck. It's an order from your Alpha."

"Wow, way to go being a dick, little bro." She cusses me out under her breath and then starts speaking again. "Fine. I'll make it happen. But you better remove that fucking stick out your ass before you see her because you're going to ruin this day for her before it's even started, and it's supposed to be the best day of both your lives, you douche canoe."

My eyes snap shut, and I run a hand over my face. "I'm sorry, Em. I didn't mean to be a dick to you. I received some news, and my wolf is getting stir-crazy. I'm going to fucking shift and ruin this suit and then come for her."

"Is it bad? Should we cancel the wedding?" she whispers, her tone laced with worry.

"No, we're not canceling the wedding."

"Okay. I'll see what I can do. Don't do anything stupid or rash; wait for my text."

Fifteen minutes later, my sister ties a black scarf around my eyes and guides me into the room Ava got ready in at my mother's house.

"Hey," Ava says softly, and I feel her fumbling before she takes my hand in hers. We're both blindfolded, and I make a mental note to thank my sister later for coming up with this brilliant idea. "Please don't tell me you're getting cold feet because my boobs look amazing in this dress, and it was a bitch to get on. I think I lost a rib or two in the process." Her tone is casual. I don't miss the anguish traveling through our bond, though.

I pull her to me and inhale her vanilla and caramel scent with a hint of wild violets. When I feel her in my arms, my wolf finally settles, and my lungs expand fully for the first time since Kaiden confirmed the Kabal's implication. "No cold feet, baby. You know how much I waited for this day to finally come."

"Oh yeah, I know. I swear to God, if I heard you one more time say 'my fiancé' or 'future wife,' I would have flung myself off the balcony," she taunts, but I know she secretly loved it every single time she heard me say it. Her fingers find my jaw, and she caresses the side of my face. "Are you sure everything's okay?"

"Yeah. I just needed to see you. Well…feel you at least since I can't actually see you."

"I'm here." Her breath ghosts my lips before she kisses me. It starts slow, innocent, but not before long, we start devouring each other with undisguised hunger as I hold her like a lifeline. Ava's nails scrape against my scalp, and she moans loudly in my mouth. I swallow the sound and suck on her tongue while cupping her perfect ass.

"Don't you dare hump each other and ruin Ava's makeup and hair! Do you hear me, Logan? I'll fucking castrate you if that happens. We have only half an hour to get to the cabin," my sister shouts, barging into the room.

We break apart on a hearty laugh, and we're both breathless as I place a kiss on her forehead. "See you on the other side?" I murmur.

"Yeah," she says softly and squeezes my hand one last time before my sister pushes me out of the room.

Half an hour later, atop a high peak in the wild violet field near my cabin with the mountains as our backdrop, Ava makes her way toward me on the white carpet, wearing the most beautiful smile. My heart thunders in my chest when our gazes collide. Topaz green fire lights up my insides, and I forget how to breathe entirely. She looks like an angel and a temptress all at once. The lacy white dress hugs her curves perfectly as silky strands of her hair blow softly in the wind.

"Ava…I…" I choke on the words even through our mental link. "I… Fuck…" Taking a deep breath, I try again. *"I'm the luckiest man alive. You're so beautiful it hurts to look at you,"* I tell her, even if I know these words are not enough to describe how I'm feeling right now. Words will never be enough.

Her eyes glimmer with emotion. *"Ditto, mi amor. Are you ready for forever?"*

"Never been more ready for anything in my entire life," I say aloud as I take her hands in mine.

If you enjoyed this book, please consider leaving a review on
↓ Amazon   and   Goodreads ↓

Iris's and Kaiden's story is coming Spring 2025

Turn the page for the blurb and cover of
"A WICKED DANCE of OBSIDIAN and Light"

Book 1 in the Echoes of Darkness Series

Preorder will be available Soon

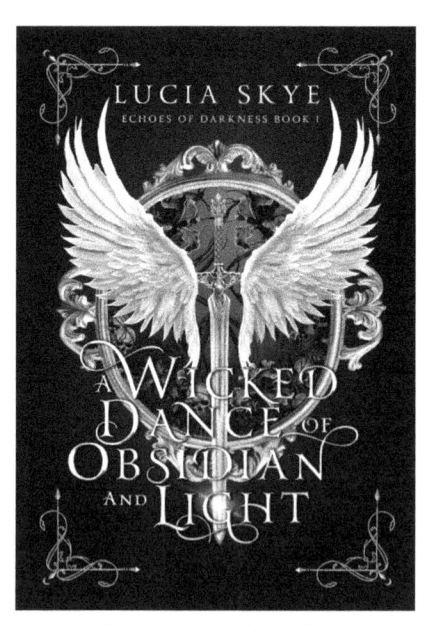

It was supposed to be another night on the job.
Hunt demons. Send them back to Hell. And go home.
Easy, right?
That's what I thought too...
Until the sky tore open.
And demons I had never encountered before started chasing after me through the forest.
There was no question...I was going to die.
But then the unexpected happened: someone yanked me back from the clutches of death.
Only my mysterious savior is nothing I expected him to be and everything I should stay away from.
Every time I get into trouble, he's there.
And it's getting harder to resist the sizzling attraction we share.
To make matters worse, the boy I served my heart to on a silver platter five years ago, only for him to crush it into a million pieces, is back.
He's all man now and claims he only wants one thing.
Me.
My life becomes a tangled web of secrets, lies, and betrayal.
And I don't know who I can trust anymore...

THANK YOU!

I cannot express enough gratitude for every single reader who took a chance on my book.

Everything I write is for you.

About the author

Lover of beautifully written words, strong heroines, anti-heroes, steamy romance, and swoon-worthy, broody MMCs, Lucia spends most of her free time, you guessed it…reading. Or better said, devouring books until the early hours of the morning because the main characters *finally* kissed after an agonizing slow burn, and she needs to know what happens next.

When she's not glued to her laptop, writing, drawing character art for her stories while listening to true crime podcasts, or daydreaming about falling through a magical portal in a mystical realm, you can find Lucia on the couch with her two fur babies, watching House of Dragon.

http://linktr.ee/LuciaSkye.Author

Find her on socials